**monsoon**books

## IBAN WOMAN

Born and raised in Sarawa[...]Iban mother and Melanau fat[...]been interested in the culture and traditions of [...]nous people. After graduating from university in Japan and enduring ten years of corporate life, the author found herself yearning for childhood evenings spent in the longhouse, sitting in a pool of lamplight, listening to her great-aunt tell tales of jungle animals or her father recount his hunting adventures. *Iban Woman* is Golda's third novel in a series of Iban novels that may be read in any order and includes *Iban Dream* and *Iban Journey*. Write to Golda at goldamowe@gmail.com For updates and news of author events, follow Golda Mowe on Facebook at *www.facebook.com/IbanDreamByGoldaMowe*.

### PRAISE FOR IBAN DREAM

'This is exactly the book I've been waiting for – a fantasy novel that draws on the legends of our land. This exciting story draws on Iban mythology as well as the old ways of life that have all but disappeared.' Daphne Lee, *The Star*, Malaysia

'Mowe, of pure Borneo ancestry, is a great talent, a mistress of the English language, who has accomplished what no one else has done. Dash and craft at once inform her novel. *Iban Dream* is an ensera, or epic, written in English. The heroic register of Iban language differs exceedingly from that in English, yet Mowe has succeeded in recreating the Iban feeling–and even hinting at Iban literary glories–by English means. She's a skilled and learned prose stylist.' Otto Steinmayer, *Borneo Research Bulletin*

## ALSO BY GOLDA MOWE

*Iban Dream*
*Iban Journey*

# Iban
## Woman

Golda Mowe

**monsoon**

**monsoon**books

Published in 2018
by Monsoon Books Ltd
www.monsoonbooks.co.uk

No.1 Duke of Windsor Suite, Burrough Court,
Burrough on the Hill, Leics. LE14 2QS, UK

ISBN (paperback): 978-1-912049-36-3
ISBN (ebook): 978-1-912049-37-0

Cover design by Cover Kitchen.

A Cataloguing-in-Publication data record is available from the British
Library.

Printed and bound in Great Britain by Clays Ltd, Elcograf S.p.A.
20 19 18       1 2 3 4 5

# 1

Ratai kept her eyes fixed on the campfire as though fascinated by the flames prancing and flickering. She was proud and stubborn, and she was right to be so, for she was the eldest child of Nuing, the warrior who had gone to the invisible world and returned alive. This was the same warrior who had fought an army of demon huntsmen and won. Ratai was also the granddaughter of Bujang Maias, the great headhunter who was raised by apes and who had met Sengalang Burong in the flesh and lived. That afternoon, however, despite her pedigree she was feeling shy and befuddled. Her ears listened with great concentration to the conversation between her brother, Mansau, and Sagan, a young man who lived in the same longhouse. Sagan was only about one year older than Ratai and at least four years older than Mansau. He and his mother had come with a group of people to join Nuing's longhouse about eight years earlier.

"Father says you are a good hunter," Mansau said for the third time since they had sat down to lunch.

Sagan stole a glance at Ratai. She still had her back to him. "Well," he started to say, "I always bring something home every time I go into the jungle."

"How do you manage that?"

"I have a charm that helps me find food everywhere. Once I even looked under a rock and found a large lizard. It was delicious. Mother dried the skin, and see, now it decorates my dart holder." He reached down, picked up a shallow bamboo tube leaning against his basket and passed it to Mansau.

The strip of skin was like an eye-catching ribbon around the yellowed surface of the bamboo holder. Mansau ran his finger appreciatively along the brown skin with white stripes. He recognised it to be the part of skin taken from the back of an angle-headed lizard. Inside the holder was a fistful of newly made blowpipe darts.

"When did you make these?" Mansau asked.

"Just two days ago. I came across a nibong palm. The bark was hard and straight, so I split it into darts. I have seen darts made from bamboo, but they are not as good. I have more at home. I can give you some if you want."

Ratai guessed that Mansau was trying to help Sagan. She liked her young neighbour but she was confused about her feelings towards him. She wanted him to be close to her, but she did not want him to speak to her. Each time he tried to do so, she would respond harshly. She felt so bad at times because she wanted to treat him better. She longed for him to think of her as being gentle, feminine and kind. Yet another side of her wanted so badly to reject him outright.

Her mother Nambi had often talked to her about the bliss of marriage, but Ratai wanted more than just the bearing of children and the planting of fertile fields. She wanted to see new places, visit new people. She had heard so many different versions of the story about how her parents had travelled to this land. She wanted to get a taste of what they had experienced. Sagan was a sweet man, but he did not have the adventurous mettle that she needed from a man who would lead the life she wanted to experience.

Ratai thought with longing to the days when she was young, when she used to follow her father to the mouth of the Rajang River, to a place where he traded jungle produce with Melanau seafarers. These visits were her annual highlights. Ships towered like houses upon the water, and the bazaar was filled with trinkets and jars and strange fragrant food. One time she even saw Melanau men swinging from a huge swing. Dozens of them jumped onto the rattan line, clinging on to it and to each other as they tried to make it swing ever higher to impress the gods. Ratai dreamed of the day when she would be allowed to ride the swing and touch the gods. However, Nuing stopped taking her with him when her womanly breasts started to show and she started attracting the wrong kind of attention from the strange men in the port. Since then, all she could do was dream of visiting the trading place again.

Mansau, made uncomfortable by the long silence, said, "You brought home a porcupine yesterday."

"Yes, I did," Sagan said and boldly looked to Ratai. He had talked to his male friends about his interest in her, warning them not to make any overtures while he was in pursuit. They all thought he was strange for liking a woman who preferred hunting to weaving. But Sagan believed that he was man enough to bring out her feminine side. He straightened his back and squared his shoulders. "My mother said the quills are straight and strong. They are perfect for weaving baskets and mats. I can ask her to give you some, Ratai."

"I don't know how to weave mats," Ratai said without looking up. She added another stick to the blazing fire.

Sagan fidgeted with a twig for a moment. "I think if you try, you will make excellent and beautiful mats."

Ratai did not reply. She was ashamed to tell him that she had tried many times, but had been unsuccessful. She was already twenty, and still had not managed to weave a single presentable seed basket.

Sagan smacked his arm and scratched it. "You are a woman. Mother says that if you put your mind to it, you can weave, and plant, or ..."

Ratai put out the fire by banging the smouldering wood noisily then stood up. "It is time to check the traps," she said without turning to look at him as she slung on her basket.

The snares had been put up the day before. They were only simple loops placed between shrubs or across branches that had telltale signs of being frequently passed by small animals. The first trap Ratai checked was empty. She undid the fibre string, because it was not right to put up a trap when you did not mean to return for the animal caught in it. The second trap had a pencil-tailed squirrel caught by its hind leg. It was quick and vigorous, jumping this way and that to get away from Ratai's hand. But the string was strong and Ratai only had to pull on it to bring the animal in. She twisted its neck and killed it. Then she tossed it into the basket behind her back. She walked along a few more yards to the third and last trap. She had caught a civet cat in this one, and again this animal was put in the basket in similar fashion.

Sagan's traps had caught two squirrels, while Mansau's had caught nothing. Sagan made a show of explaining to Mansau why his traps were empty and taught him how to set them properly. Then they checked the *bubu* fish-traps. Sagan's cone-shaped trap had one large snakehead, and Ratai's had two large catfish.

Sagan said, "These snakeheads are so greedy. It must have eaten all the other fish in the *bubu*." His ears were fast turning red as he said this. It was obvious to him that Ratai, the woman, had done better than him.

"Yes," Ratai said and nodded her head, more to save him from embarrassment than it was to agree with him. "Father always separates the other fish from the snakehead if he catches any in his nets."

"I wish I could trap animals as well as you, Sagan," Mansau said with awe and admiration expressed clearly on his shining face.

Ratai was hurt. She wished that Mansau would show her the same level of admiration. On the other hand, she also understood that he never would. She was a girl after all, and if he were to ever express any desire to be like her, he would be teased by the other boys in the longhouse.

She wished that she was with her father, Nuing, but of late the chief was reluctant to let her hunt with him. Even if she did manage to follow him, he would waste long hours telling her to spend more time with her mother and sisters. "No man will want you for his wife if you don't learn to weave or plant rice. He will be reduced to begging for rice to fill his belly and for cloth to cover his nakedness. There will be no end of trouble in your household."

Ratai stubbornly refused to listen. Or rather she pretended to be hard headed. She was too proud to admit to anyone that her last fumbling attempt at weaving a mat was finished by her twelve-year-old sister, Madu. The rice seeds she planted produced more husks than grain, and almost every *taya* cotton shrub she planted would be shrivelled and diseased before harvesting time. She had no such trouble hunting and fishing, and her basket was always full with jungle fruits and vegetables whenever she went out to forage. Yet she was not a boy. Her body reminded her constantly because each time she was with Sagan, her heart would race and she would be tongue-tied.

Today she was frustrated with herself because she did too well. Her success had made Sagan feel small. His obvious embarrassment made her feel unfeminine. Would it be better if she were an inferior hunter, she wondered. Then she stole a glance towards Sagan. His bowed back was turned to her as he placed a wide leaf in his basket and put the snakehead fish atop it.

After they cleaned their fish snares with a quick dunk and shake in the stream, they started for home. The return journey was quiet, for their senses were on high alert. They stepped lightly and concentrated on their surroundings. More experienced hunters had often warned them that sometimes a tree would shift or disappear when it sensed them coming. They must be silent when they walked in the jungle, so the plants that had guided them in would not move and make them lose their way. Here where it was shady but humid, the insects sounded loud and in between their ceaseless creaks were the sound of singing gibbons.

Ratai was relieved when they reached a well-worn trail that their community had used for many years. Any vine that had fallen over the path, or any shrub that had overgrown into it, would be cut away with a machete. They were safe in this place because the spirits here were friendly to them. As they neared the longhouse, they could hear the elderly calling out to the children to come back into the house. Soon it would be dusk, a time when things seen would be changed and things unseen would become seen.

A group of boisterous children suddenly rushed towards them as they emerged out of the jungle. The curious youngsters demanded to see what was in the baskets of the returning foragers. Mansau answered all their questions as the three of them made their way up the steep carved ladder into the longhouse. Once in her family quarters, Ratai lingered, washing and chopping the fish and meat then putting them over the smouldering fire in the main room. The clay hearth set against the wall was clean, but she busied herself with clearing away the little ash that was there.

Then she returned to the back room, washed some rice grain, and stuffed them into a wide-mouth bamboo tube. After adding some water to cover the grains, she stopped the mouth with tapioca leaves, then leaned this tube over the smouldering fire. She added more firewood, and blew on the embers until a small flame sprouted out.

Her younger teenage sister, Suma, who had been watching her said, "You've been out all day. Why don't you go wash first. I can do the cooking."

"I just want to get these out of the way first before I bath. Why don't you go?" Ratai said. She was too shy to admit to Suma that she did not want to wash in the river yet because she knew that Sagan would be there with her brother.

"I am waiting for you," Suma said with a knowing smile. Even though it was never openly discussed, Sagan's interest in her sister was no secret in the community. "I have a surprise, but you can only see it when we get to the river."

They waited until Mansau returned from his bath, which was a sign that his companion had also returned. Then the two sisters each shouldered a basket filled with empty bamboo tubes. Once they reached the bathing platform Suma reached into her basket and pulled out the *pudak* leaves that she had plucked that morning.

"Where did you find them?" Ratai asked suspiciously.

"Mother and I went across the river to look for *bemban* reeds and fern. There was a screwpine tree growing not far from the river. I promise, I picked the young leaves myself." Then she added with a frown, "I am not silly, you know. I will not just take anything that is left lying around. It might have been a crocodile or leopard trap."

Ratai pinched her sister's nose. Of course Suma should know

not to take anything that had been left by the side of the river or a trail. They had heard enough cautionary tales about people who had gone mad because they had taken pretty flowers or trinkets that they found lying by the side. Ratai remembered how she had once panicked when Suma tried to grab a yellow bloom floating past her on the river.

Now she grabbed a handful of the soft, long leaves with glee then she tore them into pieces. The mush let out a fresh fragrance and started to foam as she mixed in some water. The two sisters began to lather themselves with the soapy sap. Suma then turned her back to Ratai, signalling that she would like a scrub. As Ratai rubbed Suma's pale back with the shredded leaves, she wondered if she would be more feminine if her own skin was less dark. She envied Suma because her younger sister seemed to be more gifted as a woman. The younger girl had just started learning to beat the *taya* cotton and to spin it into a thread. Yet her work was fine and though the thread she spun was thin, it was strong and did not break easily.

Ratai said, "Mother took out the trough. Are you going to starch the thread?"

"No," Suma said. "I don't think so. I am not a weaver yet."

Ratai smiled. She was very proud of her sister. Everyone in the longhouse talked about Suma's skills and they all predicted that one day she would grow up to be a master weaver. Her skill would bring blessings and new people to their house, much like their father's fame as a headhunter and law interpreter had brought proud fighting men into their community.

Suma now turned to face her, and Ratai turned to face the other direction. The sun had faded into the treeline and the sky above was turning golden. While her sister rubbed her back, Ratai wondered if the creation god, Selampadai, had made a mistake when he formed her. How could she be so skilful in manly pursuits but be a girl? It seemed so wrong. Would not the world fall into chaos if Selampadai had made more women like her?

Suma said, "You are very quiet. Aren't you going to tell me about your visit into the jungle?"

"There is nothing new to tell. We did not meet any stranger or come across any omen this time."

Suma sighed. "I had hoped that you have come across something good."

Ratai looked to the side for a moment to get a glimpse of Suma's anxious face. She understood why her sister needed news of good omen. Suma was worried about the thread preparation ritual.

"Have you wound your thread around the *kalai* yet?" Ratai asked, referring to the H-shaped frame used to stretch threads so they would not get tangled when starched.

"Yes. Mother was very pleased with my work."

Despite herself, Ratai laughed. "You should have seen my first work. The thread got so tangled, mother had to spend days unravelling them." Then her face became more serious. "I tried to be careful, but I could not seem to get it right."

A boy swimming past splashed them with water and Ratai splashed him back playfully. Then the sisters dipped themselves into the river to wash off the fragrant foam. They changed into fresh skirts when they came out. Then they took out the empty bamboos and began to fill them with water flowing down from upriver. There was no other longhouse up there, so they knew that the water was clean and fresh. Once all the tubes were filled, they helped each other shoulder the heavy basket then walked back to the longhouse.

On entering the family room, Ratai noticed her mother

Nambi sitting in front of a large wooden bowl. She was mashing the grains of cooling rice gruel with her hand. The daughters pretended not to see, afraid that any comment they made would in some way or other ruin the starching process.

They set aside the baskets of water in a small, dark room in the back then went about to prepare for dinner. There was a flurry of running feet coming from outside. Their two youngest sisters, eight-year-old Tambong and ten-year-old Rinda, burst into the *bilek*. Coming in at a more sedate pace was twelve-year-old Madu. She frowned at the two younger girls and said, "You two are such a nuisance. I am never taking you foraging with me again." She showed Nambi her small basket, which was only half-filled with fern. "Look, Mother. This is all I could get because these two were running about and getting into scraps. I could not take my eyes off them even for a moment."

Nambi smiled up to Madu thankfully. "You are such a good daughter and a responsible sister. Thanks to you, I have finished what I needed to do."

Unmoved by her sister's condemnation, Tambong wrapped her arms around her mother's shoulders and asked, "What are you doing, Mother?"

"Don't ask questions," Nambi said, "otherwise I will not let you watch."

"Come help us call Father and our brothers for dinner," Ratai said to distract her.

Tambong immediately ran outside to tell her father and two brothers that dinner was ready. Suma spread out a well-worn mat on the floor. Then the cooked dishes were poured out into bowls and laid in the centre of the mat. Nambi covered the wooden bowl of starch with a shallow basket and placed it in a secluded corner where it would not be noticed.

By the time Ratai had placed the last dish on the mat, the whole family had sat round their evening meal. Nuing split open a charred bamboo tube, exposing the cooked rice within. Then Nambi scooped out the rice according to the needs and appetite of each member of her family.

As usual Nuing passed the first leaf plate of rice to Ratai, the eldest of his seven children. She was the first blessing that ever came into their community and, to his mind, his life had prospered since her arrival. She was the child he could never deny anything to, not even when she wanted to go hunting with him. He knew that Nambi did not approve, but like him, she too could deny Ratai nothing.

Ratai knew that she was not the child of their flesh, yet she received the best of everything they could give. She owned the most beautiful skirt her mother wove and she slept on the thickest *kapok* mattress the family had. Her four sisters adored her and her two brothers looked up to her. Even so Ratai was unhappy with herself because she could not live up to her expectations of being a woman. She was so ashamed of her lack of skill that she did not dare share her worry with her mother.

Dinner that night was a little more special than usual. The fish was buttery with fat, and the meat of the squirrels and civet cat were sweet though chewy. The pickled bamboo shoot was sour and sweet at the same time. They ate quietly, only speaking when necessary. After the meal, Nuing and the two boys, Mansau and Betia, went out to the gallery where he taught them how to weave a net from the fibre of vines. Seventeen-year-old Mansau did the job with a certain level of confidence but thirteen-year-old Betia struggled to keep the space between the knots even. Ratai gazed wistfully at them as she closed the door. She wished she could join them but she stayed behind in the family room because she knew it would please her mother.

Nambi took the bowl of starch out from its corner and placed it on the mat, which had been cleared and shaken clean of food scraps. Suma brought out a shallow basket filled with skeins of newly spun thread. Carefully she picked a bundle and held it up with two hands for her mother.

"You have seen me do it before. Put it in this way," Nambi said as she grasped Suma's hand and showed her how to wrap her fingers over the thread. Suma dipped half of the bundle into the starch then gently combed the thread with her fingers, making sure that every strand was soaked. Carefully she turned the bundle and starched the other half. She released a sigh of relief when she finally put the bundle into an empty trough.

With some urgings from her mother, Ratai picked up the next bundle of thread with dread. She held it properly but she was disgusted when she had to comb the strands. The gruel was sticky and slimy, like snot, and the hint of sourness made her nauseous.

Nambi who was watching her with a worried frown, said, "Let me finish that for you, Child." She took the bundle from Ratai's hand and began to caress it like it was a newborn baby.

Ratai was mortified, and to hide this, she got up and washed her hand. Tambong followed her to the back and asked, "Why did you stop?"

Ratai had no answer, so she was glad when her mother said, "Tambong, I let you watch because you promised not to ask questions. If you cannot be quiet, you'll have to go outside and be with your brothers."

Tambong returned to sit next to Nambi and watched the process with rapt attention. When Ratai resumed her seat on the mat, Tambong sidled up to her and wrapped her arms around her eldest sister. That night only Suma helped Nambi starch the thread while the other girls watched. When they were almost done, Nuing cracked the door open a little and asked for some blankets.

Madu jumped to her feet and picked out her father's and brothers' blankets from amongst the other rolls stacked in a dark corner. Tambong stared curiously as Madu passed them through the door. With her mother's threat still fresh in her mind, she bit down on her hand. Despite herself, Nambi had to smile. She decided to explain. "Father doesn't want to sleep in here tonight because he doesn't want to disturb the thread."

"Is that why we have to be quiet?" Tambong asked.

"Yes, that is right," Nambi said. "If the thread is angry then we cannot make good cloth out of it. The colours will not be beautiful and the pattern will not be clear."

"I will be quiet, I promise," Tambong said, much to the relief of her mother and sisters.

Nambi placed two thin bamboo sticks over the empty trough then draped the bundles of thread over them. Tambong watched the drip of excess starch with fascination. This was the first time her mother had allowed her to watch. Next year, she hoped she would be allowed to pick the seeds out of the cotton blooms. She overheard her mother promise Rinda about letting her comb the cottons before they were beaten. Tambong decided that she would be doing it too.

Her little heart was so full of dreams that saw her hands turned brown with *sebangki* dye then indigo with *renggat* dye. She fantasised about weaving patterns of rattan vines festering with hook-like thorns. She told herself that she would tie-dye designs of sleeping crocodiles or maybe flying giant snakes, like the cloth her father said her grandfather Bujang Maias had bought from a Malay trader. Tambong was so engrossed in her dreams that she did not notice Ratai and Madu climbing up a notched log to go up to the loft above. Every night she would beg her three older sisters to let her sleep with them upstairs, among the bins of rice and stored baskets, but they would not let her because she talked too much. Tonight, that quest was forgotten because she had bigger aspirations to consider.

Suma did not go up because she had to sleep downstairs with her mother that night. Nambi was proud of how quickly and passionately Suma had learned everything she had taught her. It made Nambi wish that she were a more skilful weaver. She was the wife of a headhunter, yet he did not own a single bright red *pua ngar* because she did not know how to perform the ritual of the mordant bath. There was no other woman in her longhouse who knew how to do the ritual. So her proud, brave husband was reduced to wearing brown cloth that faded over time. She wished with all her heart that she could weave for him more than a simple *pua mata*.

The emotional pressure that Nambi felt was at times unbearable. She was far better off than the other women of the longhouse, and she believed that Ratai was the reason for her status. Because of her eldest, she wished she could be a better woman. Her imperfections, Nambi felt, were the reason why her child was a tomboy. It was only natural for Ratai to desire to be perfect, and since Nambi was not, Ratai's spirit was forced to follow Nuing and his ways, she reasoned. Sometimes Nambi would go into the jungle alone, hoping to meet a spirit or to get inspiration from either Goddess Kumang or Goddess Meni. Neither one had ever come to her, not even in a dream.

Tambong's snuggling up to her startled Nambi back into the present. She carried her nodding child to the sleeping mats that Suma had spread and lay down between her daughters. Again

Nambi blessed the pig-king who had sent a python shaman to take away her curse of infertility. Since that day, her harvest had always been plentiful, and she had not lost to sickness or accident any of the children she had borne. Every other mother in the house considered herself blessed if she were to have three living children. Nambi had seven. The night sound now filled the quiet room: insects chirping, frogs croaking and bats squeaking. This music lulled her to sleep.

\* \* \*

Ratai listened to the night. As she started to drift off, she heard a wood beam creak. She ignored it because this was not the first time she had heard a suitor pass by her loft to go to his sweetheart. She waited for the creak to move on, but it seemed to have stopped. Then she heard a note struck on the *ruding*, the Jew's harp. Ratai held her breath, part of her elated, yet another part of her terrified that her parents would hear.

Another note sent shivers of excitement up and down her skin. The quiver of the metal tongue stuck to the end of a thin bamboo strip seemed to vibrate for the longest time. Ratai imagined sensing the slightest tremble in the lips that gripped the harp. She suspected that her suitor was Sagan, yet she could not be sure, and she was too shy to call out his name.

Then she felt him shake her toe. She sat up slowly, making a show of being reluctant to receive him. "Why are you here?" she asked, hoping to trick him into speaking, so she could know for sure he was the man she had guessed.

The visitor struck another note. Ratai felt Madu touch her hand: her sister was awake. Ratai tried again. "If you don't tell me your intentions for coming here tonight, I shall scream and wake my father and brothers."

Another note, this time low and sad. Ratai stifled a giggle. Then she boldly asked, "What is your name?"

The voice that answered sounded as though its owner had pinched his nose shut as he spoke. "I am the man of the week-old loincloth, the man with crocodile teeth, the hunter whose basket is never empty."

Madu squeezed Ratai's hand hard. She was trying her best to feign sleep while holding back a strong urge to giggle. Ratai pinched Madu's wrist gently to warn her to keep still. She tried another question. "Where are you from, Stranger?"

"I live in the land of many hills, where the hornbills build their nests. I live near a waterfall where the Pleiades wash. I live in the land protected by the rat goddess, where rice grows plentifully."

For the next two hours, Ratai plied question after question, and the visitor continued to speak with his nasal voice, giving endless witty answers. He was not ready to reveal his real identity to her yet, for he wanted to win her over with his wit and cleverness first. He wanted to prove to her that he had the knowledge and the skill to entertain her for years of endless evenings together.

When the drone of the cicadas began to fade, a sudden loud cough came from below. Immediately Ratai dropped down on her mat and pulled the blanket over her head. She could sense that the visitor was as tense as her, for he too seemed to be holding his breath. Then she heard the creak of the beam, and her visitor was gone. Madu shook her, but Ratai did not respond, pretending to be dead asleep. Yet sleep would not come to her for the rest of the night.

\* \* \*

Morning came too soon. Ratai cursed the roosters crowing about the longhouse. She was in a half-dream state and in her mind was still speaking with the stranger that had visited the night before. When she finally got up, her head was heavy from the lack of sleep but her body was light with excitement. This was the first time any man had shown serious interest in her. She finally understood why the other girls were always so excited about it. The feeling of being admired was a strong euphoria.

While Ratai prepared breakfast, Madu kept trying to get her attention. She wanted to talk about the previous night, but Ratai was not ready to discuss it with anybody. She was relieved that her mother had not mentioned hearing notes from the Jew's harp. Maybe Nambi had really not heard, Ratai hoped, as she listened to her mother instruct Suma on how to hold up a bamboo rod lined with damp thread. Then she noticed them walk out to the open verandah beyond the common gallery. Ratai did not want to be alone with Madu, so she too hurried outside after Nambi and Suma.

Once outside on the verandah, Nambi lay the edges of the rod on opposing upright poles. She showed Suma and Ratai how to finger the threads so they would not stick to each other as they dried. After each thread was lined evenly on the pole, they returned to the family room. By now the boiled tapioca root was ready. Madu and Rinda called the rest of the family in for breakfast.

As Nuing dipped a white tapioca root into a bowlful of dark *nipah* palm sugar, he said, "I think I must fix the wall in our loft tonight. I thought I heard a cricket upstairs."

Madu covered her gaping mouth but her eyes widened with surprise. Ratai kept her head bowed, only her ears showing red and hot.

"What cricket was it, Husband?" Nambi asked.

"I did not recognise the sound it made," Nuing said, "But I

heard it move to *Indai* Sagan's family quarters."

Tears of embarrassment formed on Ratai's eyelids because of the heat burning on her face. There was no more conversation for the rest of breakfast, but the atmosphere was thick with excitement and happiness.

# 2

Ratai tried her best to hide the fact that she had a suitor. The harder she tried to avoid meeting with or looking at Sagan, the more it felt as though everyone in the longhouse knew about their secret. She was suddenly shy to be seen anywhere near him even though they had been playmates for years. Each time she had to leave the family room to go outside, she would check to make sure that he was not nearby. She went about her usual routine; bringing water to the *bilek*, pounding rice in the mortar kept in the common gallery, and spreading peeled illipe nuts on a large mat to dry on the open verandah. The whole time she kept her head bowed, afraid of catching anybody's eye, in case they should comment upon Sagan's interest or ask something that she was not yet ready to answer.

Sagan too, she soon realised, was trying to be as unobtrusive as her. She wondered why he had not just gone out to hunt or to fish then she realised that he might be trying to avoid hearing bad omens. A sudden tightness gripped her chest; what if they were not meant to be? What if the omen animals cursed their union? For the rest of the day, Ratai was torn between hope and despair. Evening did not come soon enough.

Ratai continued her silence throughout dinner. The day was so hot the thread was dry before sundown so after dinner was cleared, Nambi lay out the threads to be rolled. Ratai was extra careful while rolling the thread into balls with her mother and

Suma. It was almost as though Sagan's visit had breathed new life into her attempts at weaving. The perfectly round ball of thread she finally put into a halved coconut shell suggested to her that she would one day be the perfect woman. Nambi was pleased with her handiwork for the first time. Even Suma said her ball of thread was not as well rolled as Ratai's.

When Ratai finally made her way to the loft with Suma and Madu, she felt feminine and beautiful. Tambong as usual tried to join them, but Nambi would not let her, using the excuse that she needed someone to help her make sure that nothing disturb the balls of thread.

The sisters immediately feigned sleep. There was none of the usual conversation and planning for the following day. Not long after, the longhouse too fell into quiet slumber. Though the girls were motionless under their blankets, none were asleep. Soon they heard a beam creak. Suma and Madu involuntarily squeezed their shoulders as though wishing to melt into the floorboards.

Ratai felt her toe being shook. She sat up slowly. There was a soft musical note coming from the shadowy silhouette sitting in front of her. She knew that the room was too dark for him to see her face, yet she still tried her best to hide her excitement at seeing him.

"Why have you come again, Stranger?" she asked.

"I come because I wish to know if you will marry me," he said in the same nasally voice of the night before.

"Tell me your name and I will give you an answer."

"I will tell you, after you tell me first if you will have me as a husband."

Ratai covered her mouth to stifle a rising giggle. Then she said, "I cannot agree to marry someone I don't know."

The visitor continued to pester her for the next few hours,

and each time Ratai would neither say yes or no. Yet it was clear to everyone who listened that Ratai was agreeable to his suit because she did not tell him to leave, or call out to her father. The teasing continued back and forth until the first rooster crowed. Reluctantly the stranger left, and Ratai lay back on her mat. But she could not sleep. Her sisters had fallen asleep hours before, so there was no one she could discuss her excitement with. Her cheeks felt so hot it was like she was having a fever.

*\*\**

Ratai could not see Sagan anywhere during the day while she went about her routine. She decided that he could just be getting something for his mother. That evening she was relieved when her brother Mansau told her that Sagan had been fishing. She tried not to show her interest, but again she felt that hotness on her face.

Nambi and Nuing watched their daughter's swinging mood with joy. It had been a long time since they had seen her this happy. Whenever they could they would talk about Sagan's industry and skill within her hearing. Soon after dinner, Nambi sent her three elder girls to bed, with the excuse that she needed them up early the next day. None of the girls questioned her, for they too were eager to be in bed.

Even though he was caught up in the joy and the excitement, Nuing could sense that something was worrying Nambi. He followed her to the back, where their food was cleaned and stored.

"Our first child will be marrying soon," Nuing said as he sat next to her on the floor.

"Sagan's mother has not come to me to speak about his interest," Nambi said.

"Maybe she is waiting for the right time."

"But he cannot keep coming to our daughter every night. It will ruin her reputation."

"Tonight is the third night. When he comes tonight, I will grab him and demand that he makes his intentions public."

"But you will hurt him," Nambi said with a frown.

"Of course I won't. Put your *belia* by the side of the door. I will use the loom beater instead of my sword to catch him."

"Make sure you don't bend or break it. I need to teach Suma how to weave. She is of the right age to learn."

Suma was fifteen, Nuing thought to himself with a pang of both pride and anxiety. It seemed too soon to consider her a woman, but he was not so blind as not to notice the interest of other bachelors in his second daughter. None had approached her yet because she had not woven her first skirt. Yet he knew that she would be weaving it soon.

Nuing received the thread beater from his wife reverently. He marvelled at how much it looked and felt like a sword. The only difference was that the blade was straight instead of curved so that the weft thread could be beaten evenly into place. He laid it next to his sleeping mat, which he moved to the bottom of the ladder leading to the loft.

Tambong as usual noticed these variations and asked why the *belia* was not at its usual place.

Nambi said sternly, "I have told you many times not to ask questions, unless I am teaching you something."

Undeterred, Tambong persisted. "But what if Father breaks it and make the Goddess Kumang angry? Isn't that why you say I cannot play near your weaving things, because I might break something?"

Nambi let out a sigh. Tambong was right. "Well, Father is not like you. He is careful, and he will not break it."

The young girl was not happy with her mother's answer but she could not think of anything to say to counter Nambi's reply. She tried to lie next to her father, but her mother pulled her away. Tambong was disappointed. She had meant to touch the *belia* while her father slept.

The night soon fell into its usual jungle quiet. Nuing listened for the telltale creak in his rafters. When his eyelids grew heavy, he sat up quietly. He listened hard but no one came to his loft. Then he heard another sound above the sound of singing insects. He heard a young woman sobbing. He knew in his heart then that his daughter had realised something sooner than him: that the suitor was not returning.

\*\*\*

Nuing turned his gaze everywhere but on his eldest child. Her face was swollen from weeping and she was quiet when she came down to prepare breakfast that morning. Sensing that something was amiss, Tambong asked what happened to her face, and Ratai told her that she was not feeling well.

"You should lie down," Nambi said, pretending that nothing was out of the ordinary.

"I am all right, Mother," Ratai said. "I shall be better in a little while."

"I can bring you some water, to cool the redness," Suma said, her voice trembling with emotion. But Ratai shook her head.

Nuing was bitter for her sake. How could Sagan have put so much hope in her heart only to break it? Was it his way of punishing her, for ignoring him this past year? Yet he had come and she had not chased him away. Surely he must know that she liked him, and that her aloofness was only due to her shyness. Even though Nuing had spent many happy years with Nambi, Ratai's suffering now brought back to him all the hurt that he had experienced in his old longhouse. He knew from that experience that there was no word of comfort he could give his daughter. Finally he decided to do what his wife was doing. He pretended that nothing was amiss. If he could not comfort her then he should at least help her save face. After all, she had never confided to either himself or Nambi about Sagan's possible interest.

After breakfast Nuing said, "I am going fishing. You boys must come and help me." Then he turned to the two youngest girls, Rinda and Tambong. "How about you? Do you two want to help me look after the fish basket?"

The sisters jumped to their feet with squeals of delight and immediately set to fill their little personal baskets with tiny playthings and carved wooden tools that they thought they would need for the afternoon.

Nambi smiled with relief because the excited chatter and noisy preparations of her children masked Ratai's bitter silence. Nuing gave his wife a meaningful look as he walked out of the room. He understood that this was something beyond his skill and experience to handle. He was taking the younger girls away so Nambi could concentrate on Ratai.

Nambi and her three eldest daughters went about their daily duties silently. Ratai was never alone, though no one made any attempt to talk to her. It was a shameful thing to be rejected by a boy who had shown interest first. Nambi also worried that the rest of the community might be aware of Sagan's visits. Usually, a young man would tell his friends of his intention in pretence of asking for their advice. But actually he was telling them not to show their interest to the girl before him. Both nights Sagan had stayed till late, showing all who noticed that Ratai had not rejected him. His rejection, however, by discontinuing his visit and by not making a formal engagement, gave the impression that there was something lacking about her.

The more Nambi thought about it, the more she felt the need to find out what had gone wrong. Maybe Sagan was ill, maybe he had had a bad dream or had heard a bad omen. For her child's sake, Nambi needed to find out why Sagan's mother had not talked to her yet about the wedding arrangements. She spent the whole morning thinking about what she should say, and how she should approach Sawai, or *Indai* Sagan as she is called, about the topic.

By the time Nambi went out to the common gallery and saw that Sawai had just entered her family room, she was still undecided about how to broach the subject. In spite of her trepidation and shyness, she walked over to her neighbour's doorway. She was relieved to see it open because that meant that the occupant could receive visitors. She called a greeting from outside and entered when she heard a reply.

Sawai was sitting in front of the hearth and was laying square palm-sized pieces of beaten cotton on top of each other. She looked up and said, "Oh it is you, *Indai* Ratai. Please come in."

"You will be spinning thread soon," Nambi said as she folded her legs to the side and sat on the mat.

"I have only just finished beating the cotton. Unlike you I have no daughters to help me, so work is slow."

Seeing a way to open the subject, Nambi said, "Maybe there will be someone to help you soon."

Sawai turned back to her work, clearly unwilling to continue the conversation. Nambi reached out and peeled off a square of cotton from the nearest pile. She rolled this tightly, like it was a cigarette then placed it in a tray of similar rolls.

Nambi persisted. "You have collected quite a good amount of cotton. This should make thread enough for two skirts."

"I would like it if I had someone like Suma to help me weave a blanket, for my son."

Nambi's breath caught in her throat, and her stomach knotted with pain as though she had been punched. Could Sagan have made a mistake that first night? Then she remembered that Suma had slept with her on his first visit because they had just starched the thread. So if it was a mistake, he must have realised it.

Maybe Sagan's mother had misunderstood his interest, she decided. To keep the conversation moving she asked, "Is Sagan out hunting? I have not seen him today."

"Yes," *Indai* Sagan said without looking up. "I told him that I was craving some meat. A pheasant at the very least, if not a wild pig or a deer."

"He is a good hunter."

"I only need one good hunter."

Nambi's heart ached. This was the second time that Sawai had indicated that she did not want Ratai as her daughter-in-law.

Then in a more kindly voice Sawai said, "My family's sacred rice has never failed me. My son and I have always had enough for our needs. When my son marries, it must be to a woman who will also please the rice souls. You know how fragile they are. If they stop blessing my family, we will starve."

Nambi understood what Sawai was trying to tell her. The first time Ratai planted the rice seeds, the harvest was so bad, her family had to live on sago and tapioca roots for most of the year. In the following year Suma started to help and the harvest was better, although they lost a quarter of the crop. Rumour started to spread in the longhouse that Ratai's tomboyish ways had made the rice souls reject her. People even went as far as to say that all the seeds that failed were the ones that Ratai planted.

There was no way out of the predicament. In a way, Nambi was thankful to Sawai for not making her rejection public. By telling Nambi who she thought was the ideal choice for her son, she had not openly rejected Ratai. Instead she had given both families an opportunity to pretend that Sagan had never visited Ratai, but was waiting to talk to Suma instead.

After staying for a few more minutes to talk about where to get dye for the thread, Nambi left the room. She imagined a dozen pair of eyes watching her and trying to read her face as she returned to her family room. She found Ratai alone in the back room, busying herself with the firewood.

Nambi sat behind her, watching her back and debating about how she should explain the situation to her daughter. Finally she said, " I have just come back from *Indai* Sagan's room."

Ratai stopped piling the wood for a moment then she resumed her work. "Was there anything you needed from her?"

"No, we just had a little talk."

Ratai's hand started to shake. Half of her longed for good news, yet another part of her, the part that had accepted Sagan's rejection, longed to end the yearning.

Nambi waited for Ratai to turn and look at her, but the other now moved on to rearranging a pile of rushes. Nambi took a deep breath and continued, "*Indai* Sagan will be spinning thread soon. She has just finished beating the cotton. She wished that she had someone like Suma to help her."

Ratai was suddenly still. She stared up at the empty wall in front of her. The message could not be any clearer. She longed to talk to Sagan again, to hear his voice, to scowl at his silly laugh. But she knew that she could never do that again. They could never go hunting together anymore because she would rather die than be accused of forcing her attentions on a man. Her reputation would never recover if there was even a hint that Sagan had set the mortar upright, that the reason for her obsession was because she had had sex with him. He rejected her, even after she had encouraged his attention. The embarrassment was awful enough because Suma and Madu knew about his visits. And now, her mother seemed to know too. Ratai wondered who else knew. She felt humiliated by her predicament and she wanted to leave the house, to go to a place where nobody knew her.

"I need to go out later," Ratai said.

"Why? I need someone to help me find materials for the dye."

"You have Suma," Ratai said, trying her best to keep the bitterness out of her voice but failing.

"I need both of you," Nambi said tenderly. "Suma needs someone with her. Remember how you used to wish that she were with you the last time you helped me with the dye? Suma will want company too."

Ratai felt comforted. Then the feeling turned to one of sadness. She had disappointed her mother for the last two years, and now her younger sister was going to watch her fail. Then she decided that she was not going to fail this year. She was going to prove to everyone that she could weave. The moment she came to that decision, she suddenly felt that she could be the best weaver alive. The hope was so strong she could almost feel the finished cloth in her hand.

To Nambi's relief, Ratai said, "You are right, Mother. I will help you with the dye. I will also tie the thread this time."

Nambi smiled. "It is time for you to weave your own skirt. You are a woman now, so you must prove that you can take on womanly responsibilities."

Her mother was right, Ratai thought, she was no longer a girl. She must prove this by weaving a skirt on her own. She had caught her first pig three years before, but that did not matter because that was a man's rite of passage. Ratai understood that not every woman in the longhouse would insist that her daughter-in-law could weave, but she just happened to be in love with Sagan, whose mother was an avid weaver. Ratai's spirit rose to the challenge. In her mind she knew exactly what she needed to do. She told herself that if she were more careful and more delicate in handling the thread, she would make the most beautiful skirt. Something she would be proud to wear, its design would be imitated by other women.

Nuing was pleased to see Ratai's improved spirits that evening when he returned with a basket filled with freshwater fish and prawns.

\*\*\*

Early the following day, Ratai went into the jungle with her mother and Suma to look for dye materials. First they went to the neesia trees, which were growing a short distance from the longhouse. Many of the trunks had nicks on them, from when the barks had been stripped. Ratai picked a tree that was relatively unscratched. She began scouring the thick bark then used the edge of the machete to pry the bark loose. This *sebangki* bark would make a lovely brick red.

Suma looked out for the indigo vine. In the past, Nambi had planted these vines close to the neesia trees so that the weavers need not go too far to look for them. Before they left the house, Nambi told Suma that back in her parents' home, they used a smaller leave called the *tarum*. But the *renggat* here was just as effective.

It was a good day for them because Ratai managed to fill her basket full of the tough neesia bark, and Suma filled hers with the large dark green leaves of the indigo vine. As they made their way back, they also picked some lance-shaped *lemba* leaves to tear into strips to dry. Nambi had dried enough of the raffia-like string for her cloth but since Ratai intended to weave her own skirt too, she thought that they might need more.

Ratai's heart danced as she daydreamed about tying the strings around the warp thread. She already knew how to seal portions of thread with the waxy strip, but she had never been able to arrange a proper pattern before. This year she resolved to be more careful when counting the thread into warp columns. She reasoned that it would help her tie a symmetrical design onto the weave. The design in her mind was a pattern she had seen many years ago when she followed her father to the trading port at the mouth of the Rajang River. She had been standing next to a woman who was selling rice and illipe butter, and had overheard her telling another woman that her skirt was called 'Dry Bamboo by Meni's Lake'.

Ratai had committed the pattern to memory because her name 'Ratai' meant dry bamboo. The design was simple enough, straight vertical lines that peaked into a sharp point at the top. However, instead of running along the length of the warp thread, the standing bamboos were tied crosswise across many strings. Then there were the alternating leaves radiating out of either side of the bamboo poles. Each leaf ended with a tight curl.

She could not stop thinking about the design, so that when her mother was ready to teach them how to count the thread and to fix them to a tying loom, Ratai already had an idea of how she was going to arrange the pattern. Her mother, however, was not pleased when she saw a sketch of Ratai's plan on the wooden floor drawn with charcoal.

"This is only your first skirt," Nambi said. "Why don't you try a simpler design?"

"The tying is the most difficult part," Ratai said, "After that all the steps are the same regardless of whether the design is simple or complicated."

"But there is so much room for mistakes in this design. For one, we have to tie the bamboo poles crosswise. That means we must be extremely careful how we space them apart. We can't use the thread count to help us. If the bamboos are unevenly spaced they will not look symmetrical. Also, if we are not extremely careful when we move the dyed thread to the weaving loom, the poles will look crooked."

"This is my design, Mother. I will make sure that it is symmetrical," Ratai insisted. She had not told her mother that she had seen the design on another person. If her mother found out, she would insist to know more about the story behind the design before she would allow Ratai to weave it. "It is just a plant, Mother."

Nambi released a sigh. Maybe Ratai had received the design in a dream, she told herself. "You are right. Plants are gentle beings. They will not weaken your spirit."

Ratai smiled and it made Nambi happy to see her so driven and so confident. She hoped it meant that Ratai was no longer broken-hearted.

# 3

Ratai stretched her arms and felt her stiff shoulder muscles pull back in protest. She had tied and retied the *lemba* strings over the thread so many times she was getting a headache. She felt sick to her stomach because she had been so tense the past few days. Everything she ate or drank felt as though they had turned into lumps of rock in her belly. Today was the worst day by far. The suffocating heat, coupled with her headache made her feel dizzy.

Her family had gone to sleep hours ago, but she was still up, burning the lamps. She knew she should not be doing that because it usually took her father days to collect the resin to fuel one lamp. But she did not want to admit defeat. The ties were a mess. Her mother was right, it was extremely difficult to make the geometric design symmetrical.

"Are you still up, Ratai?" her mother's sleepy voice said behind her.

Ratai quickly covered the ties with a cloth, afraid that her mother would see what a failure her plan had turned out to be. "I am almost done, Mother."

Nambi raised herself up on an elbow so she could look over her husband's sleeping form. "Go to bed, Child. You can continue tomorrow. Take your time. I will wait for you before I start dyeing the other cloth."

Ratai pretended to fuss about the tying loom and the thread

stretched over it, but she was actually collecting the many *lemba* strips that she had ruined. She was worried that her mother would see them in the morning and begin to suspect what she was trying to hide. Then she again checked that the work was properly covered. She had told her family that they must not look under it because the design could be ruined by a careless comment. Even the youngest, Tambong, had taken her warning seriously and had never peeked.

Her mother had offered to help many times, but Ratai's sense of inadequacy made her stubborn. She was worried that she would let her mother down again. So she only did the ties when she was alone in the room or when everyone had gone to sleep. At that moment, Ratai wished that she could release a loud sigh to vent her frustration but her mother might hear. Instead she only blew out the lamp. Then with the help of the dim hearth light, she made her way to the ladder and climbed up to the loft. Suma and Madu were already deep asleep.

Ratai lay down thankfully. But she had been bent over the tying loom for so long that lying flat against the mat caused pain to shoot up and down her back. Her breath caught in her throat for a moment. Then her tense body slowly relaxed and she fell into a deep sleep.

\*\*\*

The light was so bright it was like being hit with crystal shards. Ratai covered her eyes and turned her face away from the beam. Despite the pain, she felt compelled to move forward so her other hand groped in front of her. She felt the rough texture of bamboo leaves then behind this, the trunk of a bamboo. The fine needles on its surface stuck to the tips of her fingers. She ignored the pain as she steadily made her way forward.

Soon the sound of a woman singing and a fast-flowing stream reached her. She kept her eyes down and made her way towards the direction of the sounds. Her skin burned, as though she was standing too close to an open flame. She must get to the stream; maybe the water would cool her. The ground beneath was sharp with dry thorns and splinters of broken bamboo. Her feet started to bleed but Ratai was thirsty and hot. Her need for water was more acute than the pain of piercing thorns.

When she finally reached the stream, she saw a long row of women washing thread. They were all singing, yet it sounded as though there was only one voice. Each time the women raised their skeins of thread, Ratai could smell ginger. So she knew that the thread had just gone through a mordant bath.

"Please let me through. I need some water to drink," she begged two of the closest women, but they ignored her. Ratai begged another woman and another, but none would let her pass. She started pushing and pulling but the women could not be moved even an inch apart. She begged and wept and pushed but everyone ignored her, as though she was nothing more than a breeze that brushed their shoulders.

Ratai finally crawled back into the bamboo forest. She found a line of symmetrically spaced bamboo and she reached out a hand, but each time she was about to touch a stem it would move out of reach. She struggled to stand upright. Her head and her eyes throbbed and she felt dizzy.

"Help me!" she called out.

"Why?" a woman said behind her.

Ratai turned and saw a beautiful woman with golden skin and long wet hair that was as black and as sleek as river grass. "I don't want to die," Ratai said. She looked down at her skin and saw boils forming on the back of her hands and arms.

"You should not have done a *pua ngar* design on a *pua mata*," the woman said.

Ratai's fevered mind struggled to digest what she heard. A *pua ngar* was woven with thread that had gone through the mordant bath. This was the only kind of thread that the maroon *engkudu* dye would hold fast to. Then she remembered that her thread was *mata*, unripened. It was untested because it had not gone through boiling water and burning ginger. But it was not her fault, she wanted to protest. She did not know how to do the mordant bath. Nobody in her longhouse knew.

"Help me, please," she begged again, her voice now sounding old and frail.

The woman came to her, unplugged a gourd bottle, and brought the drinking water to Ratai's mouth. Ratai drank in long and deep. After she had finished every last drop of water in the gourd, the woman said, "This is the best I can do for you. You must find Kumang and ask her to save you."

"Are you not Kumang? You are beautiful," Ratai said, her normal voice now returned to her.

"I am Meni. My home is in the lake," she said and turned to go.

Ratai grabbed her hand. "Please, Goddess. You must give me a charm to help me weave."

Meni turned to gaze into her face for a moment. "You will never weave, even though you are a woman. You were a child given by Sempurai to Nuing. He is a half-demon. So you too are like him, strange in nature."

Tears began to flow down Ratai's cheeks. "No," she said. "I must become a perfect woman, a whole woman, or I will never be happy."

Meni looked upon her with pity. Then she said, "I do not have the gift of weaving for you. But since your spirit grows strong in the same familial cluster as the warriors Nuing and Bujang Maias, I will give you this." She unslung a small basket by her side. Inside was a finger of ginger, a *kepayang* nut and a lump of *nipah* salt. "A basket of ginger, and a coconut bowl each of salt and *kepayang* oil. Boil the ginger water for half a morning then pour it into a trough. After you add the salt and oil, float my slave the porcupine quill on its surface. If it feeds on the blunt end, pour in more salt. If it feeds on the sharp end, pour in more oil. That is how you make a bath for the thread."

Ratai received the basket with both hands and studied the items inside. Her senses felt numb and she could not understand what they were. When she again looked up to ask, Goddess Meni was gone.

\*\*\*

"Mother! Mother!" Suma called down from the loft.

Nambi left the side of the hearth and went to the ladder to look up. "What is it, Child? Why are you shouting inside the *bilek*? What is the matter?"

"Something is wrong with Ratai. She won't wake up and she is all hot and sweaty."

Nambi climbed the ladder and hurried to Ratai's side. She felt her face. It was burning with fever. She turned to Suma and Madu. "Bring me some water and a roll of cotton."

The two sisters dashed down tearfully. Moments later they returned with what their mother had requested. Nambi fed some water to Ratai. Then she wet the roll of cotton and wiped Ratai's face, neck and shoulders with it.

Nuing's head poked out of the trapdoor. "What is wrong? What has happened?"

Nambi said, "Ratai has a fever, we need a shaman."

After telling her daughters not to leave Ratai's side Nambi hurried downstairs to help her husband pack for the journey. As she folded a blanket and stuffed it into the travelling basket, her gaze fell on the tying loom. She went to it and pulled away the cloth cover. "No!" she screamed, her horrified eyes running up and down the design. It was a mess of jagged lines and asymmetrical poles. Could the spirit that had inspired this design be angry with Ratai? Could it be trying to make her pay with her soul because she failed to bring it to fruition properly?

Her scream brought Nuing to her side. He looked down at the thread, parts of which were frayed from numerous tyings and untyings. His face scowled with grief. He turned and threw a machete into his travelling basket.

"I will go now," Nuing said from behind her shoulder. Then he grabbed a paddle hung on the wall, and ran out of the room.

Nambi's legs crumpled beneath her, and she stared down dumbly at the floor in front of the loom. She began to weep. It would be another three to five days before her husband returned. Even though there were now more longhouses along the great river, the closest community with a shaman was at least a day away. If he happened to be travelling, her husband might be forced to wait for his return. She started to pray in her heart that a spirit would send a message to a medicine man and persuade him to come to their longhouse. She returned upstairs to her eldest's side. There she pressed her cheek against Ratai's. Her child must not die.

\* \* \*

The day grew hotter and hotter in Ratai's dream world. She kept her sights set on a hill in the distance, but she seemed to be walking on the spot. When she tried to quicken her pace, the hill moved farther away. She walked until her lungs burned and her feet blistered. The hill became unattainable, so she turned her gaze down to a line of trees at the edge of the clay desert. When the clay under her feet started to feel like fine sandpaper rubbing against her sole, she stopped.

Ratai let out a frustrated growl then dropped down to the ground in exhaustion. The line of trees was not anywhere nearer. She breathed heavily but the air barely filled her lungs. It felt like she was drowning. She let out a yell – loud, defiant, and strong. She shouted like a man going to war. She screamed and tore the world of clay to shreds. Nothing would stand in her way, no demon, no heartbreak, no distance and no time could touch her. She would weave; she would be the perfect woman. And she could have anything she wished for. Everyone would grow to admire her and praise her. No man would ever reject her again. The shame, oh, the shame – a hundred of her voice called from the air about her. She couldn't decide if she was more hurt by her heartbreak or by her shame.

After what felt like days, her spirit returned to its senses. She got up to her feet and saw that the land she had torn apart had only been broken to reveal another land of clay. It was still hot, burning hot. It felt as though flames were burning under the soles of her feet. She must not stop, she must not give up. She did not care if the ground burned her feet off, she was going to become a weaver. The smooth ground began to feel bumpy, like it was covered with large round rocks. Then something grabbed her foot and brought her down to her knees. Ratai looked down and saw with horror that a twine-like root had wrapped itself around her ankle.

A face suddenly formed on the ground. "Who is this girl?" it said. Another face appeared. "Another girl who wants our secret."

"No more, no more," a tiny face to the side said.

"Let me go," Ratai growled fiercely. She kicked her foot hard and pulled it free. Then she walked away. Each time she felt a root reaching for her ankle, she would stomp on it. The pain under her feet was excruciating but Ratai didn't care. She was so intent on gazing down and stomping at each outreaching root that she was startled when she bumped into a wall of green. The leaves were so dark they were almost blue. She dug and clawed her way inside.

Thorns scratched and clawed her face back with equal ferocity, and she pushed and pulled to get them off. Finally she let out a loud shout and the plants shrivelled before her. She lifted her arms and bent her legs. She let out another shout, for she would stand her ground. The branches returned and began to claw her again. Ratai grabbed a branch and gave it a hard pull. It broke free. She used it to whip the other grappling branches away from her. One by one, the plants receded and a path soon opened before her.

Ratai looked down at the branch in her hand and saw that it was now straight and cleaned of leaves and bark. It looked like her mother's heddle stick. She held it in front of her as she walked forward. Each time there was a bush in her path, she would whack it to the side with the stick.

By and by she came to a wall of cobwebs. She pressed her hand against it, sinking her fingers into the web. Then she grabbed a fistful of the stuff and tore it away. More spider silk formed to cover the hole she made. She thrust the stick into it and moved it to the side. The cobweb yielded but the wall would not open.

Ratai grunted and growled fiercely as she started attacking the web. She tore, she whipped, she kicked and she punched. But the wall stood unmoved.

\*\*\*

Nambi grabbed one of Ratai's wrists, as Suma grabbed the other. Ratai's fever had escalated and she was starting to claw her face again. *Inik* Jambi, an elderly woman from next door, came into the room. Her sons had helped Nambi carry Ratai down to the main room the day before. She now handed Nambi a tube of bamboo filled with warm water.

She said, "I have boiled this water with the *tamawai* leaves. It is cool enough to feed to her now. It should help bring down her fever."

Nambi gratefully accepted the tube of arrowleaf sida tea. She poured some out into a halved coconut bowl. The smell of the tea was strong and refreshing. She tried to feed some to Ratai; but her daughter's mouth was shut tight. Nambi poured some tea onto a fistful of cotton then she rubbed the moisture over Ratai's face, neck and shoulders. Ratai began to calm, and her face relaxed.

Nambi tried once more to feed Ratai some of the liquid. This time Ratai drank the tea. Once Ratai was lying quietly on her back once more, Nambi turned her gaze to the door. Her heart yearned to see her husband stride into the room with a shaman. He had only been gone for two days, so it was too soon to expect him back. Yet her spirit pined for a miracle, for a chance encounter with a kind spirit during his journey.

Nuing had been to the other world before. Surely he could find a way to return there and save Ratai. Then she recalled that the last time he went, he was away for over two years. Nambi wept.

\*\*\*

Nuing listened to the shaman with mounting despair.

"I am sorry," the *manang* again said, his face sad but resolute. "I cannot cure her, so says Ketupong."

"Please, *Manang*, please come. You are already in my boat. Your travelling basket is packed. I can give you a painted Chinese jar or a Malay iron knife for your trouble. Please come and heal my daughter."

The shaman shook his head. "The rufous piculet has spoken on behalf of his father-in-law. He has warned me not to waste my efforts. Sengalang Burong, he says, is telling me that my skill cannot heal your daughter."

Nuing gripped the straps of his travelling basket hard. This was his third day away from home. He did not know if his daughter was still alive. Then a new thought entered his mind: Could she have died? Was that why Ketupong called this morning while they were still near this house? Was it to tell him that his daughter had died? How he wished that he had his father's gift of speaking with animals.

"You should go home now," the shaman said.

"Is there nothing you can do? Is there no medicine you can give?" Nuing begged.

The old man turned to a woman and said, "Bring me some water." Then he took out a bunch of charms from a small pouch. When the woman returned with a half-filled bowl, he dropped the charms inside the water. He mumbled some incantations over the bowl. Then he took out the charm and poured the water into a gourd bottle, saying, "Feed this water to your daughter. This is the best I can do for you now."

Nuing received the gourd with both hands. Then he left the longhouse with a heavy heart. The old man was the only shaman in the whole area along the Rajang and Lebaan. Maybe the water would help his daughter become stronger, he consoled himself, and a new hope rose in his heart. If she became strong enough to travel, he could take her to the trading port at the mouth of the river. He had heard that there were many healers there. Some got their power from the sea, some from the sky and some from strange, magical plants. If he could bring his daughter to them, he would offer a sacrifice to any god they called upon. But first, he must return home. Nuing set to his paddle, working hard upon it as a new sense of urgency filled him.

***

Ratai was drenched in sweat, and she struggled to breathe. The wall of spider silk had not yielded an inch.

"Oh, what a silly girl," a little shoot behind her said. "Even I know what to do, and I've just come out of the ground moments ago."

Ratai turned to the shoot and asked, "What am I doing wrong? What must I do to get to the other side?"

"Poke the pickled spider, silly. Didn't your mother teach you how to do it?"

Ratai thought hard for a moment. She stared at the web and saw that it was jumbled like loose thread. There was no order. How could she poke the web when there was such a mess. What would her mother do, she wondered.

"Don't be so impatient, Child," her mother's voice came to her as though from a great distant memory. "Count the thread in threes then tie them down to the heddle stick. Take your time. The threads will eventually line up, you'll see."

"I don't have time," Ratai shouted to the sky above her. "It is hot. I am thirsty. I need to get to the other side now."

The little shoot said, "Just count the thread. It is the only way through."

"Shut up or I will pull you out."

"You can't hurt me," the little tree said, "I am an ironwood tree."

"You are so tiny, you are not even a sapling," Ratai retorted angrily. She wrapped her hand around the shoot.

"I shall be a great tree," the shoot replied. "Because I come from a line of great trees."

Ratai released the shoot and fell back on her haunches. She was the daughter of Nuing and the granddaughter of Bujang Maias, yet she did not want to be either one of them. She wanted to be a desirable woman. She wanted to be admired for being skilful in weaving, planting and in dyeing. Her heart pined for Sagan, yet another part of her hated him for rejecting her love.

Then a strong wave of stubbornness filled her chest. She didn't care if Sagan failed her, she didn't care if the whole world failed her. She was not going to fail in her quest. With this new resolve in her heart, Ratai looked about her and saw a creeper plant spread over the ground. She pulled it free from the soil root by root so as not to break the line. Then she looped it into a circle like she had seen her father do with rattan vines.

Ratai returned to the wall. With the straight stick in hand, she counted the first three silken threads. She fixed the group of threads to the stick with the vine. She counted three more and fixed these to the stick by overlapping the vine on them. Over and over she did this, pulling the stick forward and unlooping the circle of vine as needed. When she stopped for a moment to stretch her back and neck, she realised that she was deep inside the wall of cobwebs.

Her mother was right, Ratai suddenly thought, it was not brute force but patience that would help her arrange the thread. She returned to her task, mindful to count each group of threes twice. Soon she felt fresh air coming through the opposite side of the wall. Before long, she stepped out of it.

Ratai breathed in deep, gulping the air in mouthfuls, as though she had been running a hard race. The air here was fresh and cool. And it was quiet. Not a devoid-of-life type of quiet, but a deep sleep kind of silence. Warily, she looked about her at the forest of bushes and vines. Soon she noticed women sleeping in between the plants. Some were lying flat on the ground, some slept with their backs leaning against a trunk, and others were draped like cloth over a log or a rock.

Ratai soft-footed her way forward. She did not want to disturb the sleepers because they could be receiving messages from the gods. She passed three rows of monitor lizards in groups of threes and she saw fireflies moving up and down three identical trees. She saw row upon row of six jackfruits, each of them weeping or gnashing their teeth. Then she saw Genali, a water spirit in the form of a crocodile with two mouths. It was being reflected to either side by copper mirrors, making it appear as though there were three Genalis.

The way grew stranger, yet Ratai did not feel out of place here. Her spirit was comfortable in this world, as though it was a familiar place. It felt like home.

\*\*\*

Nambi had been up since the night before. She would not trust anyone else to look after her eldest child. Now her body felt feverishly warm with exhaustion.

Suma said, "You must rest, Mother. Ratai is calm now. I can look after her."

"But she might have another fit. You won't know what to do then."

"I will wake you," Suma promised. "At least please lie down."

Nambi finally gave in to her daughter. She lay down on a mat and closed her eyes. Yet she could not sleep because the adrenaline from her anxiety and worry was still thick in her veins.

# 4

Nambi looked up expectantly when Nuing came into their family room. Then she saw his forlorn face. Hope had filled her heart when Betia their younger son had run into the room to tell her that his father could be seen coming up the river. Now that hope was dashed because the look on Nuing's face clearly showed that he had failed to bring back a shaman.

He put down his travelling basket and pulled out a water gourd, saying, "The shaman incanted over this water."

Nambi did not reach out for it. "Why did you not bring him with you?"

"He was about to come but the rufous piculet warned him that he cannot cure our daughter."

Nambi started to sob, so Nuing quickly added, "But he gave me this," and he thrust the gourd bottle into her hand. "He gave me this," Nuing said again, with more vehemence.

Slowly Nambi nodded and regained her composure. The shaman had offered hope, who was she to reject it. She pulled out the stopper and put the mouth of the bottle to Ratai's chafed lips. Her daughter had not woken in four days. Her ruddy cheeks were now sunken and her usually moist skin and lips hot and dry with fever.

Ratai's jaw was locked tight, but there was enough of a crack between her lips for Nambi to pour in sips of water. Then she watched Ratai's neck, waiting for her to swallow before she gave her more water.

\* \* \*

Ratai could feel a little coolness wash over her. She coughed and ran a hand over her face. Her head hurt, her skin burned and her stomach cramped. The sleeping forest was hours behind her, yet even in that place she could see nothing to eat or drink. The ground here was hot, and sinkholes gave out puffs of smoke. She had learned to test every step in front of her because she had almost fallen into a hole filled with embers when she first came out of the forest. The experience had almost made her return to the cool shade of the canopy, but she wanted so badly to see her family again. She knew that they were not behind her, so she must continue to move forward.

A little revived by the coolness, Ratai stood up and began to shuffle forward. Soon she heard the sound of hammering. She made her way towards it. Maybe there was someone there who could help her, tell her what to do or where to go. After about half a mile, she started to notice clay shapes of people lying on the ground about her. Ahead was a large man working in front of a giant furnace. From the metallic ring of hammerings, Ratai guessed that he was a blacksmith. Instead of a hammer with a stick handle, the man was grasping a smooth stone in his right hand and smashing it down with great force.

The closer Ratai got to him, the more she realised that he did not look human. His skin was covered in so many layers of clay that it appeared scale-like. He must have been bent over his work for many long years because his spine was curved into an arc. She could also see that his right arm, and the right hand that held the rock, was far larger than the left.

Yet the loincloth he wore was the most brilliant red that Ratai had ever seen. And it was so long that the front and back flaps curled about his feet in billows. Ratai was terrified but he was the only living thing for miles around. She took a deep breath to fortify the little courage she had.

As she drew nearer, the heat emitted from the furnace grew stronger and soon became unbearable. Ratai froze when a clay figure in front of her suddenly got up and walked towards the blacksmith. The form he was working on rose from the slab. Ratai could see that it was a man. He walked to a row of sticks and took one out. Then he went to a table and stood in front of it, undecided.

The blacksmith's voice boomed, "You said you wanted a spear!" The man form chose a triangle-shaped piece of iron from the table and walked away. Then the other clay form climbed onto the slab.

"What do you want to play with?" the blacksmith asked. "A spear or a spindle?" Then he cocked his head towards the clay form and listened for a reply that Ratai could not hear. "A spindle you shall have then," he said. He turned aside and grabbed a handful of iron ores. He threw them into a stone bowl and put this into the furnace. Then he pumped the bellows, sending flames shooting out of the smoke stack and up into the sky. Once the flames receded back into the furnace, he thrust his giant blackened hand inside and took out the red-hot bowl.

He then returned to the clay form on the slab, and with his free hand pressed a straight line down the length of the centre of its torso. Next he poured the molten iron into the channel he had just made. Sparks sputtered and hissed as the liquid ran along the groove. He blew on it before picking up the stone again and started to hammer the hardening iron from end to end. He dipped a coconut bowl into a jar of warm oil and poured it over the full length of the iron inside. The oil bubbled and smoked. Then he beat on the iron some more, making the air sparkle and steam about him. More oil was poured into the clay figure. He repeated this process over and over until the iron gave off a sharp ring when he hit it. Then he poured in water before he smoothed back the clay over the iron to hide it. The clay took on the form of a woman.

Ratai watched him work with wonder. Was he a god? Or was he a demon? Ignoring the heat of the furnace, she moved in closer to learn what he was doing.

Suddenly the blacksmith turned his red eyes to her and said, "You have been made. Why are you still here?"

Ratai swallowed back a scream. His fierce gaze had forced her to take a step back. Then he squinted his eyes and said, "You are that girl who stole a spearhead from me."

"You are the creator god, Selampadai," Ratai blurted without thinking. She knew him because each time in the evenings when she heard the chirping of the millipede, her mother would tell her that it was Selampadai hammering a new human into existence.

The clay woman got off the slab and went to the rack to choose a stick. Then she went to the table and picked a needle, which she fixed to one end of the stick. Another clay form climbed onto the slab. Selampadai said to Ratai, "I cannot unform you, if that is what you want." He turned to the clay form and asked what it wanted to play with.

"Why do you say that I stole a spearhead from you?" Ratai asked, feeling hot with embarrassment, for being called a thief was no light matter.

As he worked on the clay figure, Selampadai said, "You told me you wanted a spindle, so I made you into a woman. When you got to the table, you wanted a spear but I insisted that you take the spindle needle. I did not realise that you had taken a spearhead until I started to count them."

"It was only a spearhead," Ratai said.

Selampadai snorted. "It confused you because you now have the wrong toy to play with. You become restless in everything you do."

Ratai was quiet and thoughtful the whole time Selampadai busied himself in front of the forge. When he returned to the clay, she said, "I am sorry. Can you take it back, and give me a spindle in its place?"

"No, I can't. It will follow you to the afterlife because it has become part of you. But you are not dead," he said with a quick turn of his head, as he reconfirmed the suspicion in his mind. Then he asked, "Why are you here?"

"I don't know. I want to go home. Can you help me?"

He studied her face again for a moment. Then he said, "You are *busong*. You are cursed because you broke a taboo." He shook his head. "You should never have tried to weave a design that you are not ready for."

Ratai looked down dejectedly for a moment. Then she realised that she was standing before the creator god. She said, "You must know how to undo the curse."

Selampadai turned away from her with a shake of his head. "I cannot help you. Only the Goddess Kumang can free you."

"How do I find her?"

He pointed to the diminishing horizon in front of them. "That is the way you must go."

Ratai looked at the great expanse with despair. How was she to cross that? She was exhausted, hot and thirsty. She had walked so far, for so long, yet her destination was still beyond sight. She dropped down to the ground and wept.

Selampadai returned to his work. Ratai's quiet sobbing soon

grew to a wail that overwhelmed even Selampadai's hammerings.

"Woman! Why must you weep here?"

Ratai's wailing stopped and she whined, "Because I don't want to stay here but I cannot go home."

"Just go to Kumang and ask for her help."

"She is so far away. I will die trying to reach her."

"You will die if you stay," the blacksmith god said with a growl. "Because I will smash your skull myself."

"At least my body will not be in an isolated place, with no one to care for it."

"It would not matter," Selampadai reminded her. "Only your spirit is in this land. Your body is back in the world." After saying that he turned back to his work again.

Ratai watched his rippling back for a long while as she debated over what she should do next. If she stayed here, she would definitely not be able to return home. But if she went, she might die. A sudden new hope entered her being making her say, "My father will look for a shaman. He will find me here and show me the way home." She had seen a soul retrieval rite before. She remembered how a shaman described the lands he was travelling through as he sought for the lost soul. This land looked like one of the places he had passed. Then she remembered that he did not manage to find *Indai* Tandok's soul, so the lady had continued to fade away and died a week after the ritual.

"No one is going to come for you," Selampadai said. "You have disregarded a taboo. Hasn't your mother taught you that you must learn how to properly weave first before you can do a work that had been inspired by a goddess? Trying to do it without skill is an insult."

"But it was just bamboo," Ratai said.

"Foolish girl. You have no respect for rules. You should have learned where the pattern came from before you even attempted to tie the first knot."

Ratai looked down at her dusty feet. She was never good at listening. Her mother had always reminded her to be feminine in thought and action. Her sisters, even the youngest, had never had any trouble following Nambi's advice. Ratai often wondered what was wrong with her, why she was so different. Now she understood. If only she had not taken the spearhead.

The noise of hissing water startled Ratai out of her thoughts. She looked ahead of her at the great expanse. Then she got up and began walking towards the horizon. Part of her wanted to stay or at the very least ask for a charm from Selampadai, but another part of her was angry and stubborn. She did not want to say goodbye to him because she felt that it was his fault that she was in this predicament.

As she passed him, Selampadai looked up from his work. He called her back. Then he took a hot coal from his forge, put it in a small bamboo tube and gave it to Ratai. He also gave her a small flint knife. His voice was kinder when he said, "Take these, Child. The coal will help you light a fire even on a piece of water-soaked wood. This knife is so sharp no sap is too sticky and no wood is too hard for it to cut through." He helped her tie the tube and knife to her waist with a string then he returned to his work.

Ratai accepted the gifts wordlessly, as though she was already dead and was unable to vocalise her gratitude. She walked away, looking down at the ground, taking one step at a time. She did not want to look up because she was afraid that the sight of the distance would weaken her resolve. The ground beneath her started to change. First a net of thin dry roots then a single blade of grass. More grass until finally there was a carpet of turf under her feet. Ratai looked up and saw that she was at the foot of a hill.

She had reached Gelong, the invisible land. She had heard many times from her father the story of how her grandfather Bujang Maias had met Kumang on this very hill. It was never clear to her whether he had met her in the flesh or in a dream.

The trail going up was all limestone clay, and the plants to its left and right seemed to have been placed atop the surface, instead of having roots growing into the ground. She imagined the bushes and trees tumbling over in a storm, then she imagined an *orang Gelong* putting them upright again. This harsh place felt so comforting after the arid landscape.

The higher up she went, the more languid her body felt, and her eyes began to droop. Groggily she wondered what would happen if she fell asleep in a dream. Would she need to find a way to wake up from that dream too?

The ground started to level but a few yards later it began to slope down. Ratai looked and saw a wide black lake below. Barely a ripple disturbed the surface. Along the banks were a multitude of bathing platforms. Bards had sung that the spirit beings of Gelong were so industrious each family had built their own bathing platform. She walked down the slope and approached the closest platform. There was no one about. She looked up the slope again and saw tall pillars holding up a longhouse high in the clouds. She had passed right under it thinking that the pillars were living trees.

She looked down at her clothes and realised how dirty she was. It would be rude for her to go directly to the house. There were some fragrant screwpine leaves growing by the side. She tore a few strands of the young soft leaves before going to the platform. Cautiously she lowered herself into the strange lake. She looked about her for a few moments more, feeling somewhat unnerved by the silence and stillness. Then she tore the leaves and used it to scrub off the dirt and grime from her body. While still in the water, Ratai unwrapped her skirt and scrubbed it clean. She put the skirt back on again before climbing back up on the platform. There she wrung the hem and tried to get as much water as she could out of the skirt. Water was still dripping from her when she made her way up a different path leading to the main ladder of the house. The garden that she passed was filled with cotton bushes and *lemba* plants. Here and there were also neesia trees that provided the bright red dye that was beloved by all Iban women. She breathed in deep the stench of the ripe noni fruit, which was fragrant with expectation.

When she neared the ladder, her steps slowed. She could still not see anyone anywhere. Yet the place could not be abandoned because the garden was well tended. Then she heard a faint sound coming from above, like the sound of pestle hitting mortar. She approached the ladder with more confidence. She looked up and noticed for the first time that the house itself was made up of so many stories that she could not see the roof.

She touched her foot to the first step and called out. "Is this house free of taboo? Are you free to receive visitors?"

An old woman with an ugly face looked down from the entrance above and said, "Come, come. No taboo binds this place, no barrier prevents visitors from coming up."

Ratai started climbing the ladder. The steps were nothing more than notches cut into a long single piece of log. There was no handrail for her to cling on to. After some time climbing, Ratai felt the wind on her face. She looked down and saw that she was now so high above the ground, the black lake she had bathed in looked only as wide as the palm of her hand. Her heart fluttered fearfully within her and her legs began to shake. She had the unexplainable urge to jump, to fly. Instead she fell on the log on all fours.

Ratai again looked up and saw that the doorway had receded into an inestimable distance above her. Rage began to fill her being. The gods were not fair. They gave you hope then they took it away. The gods were unreliable. Their words were like smog, smothering you and limiting your vision with their unclearness. Ratai became so enraged she stopped fearing death.

She stood up, looked up defiantly at the entrance and resumed her climb. Slowly the receding doorway began to move back towards her. A few more steps and she walked through the threshold. The moment she stepped into the house, her rage immediately turned to relief. She took deep breaths to calm herself. Then she noticed a solitary old woman sitting on a colourful mat. In front of her was a small jar of rice wine and a woven tray filled with betel vine leaves and lime chalk. She was using a stylised guillotine knife to peel a betel nut, which she then cut into thin slices.

"Come sit, Child," she said, "Who are you? Where are you from and why are you here?"

Ratai lowered her hips on the mat thankfully. Her legs were weak with relief. "My name is Ratai," she said. "My parents are Nuing and Nambi of Lebaan. My grandfather is Bujang Maias. I am here to ask for help from the Goddess Kumang. I need her to show me the way home."

"But this is the world of dreams," the old woman said. "She cannot help you here unless she goes to sleep in the other world."

"But you are here," Ratai said, perplexed.

The old woman frowned. Then she said testily, "That is because I am asleep in the other world. I am an old woman, I need my naps."

"Who are you, Grandmother?" Ratai asked.

"I am *Indai* Lipai. I am Kumang's chief servant."

"That means you can help me."

"No, Child, I cannot. Because you are *busong*. You are under a curse. Only the goddess can help you."

"But it was only bamboo," Ratai said, once more pleading her case. Plant spirits are supposedly cooler, less harmful than animal ones. "How could the design have harmed me? How could it have cursed me?"

"The design was a gift from the Goddess Meni to a weaver of the old land. One of her conditions was that the design must be woven with a processed cloth because the red dye must be of the colour of dusk reflected on her lake."

"I met the goddess, but she wouldn't help me," Ratai said as tears of frustration began to run down her cheeks. She hung her head and stared at the mat.

"If she had wanted to punish you, you would be dead now. Has she not given you materials for a mordant bath?"

Ratai's hand immediately went to the small basket hanging from a rope slung over her shoulder.

*Indai* Lipai explained, "She could not set you free because you broke her rule. Instead she sent you across the dreamscape to this place. If you had been weak and not worthy of her gift, you would have died during the journey."

"Can your mistress truly help me or will she send me to another being?" Ratai asked petulantly.

"Do not be arrogant, Child," *Indai* Lipai said, her voice slightly raised. "She is the patroness of weavers and headhunters. If she cannot help you then you will be lost in this land forever."

"What happens to people who cannot leave this place?" Ratai asked.

"Your body will die because no one can live long in the other world without eating and drinking. Your soul will continue to suffer from hunger and thirst until you go mad. Maybe you will find a way back to your world but you will return as a demon."

Ratai was quiet for a long time. She had not eaten or drunk anything that *Indai* Lipai had served her. Nothing was going to quench her thirst or satisfy her hunger anyway. She needed to go home. The longing to see her family once more was so strong, her chest felt tight.

"It will be dark soon," *Indai* Lipai said. "You should start climbing up to the top floor."

Ratai went into the room that *Indai* Lipai pointed to. Inside, the room was wide, far wider than the spacious common gallery outside, and the floor was polished to a mirror finish. No wonder Keling was such an unbeatable headhunter, Ratai thought. The floor of the room was perfectly clear of any object or liquid that would make him stumble or slip. Rolled mats and Chinese jars lined the walls on all sides. She looked about for a moment then noticed a log leading up to a trapdoor. The log was smooth and slick with *kepayang* oil. She tried to climb it a few times but she kept slipping down. Then she saw a ripe jackfruit placed next to the fire hearth.

A sudden idea entered her mind. She handled the flint knife that Selampadai had given her and started to peel the fruit. White sticky sap oozed out and covered her hand. Disregarding the ripe golden flesh, she cut the rind into smaller pieces to get as much of the sticky substance as possible. After both her hands were covered with the sap, she returned to the log and rubbed the sap on her knees and the sole of her feet. She tried to climb again. This time she did not slip. The sap began to soften and peel as it became mixed with the oil, but it gave her just enough traction to climb the log.

She reached the upper floors just as the oil started to penetrate under the sap covering her hands and begin to separate the sticky substance from her flesh. With her feet dangling down the trapdoor, she scraped up more oil from the log and rubbed it onto her palms, knee and soles. After she got most of the sap off her skin, she looked about her.

On this floor were sheet upon sheet of underlayer bark. Some were still hard but to one side of the room were rolls of bark that had been pounded soft. There was a half-finished bark basket, and a partially embroidered loincloth at the bottom of the next log pointing upwards. When she reached it, Ratai noticed that the log was a thorny *nipah* stem. The thorns were as long as needles and if one were to pierce the palm of her hand, the point would penetrate through to the other side. Ratai despaired about climbing it.

She searched for another way up. There was none. Then a thought occurred to her. She picked up an unbeaten hard bark and draped it along the length of the log, as far up as she could reach. When she dragged it down, it snagged some thorns and broke them off. She started to climb. The broken thorns pressed hard against her callused soles but they did not cut into her skin. Holding the square bark in front of her, she snagged and broke off more thorns until she reached the floor above.

The room here was dark. With the little light that came from above and below, Ratai could barely make out the forms of fresh resin lamps lying on the floor. She groped her way towards the square of light above her. The log leading upwards was solid and had notches cut into it but it was swarming with red fiery ants.

Ratai immediately jumped back with terror. She had been bitten by a nest of ants a few years back and the pain still haunted her. Her mother told her that the insect was still trying to get her because when she was a baby they had tried to eat her but her father had saved her. Surely the ants would get her this time. Ratai looked about but the only thing in the room were the lamps. She returned to the other trapdoor but the nipah log was gone and the floor below seemed to have dropped to a great distance. If she were to jump, she knew it would be instant death.

She decided to light one of the lamps; maybe the light would help her find a tool or another way up. She opened the bamboo tube Selampadai had given her. The coal inside was still red-hot. She slid it out to the edge of the tube and touched its ember surface to the wick of a lamp. The resin lamp burned and emitted clumps of sooty smoke. She brought the lamp to the log to try to see better. When she lowered the lamp to look behind the log, the ants began to scatter away, to get away from the smoke.

Ratai almost let out a shout of triumph. She quickly clasped a hand over her mouth because a shout of victory in another person's *bilek* would be misunderstood as an attack upon the owner. She did not want to be assaulted by the rest of the inhabitants of the longhouse. Ratai began to move the lamp up and down the notched log. Soon it was all covered in soot but free of ants. She climbed the ladder.

On reaching the floor above, she blew out the lamp and set it down. Here the room was so bright it hurt her eyes. It was empty though, and there was only a rope ladder hanging a quarter of the way down from the trapdoor above. She jumped as high as she could but the lowest rung was at least a foot beyond her reach.

Ratai stood under the ladder and called out, "Is there anyone up there?"

She listened for a reply, but there was none. She called again. Once more there was no reply. There was, however, a different sound coming from the walls. She pressed her ear against a panel.

There it was again, the tiny tap-tapping sound as though there were a thousand blacksmiths hammering with the points of needles. Parts of the panel were soft to the touch, she realised. They broke under her fingers when she pressed them and a sprinkle of pale termites spilled out. She looked down and saw that the bottom part of the panel had been eaten away.

Ratai squatted down and thrust her hands into and under the wall plank. Then she pulled the piece out. The sides were not fixed, so she could pull it back until the top where it splintered free from the brace holding it in place. She pulled out the flint knife from her rope belt and cut away a "V" shape to either side of the plank to form hooks. She also scored the smooth surface of the plank with her knife to make it rough. Then she slid the cut end into the bottom rung of the rope ladder and hooked it in place. Gripping the sides tightly, she began her climb. The plank wobbled with every step, and crackled when she put her weight onto a soft part of it. Her shoulder muscles were stiff from trying to hold herself steady, and her hands burned with the effort of gripping the smooth wood. When her hand finally grabbed the first rung, she let out a loud sigh. She clung on a few moments more to catch her breath then she resumed her climb, this time on the rope ladder.

By now Ratai was ready for the next test. She remembered love poems of how the warrior Keling had to go through seven tests before he could finally get into Kumang's bedroom. Was she going through a similar trial? She looked about her with a stronger sense of purpose. This new room was filled with whole and stripped rattans. She spotted the trapdoor immediately because there were half a dozen loose rattan vines hanging down from it. She studied the vines and realised that they were too smooth for her to climb. Not only that but when she tried to climb one it began to swing her like a pendulum. She had always fancied herself to be as audacious as a Melanau riding a Tigaw swing, but today she felt too tired to even get a proper grip. She tried holding two vines together but she only managed to get a little higher because the energy needed to keep both vines together was too hard for her.

She looked up longingly, wishing that she had the strength to climb. There must be something she could do. Then it occurred to her that she could tie the vines together, like she had seen her father tie halved bamboos together to make a latticed floor.

She found a roll of rattan strips that were soaking in a bowl of water. She brought this bundle to the vines. Then she pulled out a softened strip and proceeded to tie a knot on one vine. Then, without cutting the strip, she tied another knot to the next vine. She did this until she had tied all six vines side by side to each other. Then she tied the next row of knots with a new strip, about two feet above the bottom row. She repeated this until the new row was beyond her reach. She climbed, tying the new rows as she progressed up.

When she reached the sixth storey, her heart skipped a beat. It was a weaving room. There were balls of spun cotton in shallow baskets. There was also a wall lined with rolls of unspun cotton and in the middle of the floor was a spindle that glistened from years of use. Next to this was a tying loom. Its thread was covered with a piece of cloth so Ratai knew that the goddess was working on a new design. To one side of this was a pile of woven cloths. Ratai touched the pile with awe, and ran her hand over some of the intricate designs. The patterns of animals, spirits, and curving claws or hooks inspired her with imagination. The colours of red, yellow and indigo were so brilliant they seemed to give out their own light.

Then Ratai turned her eyes upward longingly. She could sense the presence of the goddess in the floor above. Leading up to her chamber was a weaving loom. The warp threads had been fastened to the loom and upon it was a design of one and a half giant snakes. The other half of the design was on the underside of the loom. She looked the loom up and down but could find no way to climb it. The side beams were too smooth. The threads had been dyed and were free of their ties so trying to climb over that would be impossible because the strands were loose. The goddess would soon start to weave, she thought, because the heddle stick had been tied to the thread.

She looked behind the loom and found a basket of laze rods. Could she use these to climb? Would she dare step on the goddess's handiwork? But there was no other way up. Ratai grasped a handful of rods and returned to face the loom. After begging for forgiveness under her breath and explaining to the thread as to why she needed to see the goddess, Ratai weaved the first laze rod over and under the thread. Then a foot above this, she weaved in another rod, this time in the opposite over-and-under direction. She did this over and over until she could reach no farther. Then she grasped a fistful of rods, took a deep quacking breath and started to climb. She continued to weave the rods in until she reached the upper floor.

On reaching the room, the first thing she sensed was the cool breeze blowing in from an opened skylight. She looked up but there were no stars in the night sky. It was empty and black, like a pit with an unfathomable bottom.

"Who are you, Child?" a woman's voice asked in a dreamy trance-like manner.

Ratai turned her gaze to the darkness within the room and said, "I am Ratai, daughter of Nuing. I am from Lebaan."

A light started to glimmer from within the darkness. The light soon spread to illuminate the whole room. Ratai looked about her with wonder because everything – the walls, the floor, the baskets, the jars – was reflecting the light coming from inside many layers of mosquito netting.

She could see the layers being peeled away from the inside. When the light reached the outermost layer, it was so bright that it engulfed the fabric of the netting. Ratai covered her eyes but as the last layer was opened the light dimmed enough to allow Ratai to open her eyes once more. She stared with awe, for she had never imagined that anyone could be so beautiful. Her legs lost all strength and she fell down on her knees in terror.

Time seemed to stand still. Kumang sat down across from her and smiled reassuringly. Ratai could feel power emitting out of her, a strong independent power. Kumang's lovely face was proud and fierce, as any perfect woman should be. Now sitting before her, Ratai felt shame. She knew what she had to do as a woman, all the skills that she should have learned but never did. She had grown up believing that weaving and planting were inferior to hunting. But now, sitting before the goddess, she realised that her role as a woman was to support life, to grow life. Planting, birthing and weaving were in no way inferior to any other role. Ratai hung her head, believing that she did not deserve to look upon the goddess's beauty.

Kumang said, "You are *busong*, yet you have managed to reach my bedchamber."

Ratai's tongue felt fused to the roof of her mouth. There was nothing she could think of to say to justify her actions. Her own arrogance and vanity had brought her to this place. She should have submitted to her fate and die, but she had kept asking for help. It was taboo for the spirits to refuse her help because she was a desperate soul seeking to live.

"Eh! What a horrible mess," *Indai* Lipai said when her head poked through the trapdoor. "You have made me work harder than any other visitor before you."

"I am sorry," Ratai said. "I did not know how else to reach this room."

"Most people would just tolerate the ants or the thorns. Or if they were truly worthy to meet the goddess, they would have been able to jump up. But you? You dirty the ladders with sap and soot. Then you break a wall and use up *Endu* Kumang's rattan strips to tie the vines together. She was saving it for a special basket for Keling."

*Indai* Lipai's bulging eyes made her face appear uglier than usual. She was speaking so vehemently that spittle flew out from between her sharp teeth. Despite herself, Kumang laughed.

The room swayed and the hanging beads and gold or silver leaves tinkled like raindrops, echoing her laugh. When Kumang finally moved her hand away from her mouth, Ratai could see that her teeth were perfectly black. Again her heart pined for that beauty, and wished it for herself.

Kumang said, "You are very resourceful, *Anak*. You will be an excellent mother and wife."

A tightness began to fill Ratai's chest. She said, "I cannot weave. I am not marriageable."

"That is nonsense," *Indai* Lipai said. "If your *padi* grows well, you can have any man you wish."

Ratai shrunk away from their gaze. "My *padi* stalks will not bend with the weight of rice grains. Most die. My family would starve if I was the only person they relied on to plant the seeds." Ratai began to sob with self-pity. The other two women waited in silence until she regained her composure. "My sister," Ratai started to say but then stopped to pull in a deep breath. "My sister Suma is as perfect as I am flawed."

"Does your mother reject you?" *Indai* Lipai asked. "Does she ignore your needs?"

"No, she loves me as though she had birthed me herself." Then Ratai added, "I think my troubles may be because I stole a spearhead from Selampadai."

"No wonder you are confused," *Indai* Lipai said with a snort of derision. "If I had known that, I would have chased you out of the house."

Kumang, however, studied Ratai's face with interest. "You are very much like your father Nuing. He too was lost even though he was loved and protected by a strong headhunter and a gifted weaver."

"He is happy now," Ratai said.

Kumang nodded. "And you too will find your happiness."

"But how can she?" *Indai* Lipai said. "She cannot weave and her rice does not grow abundantly."

Kumang straightened her back and the room grew brighter. Then she pronounced, "The child will prosper." And before *Indai* Lipai could make a list of how impossible that prophecy was, Kumang said, "The spirits will bless her because I am adopting her."

The goddess turned her gaze back to Ratai, who was now staring at her wide-eyed. "You asked for a spindle from Selampadai then you stole a spearhead. I am the goddess of the weave and the patroness of headhunters. I am the only one who can make you prosper."

Ratai prostrated herself before the goddess in gratitude, in awe of her generosity. She wept with relief. When she opened her eyes again, she found herself in a dim room and lying on her back.

She was exhausted and could barely move. Even breathing was a struggle. She tried to speak but could only manage a moan.

Suddenly she felt a movement by her side. She looked up and saw Suma's face. Her sister called out, "Mother! Mother!"

Nambi was instantly by Ratai's side. She wept with joy on seeing that her child's eyes had opened. "Where have you been, my child? Where have you been, my heart?" she said over and over.

Suma brought some water, and Nambi brought the halved coconut husk to Ratai's lips. This time, Ratai drank. By now Nuing and other women of the longhouse had also come into the room. They helped Nambi cooled Ratai's face and shoulders with wet cotton.

While feeding Ratai some thin rice gruel, Nambi sang, "My child is returned to me. I feed her rice gruel now, like when she first came to me. When she was a babe in my arms. I was confined to my room for forty days, as though she had come from my own womb. Oh how awful were those forty days when no news came about her father. She was my only solace. For two years she was my only joy. She has been my solace for twenty years. She is the reason I am a mother, she is why I have my field and my children."

Nuing wept as he listened to his wife's song. The day before, he had chopped up Ratai's tying loom and cut the thread she had worked on. He had killed the spirit that demanded for her blood. Then he burned the pieces in a place far away from the longhouse. He had also made an offering of food and wine to the spirit of the thread, and he had sacrificed a prized rooster to the spirit of the design. He did not know if what he was doing was right or wrong but he did not care because he was desperate. He was desperate to have the gods return his daughter to him.

And here she was now, awake and eating from Nambi's hand.

# 5

It had only been two weeks since Ratai woke up from her long sleep. Sagan watched her lethargic frame from a distance. He was ashamed and afraid to approach her. Though they had been friends for years, Mansau, her brother, would not talk to him. When Sagan had asked him about Ratai's condition, and whether there was anything he could get for her, Mansau had turned and said, "It is your fault that my sister almost died. You shamed her. You destroyed her character and reputation."

"I am sorry. My mother insisted that she did not want Ratai as her daughter-in-law."

"Why did you not ask your mother first? Ratai was trying to redeem her reputation because of your rejection," Mansau said, "She became cursed because she tried too hard."

Since that conversation, Sagan had never been within three doors of Ratai. From the signs and words that they gave him, he knew that her father and brothers no longer wanted him anywhere near her. Mansau was right, Sagan chided himself, he should have asked his mother about her feelings for Ratai first. But he was afraid that Ratai would reject him after he visited her. What would he say to his mother then? His mother had never spoken badly of Ratai before, so her vehement disagreement came as a surprise to him. He was caught between a rock and a hard place. If he were to float onwards, he would be eaten by a crocodile. But if he were to run aground, he would be swallowed by a python. The best solution he could think of was to set aside his intentions for Ratai first while he tried to persuade his mother to accept her as his wife. He had never expected Ratai to overreact the way she did.

Now, living in this place was becoming intolerable for Sagan. He still loved and desired Ratai, and not being able to speak with her was unbearable. He felt like a pariah in his own home. Maybe he should go with Bantak to the trading ports at the river delta. Work with a trader or a ship so he could afford to buy some beautiful Chinese jars for both his ladylove and his mother. Maybe that would appease both women and bring peace back into his life again.

As he thought over the idea, it slowly dawned on him that a jar was the very thing that would persuade Nuing that he was serious about being married to Ratai. It would also prove that he was a capable man and a good provider.

That evening after dinner, Sagan told his mother about his decision to go with Bantak the next time he travelled. She knew why he wanted to go. She turned in the direction of Ratai's home and sniffed with scorn.

"You should never have gone to that girl," she said.

"It is not her fault."

She turned her gaze back to glare at him. "She is a foolish woman. She is *busong*. Even the shaman would not come to heal her."

"Mother, I do not wish to argue with you. I must do this to gain back the chief's trust, to show him that I am truly earnest."

"There are other girls who will have you," Sawai said imploringly.

Sagan looked towards the door for a moment, his face flushed red with frustration. Then his angry eyes turned back to her. "Don't you understand? There is not a single family in this house that would allow me to visit their daughter anymore. The only man who talks to me kindly is Bantak, and it is only because there is no unmarried woman in his *bilek*."

Sawai hung her head down with sorrow. Then she said, "Maybe you can find a girl from another longhouse."

"You wish for me to *nguai*?" Sagan asked, his voice tinted with surprise.

"No. Not at all. Bring the girl home. You don't have to move into her family. Bring her here."

Sagan let out a heavy sigh. "But I cannot stop thinking about Ratai."

"She has enchanted you," Sawai said, her eyes bulging wide with horror and sudden realization. "You must fight this feeling or you will become mad."

Sagan stared at his mother with disbelief as she continued her ranting. "See!" she said, pointing a finger at his face. "See, even now you are thinking of leaving your old mother alone, so you can bring home a Chinese jar for her. You could be gone for years. I will have died before you come home. Who will bury me then? Who will weep for me?" She started wailing and beating her chest.

Sagan got up and left the room. Yet even outside he could not escape from her. Her wails permeated the common gallery, turning many heads and making Sagan's angry flush even redder with embarrassment.

A woman came out from the room next door and went into his family room. Then another woman went in to inquire about his mother. Sagan lay down on his bachelor bed and turned his face to the wall. He traced the roughly hewn plank with a finger. He was familiar with those lines, for he had traced them many times before, especially when he thought of Ratai and fantasized about their life together. A hand shook his arm.

He looked up and saw Bantak returning his gaze. Sagan rose to make room for Bantak to sit next to him. They both sat facing the now open door of Sagan's family room.

"You have told her?" Bantak said.

"Yes," Sagan replied and let out a heavy sigh. "I thought that she would be sad, but I never expected her to embarrass me like this."

"You are her only child," Bantak reminded him. "I am the youngest in my family, and my mother caused a scene two years ago."

"But it was not as bad as this though."

"That was because my brothers and sister were there to calm her. But she doesn't cry anymore when I leave. I have proven to her that I can watch out for myself."

Just then Bantak's mother Umoi was seen entering the room. A few minutes later the loud wails were reduced to sobs. "Don't worry," the neighbourly woman's voice could be heard saying. "My son Bantak went to look for work many times and he always came home with wonderful things. Have you seen the Chinese jars that line my walls, or the silver belts holding up my skirt? Your son will come home with these things for you too."

Another woman said, "You will become rich and happy. Your son will become like a prince. Every man will admire him. Every mother will envy you. Then we will all tell our sons to be brave and industrious like him."

While this was still going on, a group of men led by Nuing reached the longhouse. On their backs were baskets filled with palm cabbage, sago, fish and wild pig. The chief was going to hold a feast to thank the gods for allowing his daughter to live. Though Ratai had told no one about her dreams, rumour started to spread that the reason she lived was because a great spirit had shown her mercy.

Sagan wished with all his heart that he could talk with Ratai about her experience. He also wished he could explain to her that he never meant to insult or demean her. Only that he wanted to persuade his mother to accept her first. Yet all those words in his head seemed like dust now because he was not allowed anywhere near her.

None of her siblings would pass her a message from him. The tension between him and the chief was so thick, Sagan felt breathless each time he crossed paths with Nuing. He tried to talk a few times, to explain his action but he was terrified for his own life. He had no option. He must bring back a gift worthy of a princess.

*\*\**

Ratai could feel Sagan's hot stares on her back. She wanted so badly to return to her family room, to the loft, to hide herself from his gaze. But her mother was adamant. Ratai must shame Sagan more than he had shamed her. She must not show any weakness or any submission to the ill reputation that he had poured on her head. He was the shameful man, Nambi kept reminding her. He should be the one hiding from everybody like an *antu uging*, a recluse, not her.

So today, like yesterday, Ratai sat outside with her back to Sagan. While she carefully worked on a mat she half thought about her dream journey. She still remembered every item that the goddess Meni had given her: salt, *kepayang* and ginger. She tried to recall the formula for a mordant bath and how the porcupine quill was meant to swim on it.

Selampadai had said that she would never weave cloth as a

punishment for stealing the spearhead from him. But Meni had given her items for a mordant bath. As she thought through all these things, Ratai's fingers moved deftly over the weave and warp of the dry rush reed. She sang a little lullaby about a river that washes over a growing reed, about rain that runs down its spine and about the sun that burns it to a golden glow. When she looked up she was surprised to see her mother and some women staring at her and her handiwork. Was it so bad? She wondered and blushed.

"*Anak*," her mother said. "That weave is magnificent." Nambi raised the mat to better catch the light. The pattern was reminiscence of the talking ginger roots that had mocked her.

"It's the *bingka lia'*," Ratai said shyly. She had called the design by its literal name because she could not think of a more poetic form of address.

The women ooh-ed and aah-ed at the curls of the ginger roots that were linked one to the other in a long diagonal line. The thickest roots lined one side of the mat, and the succeeding curls grew ever smaller than the one before it until the last tapered to a point on the opposite side.

Ratai blushed further, proud and embarrassed at the same time when the women asked her to teach them the design. Nobody had ever asked her to teach them anything. Nambi looked on with open pleasure, for her eldest was now a woman.

As the day progressed, Ratai grew more and more confident. Her wrists and fingers began to move with the fluidity of a dancer and her voice grew gentler. Gone were the sudden tomboyish movements or the rough barking tones. Even her laughter had become more restrained.

After some hours of watching her, Nuing once more sat back and marvelled at the sudden change in Ratai's behaviour. A golden glow seemed to now emit from her, so that he asked, "Child, what has happened to you?"

Ratai instantly became silent. Nambi was perplexed that her daughter should be troubled by Nuing's question. Then she realised that Nuing was asking her about her fever and not about the day. A sudden panic gripped Nambi's heart. "What happened in your dream? Did a demon ask for a favour from you while you were ill? Did you promise to give it your soul in exchange for this gift?"

Ratai shook her head but remained silent.

Nuing leaned forward. "You must tell us, Child. Maybe we can do something to help you. Maybe we can give a sacrifice in your place."

Ratai finally said, "I met Goddess Meni and Goddess Kumang in my dream. They advised me and helped my spirit."

"Did they give you a charm?" a woman asked.

Ratai looked up shyly for a moment. "Meni gave me the ingredients for a mordant bath."

"What did Kumang give you?" another woman asked.

"She told me that I will never be able to weave but she adopted me to save my life."

The breathless silence about her suddenly burst into a cacophony of chatters. "No wonder she looked so beautiful after she woke up." "The mat pattern must be a gift from the goddess." "She is an *indu ngar,*" said a woman, referring to her new status as an alchemist of the mordant bath.

*Inik* Jambi said, "We must find a bard to praise and honour the goddess. A simple thanksgiving feast is no longer enough."

The women who had encircled Ratai now rose and began to hurry back to their rooms, calling for members of their family as they did so. That evening after dinner, everyone collected in the chief's common gallery. The consensus to invite a bard was immediately reached. This meant that they must invite their friends and relatives living within two days' journey of the longhouse. Four men were assigned the task of inviting guests. One group of two would go up the main river, and the other would travel downriver. The date of the festival was fixed at two weeks after that night.

Long strings of raffia rope were brought out and fourteen knots were tied onto each strand. Early the next morning before the four men left, one rope was untied from each rope. These ropes would be given to longhouse chiefs, who would then untie one knot for each passing day, so that his visiting party would be neither too early nor too late for the feast.

After the people had seen the messengers off, another group of men, led by Nuing, paddled out to the main river then turned downriver. It took them more than half a day of hard paddling to reach a *nipah* palm forest. On reaching the thicket, they looked for the older palms and cut them down. Then they lugged the pieces to open ground and burned them. For the next two days they continued to collect old palms and burned them in a large bonfire. On the morning of the third day they collected the ashes in bamboo tubes and closed woven baskets before making their way home.

When they reached the longhouse, half a dozen troughs were brought out and filled with water. Then the palm ashes were poured in. The ashes were swirled about with large sticks, after which the mixture was left to settle. Ashes that floated on the surface were carefully skimmed off before fresh bamboo tubes were filled with the thickened cloudy water. These tubes were placed over an open fire and the water inside was boiled until they were dry. Then they split the tubes open and pried out a knuckle of grey-green salt. The lumps were crumbled then dropped into small clay jars.

That night there was another meeting. This time the people discussed which part of the stream they were going to block. Eventually it was decided that they would go two miles upriver because the streambed there was low enough to cross by foot during low tide. The whole time during the discussion, no one mentioned the words fish or derris root. They were afraid that one of the small insects or lizards would tell the fish about their plans. Some other men offered to go into the jungle, to build pig traps along a new fresh trail that they had spotted the day before.

Early the next morning, before the sun rose, the longhouse was a din of activity. People called out loudly to each other and shook their children awake. It was going to be a busy day. Everyone had their duty: chopping wood or collecting rocks to dam up the river, cutting bamboo tubes to keep the fish in, or digging for derris roots to intoxicate the fish with. By mid-morning, the tide had become low so the people started to plant sticks and split bamboo across the streambed.

An older group of people chopped up the *tuba* roots and pounded them with rock inside a shallow boat. After the bottom of the boat was properly blanketed in white sap, the boat was dragged into the river and water was poured into it. Then the mixture was swished about until the water became milky. The boat was then overturned and the derris root poison released into the stream.

In parts of the stream, by the bank and at the barricade, everyone waited with great anticipation. A few minutes more and the surface of the river began to fill with fish. The smaller fish flopped belly up helplessly, struggling to right themselves. These were scooped into nets by the younger excited children. The older children used three pronged fish spears to pick up the large catfish and snakeheads. Any of the stronger and larger fish that tried to jump over the fence were smacked on the head with clubs by the adults then tossed into baskets. Basket after basket was filled to the brim.

After every intoxicated fish was collected, the barricades were pulled off the streambed and the people trudged back noisily to the longhouse. Not even the loudest ill omen was going to cast a shadow on their festivities now. As long as they didn't hear the warning messages, they could ignore them. On reaching the house, they cleaned the fishes' entrails. Some were splayed open and smoked over low fires while others were rubbed with salt. The women massaged the fish flesh until the juices they pressed out ran clear. Then they put the fish into bamboo tubes with brine water, roasted rice and both the *kepayang* leaves and the fruit that the wild pigs loved so much. Fragrant leaves were then stuffed into the opening to seal it. The tubes were then brought into the longhouse to be left in cool corners to ferment. They needed to be left alone for at least five days. By the feast day, the *pekasam* would be perfect for eating.

Even after all this work for the festival was done, there were still many fish left over. These were divided equally among each person. One woman was pregnant and she received a double share – one share for herself and the other for her unborn child.

The next day, the men who went out hunting returned with three live pigs. These were kept in pens and would be fed until the day of the feast. These wild pigs, however, were useless as sacrifice because their history was unknown so the divination of their liver would be unreliable. Since the feast would be one to honour two goddesses, Nuing chose a prized sow, one that had littered seven times, as his offering. This was of course one of the highest forms of offering to thank the gods, so he told Nambi of his intentions before he pledged the sow.

"Of course you must," she said. "There is no better gift for the goddesses."

The four messengers returned a week after they left and told the people that all six longhouses they invited had agreed to come. "No taboo holds them back," said the eldest man. "There is no one in mourning, and no one ill in their house. Every family will send someone to honour our house."

Great excitement greeted the news. The men were questioned for more details: How many people lived in each longhouse? How far away did they live? Then duties were assigned according to the capacity of each family. Every family must make their common gallery ready to receive guests from the longhouse allocated to them. They were responsible for building cooking hearths in the front open verandah and for providing food for the guests. These visitors were not strangers to the people, for they had helped each other clear land, and in the course of their many struggles and celebrations together there had been marriages and fostering between them. In-laws naturally got first choice of whom they would host.

Nuing, being the chief, was assigned to care for the largest longhouse. He would be hosting them together with two other families. The following morning, people again returned to the jungle to collect wood and clay for building a hearth in the open verandah. Thatch roofs were also woven, and these were placed over the hearths to shade cooks from the sun and to shelter them from the rain.

So then began the friendly competition between the families. There was an endless activity of hunting, fishing, and gathering. Any animal or fish that was caught was smoked over fires. Then a young man came up with the idea of filling an old dugout canoe with water and began to keep the live catfish he caught inside. Soon more people followed his example.

By the time the first guests arrived on the afternoon of the thirteenth day, there was plenty of food and rice wine to satisfy even the strongest appetite. The following morning, boatloads of people started arriving, each taking the time to wash and to change into their fineries before coming up to the longhouse. At the top, as they crossed the threshold of the house, a rooster would be waved over their heads to chase away bad luck and to nullify any bad omen they might have heard during the journey. Rice wine was also offered to them. Not a single person refused the drink, which was meant to wash their spiritual feet.

The guests were then led to the common gallery of their host. Many visitors instantly took on the duty of preparing the meal. Fires were built on the makeshift hearth. Even among the guests there was a kind of competition for who could cook the best food. Ideas were shared as easily as news. Each person brought their own rice from home, so that when it was time to cook the grains the day's portion were all collected together in a bamboo tube. The burden of meat and vegetables fell on the host.

A bard and his two apprentices arrived before nightfall. There was much excitement when he was recognised through the staff he carried, for it jingled and jangled with the music of charms. The elders came out to meet them at the bathing platform and asked for news of omens that had crossed his path. The bard told them that he had not seen or heard any bad omen. But just to be sure that he had not misheard or misinterpreted anything untoward, a small pig was brought out when he reached the steps and its life was sacrificed so all bad luck and sickness would be washed away.

Ratai was still unsure how to carry herself as attention was lavished on her. Yet she relished every moment of it, so that by evening she had forgotten her broken heart and her eyes no longer looked surreptitiously for signs of Sagan. The house was now filled with well-wishers because the ceremony of thanksgiving was to start in the morning. That night there was barely any sleep for anyone because it was filled with poetry sung by aspiring singers and epics told by storytellers.

Sagan watched the goings on with a heavy heart. Each moment, each song seemed to carry his beloved farther away from him. His heart ached as he watched one bachelor after another smile boldly at Ratai. His spirit shrunk as he listened to man after man boast about his headhunting or travelling exploits within her earshot. They were like the great heroes of epics, like her grandfather, like her father. While he on the other hand, had no experience and no exploit to rival theirs. Sagan decided that he could not stay.

He entered his room and began to pack. Then he went outside and asked his friend Bantak to meet him at a fishing hut that was about half a day's paddling from the longhouse. Like a thief he snuck out of the longhouse from the back trapdoor. There was no *Keduran* Ceremony for him. He would not be seeking advice or help from the spirits before he began his journey. Because of the pain in his heart, he chose to ignore their help.

# 6

Sagan again looked upriver, shading his eyes from the late morning sun. It had been particularly hot the last few days. For the past week he had been living off palm cabbage and fish caught in his bamboo hooks. He missed home, he missed human company. On some days he would wonder if a spirit had taken possession of him and turned him into an *antu uging*, a recluse. Then he reminded himself that he was not one because he was still longing to meet his friend Bantak.

Today, like yesterday, he stood at the banks shading his eyes against the light. Sagan calculated that if Bantak left the house at dawn, he would reach this place at about this time of day. He was about to give up his watch when he spotted a lone boatman in the distance. He waited breathlessly. His need for company was stronger than the pang of hunger in his belly.

As the boatman came within shouting distance, Sagan stepped to the very edge of the bank, waved his arms high above his head, and called out a loud *Ooi*. The boatman responded with a wave, and when Sagan saw that he paddled faster, he knew then that it was his friend Bantak.

He was so happy to see Bantak that he waded into the water to help pull the dugout ashore. Bantak brought with him an extra basket of supplies. As he heaved the basket out of the boat, he explained, "Your mother is sorry she made such a scene."

Sagan nodded seriously then his face broke into a smile when he saw the packets of prepared food. He was famished for rice.

When he left, he had brought no food with him. He did not even think to bring a net or a barbed spear for fishing. Though it was foolish of him to leave without a word, and so unprepared, his heart did not regret it. He carried the basket of food to the campfire, sat down and began to eat.

Bantak sat next to him and said, "You missed a grand feast." He then went on to regale Sagan with tales of the two-day-long epic poem that the bard and his apprentices sang. He described how the young women were dressed to the nines when they danced to welcome the gods. Some, he said, wore crowns that made them look like birds of paradise. Even Sengalang Burong himself would have been pleased to see them. He then went on to give detailed accounts of the war stories told over wine and food. None of the guests, however, had a story that eclipsed the adventures of their chief.

Sagan opened the second pack of rice. He said nothing throughout Bantak's story. There was only one thing he needed to know but he did not have the courage to ask it. Halfway through his second meal, Bantak said, "There were three men fighting for Ratai's attention. You should have heard them. One man claimed he could fell ten trees a day, the other that he had killed two men and the third said that he had travelled so far he had seen men with yellow hair. But I don't know any of them. I think they are only boasting."

Sagan was thankful for his friend's loyalty, but he knew that there might be a grain of truth in what the strangers claimed. For one, it was a sacred festival and there were many others who knew the men. If they had lied, someone would have reminded them to be humble because there were divine invisible guests among them. The fact that they were given free reign to boast most probably meant that what they said was largely true.

"How is my mother?" Sagan asked in the lull of silence.

"She was upset, but she could not show it," Bantak said, "So she left on the morning of the festival to spend the next three days in the hut of your *padi* field."

Sagan felt bad for putting his mother in that predicament. She should not have suffered for his mistakes.

"My mother tried to persuade her to stay," Bantak said. "But she insisted to go because she did not want to curse the feast with her melancholic presence."

Sagan kept his gaze in front of him, at the fading fire. Sadness or discontent at sacred feasts to thank the gods was an insult to the host. It would be akin to wishing that Ratai had died during the fever. The longhouse chief would then have every right to chase her out of the community. Then Sagan, as her son, would be duty-bound to treat the people of that house as his enemy.

Sagan knew that it was pointless to wish that things had been different because wishing it would not fix the problem now. So he tried to change the subject. "What work do you think we can do?"

"Well," Bantak said thoughtfully, "We don't have river or jungle produce to sell, so I thought we should go to the coast to find some shells."

"Do you want us to bring home only shells?" Sagan said, his voice thick with disappointment.

"No. I plan to sell the shells at the trading port for rice or other jungle produce. Then we can sell those food items to the ships for the jars."

"They will give us jars?" Sagan asked. It was incomprehensible to him that anyone would let go of anything as precious as a jar for food.

"Yes, they will," Bantak said. "The Chinese are so rich, they even put water in jars. They have many many jars in their ships. You can get a jar if you can fill one with rice."

Sagan nodded seriously. "What are the best shells to collect?"

"The little white ones. The women love those cowry shells. They can sew them onto the hem of their skirts or shirts into many wonderful patterns."

Sagan frowned deeply. "I have never seen anything like that."

"That is because no one in our longhouse has them. I have seen a Melanau man wearing a jacket embroidered with shell. It was magnificent. He must have been a very rich man."

"Then we shouldn't sell all our shells," Sagan said, "We should save some for ourselves to sew onto our jackets."

Bantak grinned wide, showing his handsome black teeth. "We will be so grand, no woman will turn us away."

With that the conversation began to turn to women and how they would become the most desirable bachelors in the area. Women would boldly invite them into their homes, women would openly ask for the cowry shells, and women would speak in flirtatious rhymes with them. They talked of going from longhouse to longhouse in search of the perfect wife. Yet in Sagan's mind every face was Ratai's face, and every voice was Ratai's voice. He could only imagine her making him drink the *tuak*, and only her feeding him sweetened rice. Memories of her scent now filled his lungs and her form occupied his mind. He responded to Bantak's comments with joy and exuberance, never for a moment hinting his longing. Sagan's happy response persuaded Bantak that he had forgotten Ratai.

Soon after, they decided to leave the place and camp farther down the river. Since Bantak's boat was larger and sturdier, Sagan covered his upturned dugout under layers of leaves and piled his things into the other boat. That night as they were getting ready to sleep, Sagan noticed Bantak placing a pack of food by their shelter. He understood then why Bantak was so late in coming. It was because his family had done a blessing rite for him.

\*\*\*

It was five days before they reached the trading port. Instead of stopping in that busy place, Bantak took the boat farther down by about a mile. To the bank on the portside were rows of dugouts. Bantak studied each by turn until he saw one he recognised.

"I know this man," he said. "Let us stop here. Maybe he has some news for us."

Sagan was nervous, so he scowled to chase away his own fears, as well as to appear brave outwardly. On reaching the bank, they stepped out of the boat and pulled it up onto the alluvial mud. Sagan studied the many other dugouts there. Some were plain, others were carved and a handful had a flag tied to the end of a stick. The boat that Bantak recognized had a catfish carved on either side of it.

As Sagan stood back to admire the boat, Bantak said, "Taring dreamed that he was saved from drowning by a catfish. So he carved it onto his boat and he swore to never kill or eat a catfish."

Sagan nodded seriously. He had heard of animals saving peoples' lives before. Usually as a sign of thanks, the people would promise to never harm their kind again. Sometimes a whole longhouse would adopt the totem animal. In their case, it was the python because one had come to heal their chief and his wife. Both Sagan and Bantak had been taught since young to never cause a python to bleed or else, they were warned, the blood would burn their skin and spread over their body like a cancerous growth. Then they would go mad and die. Sagan heeded this warning so strongly that once, when a python entered his camp, he abandoned the shelter he had built rather than kill the snake. He had heard enough stories about people who had accidentally harmed or unknowingly eaten their totem animal. They suffered a debilitating disease and madness for long years before dying.

The place they walked through was like a large campground. Here and there were small groups of people sitting before campfires. Sagan followed Bantak from behind and watched and listened as he greeted stranger after stranger, replying to their questions about his person and business and asking the same in return. Bantak suddenly called out and waved to a man who was about three campfires away. The man was short but stout and his skin was far darker than normal, for being constantly exposed to the sun. Sagan wondered if he had ever lived in the jungle before. There were three other men with him.

After a quick welcome and introduction, the two friends were invited to sit in front of Taring's campfire. They shared food, wine and tobacco among themselves. Then Bantak asked Taring where he was going.

"I am on my way home," Taring said with a quick laugh. "I had a very good harvest last season and I managed to exchange the surplus rice for two Chinese jars." He indicated two bulging baskets lying to the side. Then he continued, "I also got some beads for the red rattan fruits." He reached into a smaller basket, pulled out a small cloth bag, and poured out its contents.

Translucent, marble-sized blue or green glass beads dotted with black, red or white paint covered the dirt in front of them. Sagan counted twenty beads in all.

"My wife will be very pleased," Taring said. "There is another woman in the longhouse with three of these beads. My *Indai* Kong will be happy to get so many."

Sagan's resolve to be successful for this trip grew stronger. Suddenly the reason for why a man must travel became very clear to him. It was not only to gain knowledge but also wealth. It was a chance to prove his courage and trading skills.

"How are the pickings of cowry shells?" Bantak asked.

"I did not see many this time," Taring said. "People have been saying that demons roam the coast, killing people they meet. One man we met at the trading port said he found a dead body that had a hole in its head."

Bantak asked, "Was it a blowdart wound?"

"I asked the man the same question," Taring said. "He insisted it was not one. But he also said that the wound was too narrow to be caused by a spear or a knife."

Sagan said, "I have heard stories that Penans kill with darts but they don't take the heads."

"Yes, you are right, young man. The dead man still had his head. But the witness was sure it was not the work of a Penan," the oldest man Kusau said.

"It is a pity the man and his group did not stay longer to check the surroundings," another man called Ikau said.

"No," Pung said. "They were right to run. They said that Ketupong had warned them that morning. But they disregarded the voice of the rufous piculet because they could not agree on what it meant."

"If only we know what every call means," Bantak said.

Kusau shook his grey head. "The only thing we can do is hear how and from where the omen birds call. Then notice which way they fly. That is why it is so important to pay attention to your surroundings."

"Kusau is right," Taring said. "There are now many strange new happenings in this land, so relying only on the past interpretations of the elders is not enough. We must relate the behaviour of the omen animals to these new things. That is the only way to understand what they mean to tell us."

"But there are so many. It is so hard to remember them all," young Pung complained.

Taring laughed. "That is why the most prosperous man is the most knowledgeable one."

Sagan and Bantak nodded seriously. They knew two such great men – one by reputation and the other personally. The group started talking about Bujang Maias, who could talk directly to animals, and his son Nuing, who had been helped by gods and demons. They exchanged knowledge among themselves. Stories and events were also shared because these usually contained lessons learned. The two men of Nuing's house spent a pleasant evening with their new friends.

*\*\**

The noise and bustle of the men from the other camps woke Sagan from his restless slumber. It was bone-chilling cold, so he wrapped his blanket tighter over his shoulders as he sat up. He was covered in dew, and the ground was covered in dew. He shivered and drew closer to the campfire embers. He added wood and blew life back into the flames. The mist covering the ground seemed to blend with smoke from the fires to form clouds rising into the canopy.

Though the morning was still dark, he could hear a myriad of activities about him. Kusau soon appeared out of the surrounding mist grasping two tubes of bamboo. One was filled with fresh drinking water and the other with cleaned fish. They added salt, ginger and herbs to the tube with fish then stopped its opening with bamboo leaves. Sagan leaned this over the fire.

Kusau added a breadfruit atop the embers next to the bamboo. While they kept an eye on the food, turning either the bamboo or the breadfruit every few minutes, both men talked about what they thought the day would be like. As the first grey light started to filter through the leaves, the rest of the men began to stir. Soon the scent of tobacco filled the air. They had kept the fire smoky but the mosquitoes were relentless so the first thing each man did when he woke up was to light a roll of tobacco to keep them at bay.

"How was your dream last night, Kusau?" Taring asked him.

"It was good," Kusau said. "We will have an uneventful trip home."

"My dream was good too," Taring said. He turned to Sagan and Bantak. "Well. My men and I will be going home today. The omens are all in our favour."

Sagan smiled wide. He was glad these men were going home and he was also happy that he would soon start a new adventure. The two friends, Sagan and Bantak, decided to head for the coast that same morning. Neither had received any lucky dreams, but they agreed that Taring and Kusau's dreams could be a good sign for them too. After the breakfast of fish and breadfruit they started their journey.

Half a morning of paddling later, the muddy alluvial colour of the river gave way to a sky-coloured grey tint. Sagan marvelled at this change because he had never seen this colour on water before.

"Wait till we get to the coast," Bantak said. "The water there is so blue, it feels as though you are riding in the sky." The river was active with the comings and goings of other boats. Many of the boatmen who came within shouting distance asked for news and happenings. Likewise Bantak too asked for news.

Many warned them to watch out for pirates. After hearing multiple people giving the same caution, Sagan said, "Shouldn't we turn back? The coast sounds like a dangerous place now."

"Nonsense," Bantak said. "They want to frighten us off because they want to keep the shells for themselves. Besides, there will be plenty of merchant ships passing by the coast at this time. They will give us iron or beads if we get fresh water or jungle food for them. Once I received a curved sword in exchange for a deer."

Sagan's face flushed with excitement. He had seen Bantak's scimitar. It was a magnificent sword, like the crescent of the moon. He wondered that the owner would give it up for a mere deer. Maybe it was because such swords were as common in his land as the deer was in theirs.

Just as the sun reached the apex in the sky, the riverbend in front of them disappeared into nothingness. It seemed as though the sky had merged with the waters. Sagan felt that he could paddle all the way to heaven from here. He wondered if he could visit the House of Heaven, for the stories of Seragunting and his father Menggin suddenly seemed plausible to him. Did not Menggin cross a great lake to get to heaven? Was this the lake he crossed?

"We are here," Bantak said, startling Sagan out of his daydream.

The men paddled to the bank, climbed out of the boat and dragged it to shore. They lay the upside-down craft next to a rotting log and covered it with leaves. The ground here felt a little strange to Sagan. As he walked about, the mix of alluvial clay and sand crumbled under his feet. Its unfamiliarity filled his heart with adventure and the promise of a new life.

After looking about them for a while to make sure that all was safe, they shouldered their baskets and walked towards the sound of the surf. They trudged for a few yards until the clay under their feet gave way to rock and sand. Bantak looked about him then turned towards a line of mangrove trees. They placed their baskets next to the largest trunk. Its roots stuck out or crawled over the jagged rocks like a thick mat, but its sparse leaves barely kept the heat of the sun off them.

"Are we camping here for the next few weeks?" Sagan asked. "Or just for tonight."

"Let's check the beach first," Bantak said. "If there are plenty of shells in the rock pools, then we can stay for a few days."

They started walking towards the sea and began to scan the rocky beach. Bantak was surprised to find so many unharvested cowry shells. He pointed out the porcelain-like oval shapes to Sagan. Both men were elated but neither of them celebrated openly lest they attract unwanted spirits. They referred to these shells as rubbish when they talked about their plans to collect them over the next few days.

Though Sagan wanted to start collecting immediately, Bantak persuaded him to build a shelter first. They returned to the treeline and started collecting the materials they needed for the floor and roof. Even as they cut the brush, ants and sandflies bit their legs and arms. Crabs also came out of their holes and tried to nip them. They cut down a coconut tree and chopped its trunk into three parts. Then they covered the parts with bark. On top of this they layered leaves and grass for their bedding. By the time they put up the leaning thatch roof, it was dusk.

Bantak said, "We will start collecting the rubbish tomorrow."

Even though his heart longed to start as soon as he could, Sagan was forced to agree. Dusk was a time of change when things were not always as they seemed. It was a dangerous time. They slept early that night and woke before dawn. While waiting for first light, they weaved rough shallow baskets out of coconut leaves.

At first light, they started combing the beach. The rocks were sharp and jagged but in between the larger stones were cowry shells that glimmered like pearls against the grey rocks. They placed the live shells into the crude baskets. After they had collected for about half of that morning, they returned to camp and stuffed the shells into bamboo tubes with some water. While waiting for the water to heat up, they sliced more bamboo and whittled the pieces down into long pins. Just as the water started to steam, they poured the shells out onto the sand. Then they used the bamboo pins to pull out the snails. The flesh was returned to the now empty tube together with some water and herbs before being returned to the fire. The empty shells were washed then lined up on the sand to dry naturally.

For the next four days they repeated this activity, only deviating from it when they hunted for birds or squirrels to vary their meals. One afternoon they saw a grey sail on the horizon. Sagan stared wide-eyed because he had never seen anything like it before.

Bantak smiled broadly. "That is a merchant ship," he explained.

"You are sure it is not a pirate?" Sagan asked with a quiver in his voice.

"Pirates only use dirty black sails because they cannot go into the trading ports."

"Will they come to our beach?"

"I hope so," Bantak said cheerfully. "They look like a rich ship. They will want freshwater or meat. We can get something wonderful in exchange for a little work."

They left their freshly collected shells by the campfire and went to squat by the tideline. The ship grew larger and soon they could make out a man waving to them from the bow. They watched in awe as the sail was reefed and the long oars lowered to the sea. The great hull slowed until it finally stopped about ten yards out to sea. When it dropped an anchor, Sagan estimated the ship to be larger than the chief's bilek back in the longhouse.

From the side of the gunwale a rope was let down. Five men swung down and jumped into the water. Unable to contain his excitement, Sagan stood up and waved his arms high over his head.

From the deck of the ship came a sudden burst of thunder and a puff of smoke. Sagan fell back as though he had been struck by an invisible spear. Bantak, who was till squatting low, turned to stare at Sagan with surprise. Blood started pouring out of his friend's chest. He touched Sagan's arm. There was a brief shiver then Bantak felt the life leave his friend. Another boom of thunder was followed by the burst of a puff of sand near his feet. Bantak touched the lead and quickly pulled his hand back because it felt as hot as ember. He looked up and saw that the five men were now running up the beach towards him brandishing machetes and swords. The one leading them had a chain around his neck and his face was framed with thick yellow hair like a lion's mane. His skin was dark and looked like leather. He growled and snarled like a wild animal, but he had the face of a man.

Bantak turned and scrambled towards the line of trees on all fours. There was another loud boom. This time Bantak felt fire graze his shoulder. He kept on until he reached the trees. After stopping just long enough at the camp to retrieve his machete and paddle, he ran back towards the boat.

He could hear the animal-man howling behind him. He could hear them getting closer and closer. He tripped over a rotting log and shattered it, spewing out the ants and larvae within. He stumbled to his feet and ran until he felt as though his lungs would burst. When he reached his hidden boat, he turned it upright, dragged it into the river and jumped into it. With whatever little breath he still had left in him he started to paddle for his life.

Shouts reached his ears like arms stretching out to grab him, but he did not turn to look at the men. He prayed that they could not swim. But he could not be sure because he dared not look back. Then he shivered as a new terror entered his consciousness. The lead man was not human. Bantak could hear him howl and bark like a dog that had lost its meal. Then he wondered if Sagan would be fed to it.

# 7

Mansau was cleaning the insides of his father's boat when one of his friends started shouting loudly and pointing downstream. Nuing's eldest son looked up and shouted a warning, calling for the sentries. There was a man coming towards them in a dugout boat. He looked mad, for his hair was uncombed and his face covered with beard stubbles. He also looked emaciated.

Two men jumped onto the bathing platform with a loud shout, brandishing a sword and a spear. The boatman raised his oar and called out, "It is I, Bantak."

After his initial shock, Mansau jumped into the river and swam towards the boat. He grabbed the bow and turned it towards the platform. One of the sentries had set aside his weapon and was now in the water with Mansau. He grabbed the other side of the boat.

By the time they reached the platform, Nuing was already there waiting for them. The children and women had all returned to the longhouse at the first sign of trouble. When they reached the platform and Bantak crawled out of the boat, Mansau quickly swam to the other side of the platform in disgust. The boat was in a filthy condition and Bantak was equally dirty, covered in days of grime and sweat. There was also a strange kind of reek that permeated from him. A combination of sour and sweet, like vomit, like death.

"What happened to you?" Nuing asked as he helped the frail Bantak to sit up.

"Demons attacked us," Bantak said, his voice quivering with weakness.

"Where is Sagan?" Mansau asked.

"I think he is dead," Bantak said. "The demons threw an invisible spear at him. I saw him fall on his back, as though he had been impaled. He did not get up."

"Why are they here? Will they come to our longhouse?" Mansau asked.

"Enough questions," Nuing said. "We must take him back to the house. He needs food and water."

Bantak's muscles were so stiff from sitting in the boat and rowing with all his might for days that he could barely stand up. Two men lifted him to his feet and supported him back to the longhouse. His mother wailed on seeing him being carried by two men up the ladder and into the common gallery.

Then they sat him down on his plank bed in the gallery. Nuing brought a gourd of water to Bantak's mouth, making sure that he drank slowly. Now assured that her younger son had no open wounds, *Umoi* returned to her family room and came out with rice and some smoked meat. Bantak ate slowly, like an old man. After restoring some of his strength, Bantak recounted his story of how both he and Sagan were attacked by a ship full of demons.

"You are sure about what you saw?" Nuing asked.

"Yes. They could not be men. They were too strange. They were all dressed in black. The man leading them behaved like a dog and he had yellow hair. The other men's faces were covered with so much hair I could barely see their mouths. "

Graman, a middle-aged man who joined the community ten years before, said, "*Tuai* Nuing, you have fought demons before. You can lead us to take revenge."

"Yes, *Tuai*," said Bada. He was only a young boy when

he travelled to this land with his grandfather under Nuing's leadership. Now, he was a grown man with a young family. "You know how to invite the gods. You are protected by the half-demon Bungai Nuing. He will persuade the other gods to help you."

Nuing's bowed back was still as he listened to the talk about him. He might have a direct link to the half-demon but he was unwilling to invoke him. In his human form, Sempurai was charming and sweet-tongued, but as his demon form Bungai Nuing, he had a horrible temper. His fits of violence were so well known that cautionary poems and songs were written about him. He was thankful to Sempurai for helping him get the spear. Without it, they would all have been fodder to the demon huntsmen. Yet being half-demon meant that Sempurai's method of resolution could be unbearable because he had no pity for weakness and no sympathy for suffering.

Soon Nuing noticed that the noise about him had died down. The people were waiting for him to make a decision. They were waiting for him to choose the path of glory. They wanted him to bring gods to their aid, like the days when his father had fought demons. Yet a chill now gripped Nuing's heart and twisted his spine, reminding him of the horrible pain he had suffered. He said, "Those killers are far from us. We are safe from them in this place. I do not think it is wise to go out and seek them."

"But, Chief," Bada said, "They might still come. We have heard stories of raids before in the past."

"That is so," Nuing said. "But we have already lost one man. We cannot afford to lose another."

"I want my son to be avenged," Sawai said vehemently. "I want to use the heads of those murderers to cut the ties of mourning." Then she beat her chest and wailed, "Where are you, my son? Have your murderers left you at the shore for the crabs and birds. Haunt them, curse them, weaken their spirit. You are young, but you became weak because you were enchanted."

A few women rose and pulled Sawai to her feet. They led her back to her family room where she continued her lamentations, which were mingled with accusations and curses.

There was barely a murmur in the common gallery as the people listened to her with mounting misgiving. Everyone knew that she blamed Ratai for making her son leave the longhouse. She had told them that Ratai had put a spell on her son, so that he would go out and collect vain wealth for her. He would rather get jars for Ratai than help his old mother in the field, she said to anyone who would listen.

Some time later, the mourning songs and curses faded into sobs. Nuing's face was heavy with feeling when he finally looked up and said, "We must think this through carefully. A war expedition is not something to be decided lightly in the heat of the moment."

Assan, a teenage boy, said, "You have attacked a ship before. That is what my father said. You should know what to do."

Nuing shook his head. "My friend and I joined a pirate ship. We do not have a ship big enough to fight with theirs."

"We can build bigger war boats," Assan's friend Dujong said.

Nuing shook his head and explained, "There is no craft or skill we know that can build a boat that large. It has to be as big as a house." He cringed inwardly as he said this. He recalled the blast of canons and the heat and fire that had killed Fakir, the navigator of the pirate ship. It was a horrible death. Nuing would rather die by the sword or a spear to being burned alive by fire.

He suddenly felt tired and old. Maybe he had become soft. Life had been very good in the past few years. His children were all born strong and healthy. There was nothing more he needed.

What good was pride and glory if it meant that he would lose everything, including his life. But he did not want to disappoint his people. He did not want them to think that he had become weak and was no longer worthy to lead them.

"We must take care about making such decisions," he said to the assembly of people. "We must remember, Sagan left this house without a word. Without even a blessing from his mother. For all we know, this incident might have been a punishment from the spirits."

"The chief speaks wisely," the elderly augur, Nyaru, said. "He left in the midst of a feast. He left on the day we were supposed to welcome the gods into our home. He was *puni'*. He did not wait to appease the longing of his soul first. Because of that, his being became fragmented."

The people began to murmur among themselves. Nyaru was right, they said to each other. Sagan could not be in tune with his surroundings, he could not be alert because part of him was always looking back with regret. He should at least have tasted a bit of rice or a piece of meat before he walked out of the house to begin his journey.

"But we must avenge him," Ratai's voice suddenly broke through the noise and silenced the crowd. "We must. Sagan was one of us." Her face was hard and deep red with passion, as though about to burst into flames.

Nuing looked away from her towards Bantak. "This is not for us to decide." He felt his stomach cramp when he said that. He was ashamed of himself, of his own cowardice. He wished that he were as brave as his father Bujang Maias. He wished he could surmount any problem with his strength and courage. But he did not have enough of either. He had seen the death of his enemies and of his friend in equal measure. His body was broken when he had to face death. Though it was now healed, the memory of its pain had never gone away.

Then he said, "We must ask the gods for their guidance. Only they know if Sagan's death deserve revenge or if it was because he ignored their warnings."

Nuing did not look up when Ratai left their presence. He did not have to look because he could hear her cry of despair and her heavy steps as she ran out of the longhouse. He looked down at his hands. They were trembling, so he clasped them together to steady them. The scowl on his face deepened when he again asked Bantak to repeat his story. In his heart, he prayed that the gods should show them omens forbidding the war expedition.

\*\*\*

It was many days before Bantak had recovered enough of his strength to get up and work in his family field. On the first three nights of his return the people had made offerings to the spirits, to ask what they were to do. They listened to the call of the birds, they looked to the sky to watch out for hawks like the Kayans did and they even discussed their nightly dreams with other more experienced elders. None of them, not even Bantak, had received a definitive dream or heard a strong omen that pressed them to go to war.

Bantak was glad when he was finally able to be out of the longhouse. The endless discussions and questions of his experience with the demons and Sagan's death were wearing him down. Yet his serenity was cut short when voices called from the edge of the field, looking for him and his mother.

"I am here," Bantak called back. Soon two young sentries, Assan and Dujong, could be seen trotting towards them. "What is the matter?" Bantak asked with anxiety when they got close enough for him to notice the deep scowls on their faces.

"You must be careful," Assan said. "My sister and her friends said that they saw Sagan's spirit near our house."

"That is impossible," Bantak said.

"They swore they had seen him," Assan said. "They were looking for fern when they saw him walking about the jungle behind our house."

Bantak's mother said, "It is because we have not conducted a proper burial for him. His soul is confused."

"What do you mean?" Bantak asked.

"He will continue to come to us and feed off our spirits," she wailed. "We will all die!"

The sentries nodded seriously. Dujong said, "That is what the augur said too. He told us to warn as many people as possible."

After the sentries left to move on to the next field, Bantak's mother started to put their tools back into a basket. "We must go back to the house now."

"There is still much daylight."

"No!" his mother stressed. "You have just recovered. He may be looking for you. If you cross paths with him, you will become ill again."

Bantak hurried back with her. Even though they were still a mile away, they started meeting other families who were hurrying home from their fields too. There were none of the usual greetings among them because everyone was listening hard to the sounds in the trees. Their eyes scanned their surroundings as though looking for enemies. Even the younger children did not dare make a whimper.

Though the sun was still high in the sky, people were already cleaning themselves and their tools at the bathing place. This was done hurriedly. Parents rushed their children home as quickly as they could after collecting water. Then, one after another, the gallery doors to the outside were closed. The heat inside the longhouse was stifling and the air was humid but nobody cared because their terror chilled them.

Sagan's spirit might have come home because he had not realised that he had died. He came home because it was the natural thing for him to do. If there was a dead body, they would have put it in his family room so he could see it. And they would have mourned over it so he could sense their grief. But there was nothing for him to see or to know. Once the last family had returned to the house, the people all gathered in front of the chief's room. Nuing took his place at the gallery and all eyes turned to him for a solution to their predicament.

"Our home is cursed, *Tuai*," Bantak said, without naming his friend, "because we would not avenge his death."

Nyaru, the augur, shook his head in disagreement. "Nobody is ill or dying. He has only come home because it is the natural thing to do."

Bantak's father said, "But he will soon be angry and discontented. Bad luck will befall us all."

The chief turned to the augur and said, "We don't have a body so we cannot do a proper burial. What else can we do to persuade him to leave us in peace?"

Nyaru closed his eyes and moved his head slowly from side to side. It was almost as though he was looking for an answer in the inner world. Finally he opened his eyes and said, "There is an old story from the ancestors. It is about Garik, the son of Kadam. His father was killed by enemies in the field but his body was never brought back to the longhouse. His spirit, however, returned home."

"What happened to the people?"

"Nothing," Nyaru said, "because Kadam appeared to Garik in a dream. He told his son that he returned because life in the other world was hard. He had no tools to work with, no clean clothes to change into and no pot to cook with."

The people turned to each other to discuss this new information. The augur was right. If there had been a proper burial, Sagan would have his personal belongings buried with him.

"What did Garik do for his father?" Nuing asked.

"He put tools and cloths into a jar and sealed it shut. Then he buried the jar at the cemetery."

Nambi shook her head. "That is not possible. *Indai* Sagan does not have a jar, not even a small one."

"*Indai* Ratai is right," *Inik* Jambi said. "Sagan was still a boy when she moved here. She had never married any man, so her home has no jar or trophy heads."

"She is a very unlucky woman," Bada said.

"She is luckless because she never stops cursing," Nyaru said.

The people murmured in agreement. Nyaru was right, they said to each other. Sagan's mother complained incessantly. There was never any peace in her presence. If the day was hot, she complained that it would ruin the fermentation of rice wine, if it was wet, she complained that she could not dry her rice or illipe nuts. She rarely had anything kind to say to anybody. She cursed so much that people started saying that she was *tau tepang*. They became afraid of her, fearing that she would say something that would put a curse in their life.

Though the blame of Sagan's death had now clearly shifted to his mother, Nuing felt that he was still partially responsible for it. Maybe he should have said something to stop him from stealing out of the longhouse like a thief. But at the time he was worried about his own daughter's feelings and reputation. Today, he felt that he should do something. If he let this moment pass, he knew the guilt would continue to haunt him. "I will give her a jar."

The crowd fell into shocked silence. Nambi said, "Are you sure, *Apai* Ratai? Those jars are our children's heirloom."

Nuing could tell from the tone of her voice that his wife was unhappy with his decision. He did not want to discuss it with her in public, so he got up and went into the family room. His wife followed.

Once they were alone in the room, he turned to her to explain, "We must give her a jar, so that Sagan will stop coming back."

"There must be something else we can do," Nambi insisted.

"Yes, there is. But it means sending people out to avenge his death. With the jar, at least we have a guarantee that nothing bad will happen to us. If I lead an expedition, there is no guarantee that we will all live or that we will even find the murderers."

Nambi hung her head. She understood what he meant to tell her. "More men will have to be sent out to appease those who died."

"That is true," Nuing said. "I would rather lose a jar than any of my sons. Mansau is now old enough to be considered a man. If I go to war, he will have to come with me."

Nambi turned her gaze to the row of jars lining one wall. At the end of the line was a plain one that was dark brown all over. It had no embellishment at all and was once used by merchants to carry salted vegetables. She pointed to it, saying, "That one. Give her that jar."

Nuing lifted the jar. It was a good size, about the depth and width of a young girl's travelling basket. He nodded and carried it outside. Everyone who saw the jar nodded approvingly. It was neither a dragon nor a deer jar, so it was perfect for use as a burial container. This also made it good for a gift because its value would not burden the receiver.

When the jar was brought into her *bilek*, Sagan's mother stared at it mutedly. Bantak's mother began going through the male clothes and farming tools in the house. She gathered together a pair of loincloths, a faded blanket, a rusted knife and other well-worn tools. All these were laid out in front of the jar, waiting for Sawai's approval.

When she made no move to look through the items, *Umoi* said, "May we bury these things for your son?"

Sawai looked up for a moment and the dazed sorrow on her face faded away. Reason returned to her eyes for a moment. Noticing the jar for the first time, she asked, "What is this?"

"The *baya* for your son," *Umoi* explained. "He cannot be at peace until these tools are sent for his use in the other world."

"But he should not be at peace," Sawai said. "He should not be at peace until his death is avenged."

"Be reasonable," Umoi pleaded. "It will be many months, even years, before he is avenged. He should not be forced to suffer in the other world."

"What if people forget about him?" Sawai insisted. "If he stops haunting us people will forget. He has no father, no brother and no uncles to fire up the men for war."

"If he keeps coming, he will bring death and disease with him. Our people will become fearful and weak."

"Then let everyone become weak. Let everyone die. My son's death must be avenged," Sawai wailed.

She rose and leaned forward to claw Umoi's face. Umoi grabbed both of Sawai's wrists and pushed her down. Sawai fell back and kicked her knee into Umoi's stomach. Umoi let out a scream. The other women, who were watching the exchanges with shock, suddenly came to their senses and threw themselves on Sawai. Their shouts and calls brought in the men from outside.

Bantak helped his mother tie a piece of twine around Sawai's wrists. Then he wrapped more twine around her ankle. The whole time, Sawai thrashed about violently as though possessed by madness.

The augur, Nyaru, started putting the selected cloths and tools into the jar. Then he covered it with an extra piece of cloth and tied a twine over it and under the lip of the jar. He brought the jar outside to the common gallery. Nobody was sure how to conduct a *ngerapoh* ceremony because nobody had any experience of seeing one being celebrated.

After some discussion among the elders, they agreed that it should be conducted like a normal burial ceremony. Food offerings and wine were brought out. The offerings were scanty because the ceremony was rushed and Sawai was in too much distress to see to it that it was conducted properly. Yet the biggest reason was that the people were afraid. They wanted to bury the jar as quickly as possible, with minimal ceremony, because a proper ceremony would need time to prepare. They were all terrified of encountering Sagan's ghost.

By morning, everyone was bleary-eyed and anxious when they made preparations to go to the cemetery. They did not bring Sawai with them because they were afraid that she would pour a string of curses on them. Or that she would break the jar and make it impossible for Sagan to bring the items with him to the other world.

Nuing put the jar in his boat with a mixture of relief and anxiety in his chest. He was sorry that Sagan had to die, but his death had automatically redeemed Ratai's reputation. It was proof to his people that Sagan was the one in the wrong, that his daughter was a victim of his malice. Even though the Goddess Kumang had adopted Ratai, her full exoneration was only possible with Sagan's death. The night before he had listened to the others talk about Sagan and Ratai. All of them conceded that the gods had proven that Ratai was a pure and honest woman. They believed that the spirits had punished Sagan because he had ruined her character.

Now Nuing turned his gaze back to the jar. Try as he might, he could not hate Sagan. He was angry with him, but he could not hate him. He sensed that Sagan had cared for Ratai deeply. He had hoped that they would be married because then his daughter would remain in the same longhouse. If she chose a man from another house there was a chance that she might have to follow her husband.

The burial ground was some miles away on the opposite bank. Fresh vines had grown over the path leading to it. Some brush had been cleared away by the men who had reached the place earlier. The group followed this path to the edge of the cemetery. Just as the first man was about to step into the burial ground they all heard the call. A kingfisher sobbed, ahead and to the left of them.

Nuing, who was carrying the jar, suddenly made a turn away from the path and walked towards the dense jungle beyond. The people, who were startled by the sound of the bad omen, stood rooted to the spot. None of them dared move forward or return to the boat.

A few moments later the men who had gone ahead of them ran down the path towards the group. "Where is the chief?" Bada asked, his quivering voice vocalising the fear on his face.

"I don't know," Mansau replied. "Father ran that way without saying a word." He pointed to the direction where his father had gone.

"Why are you standing here then?" Bada asked. "Why are you all not with him?"

"He has gone off alone without a word, " Nyaru said. "The kingfisher has just foretold that we will fail if we fight. This is the sign we have been waiting for. Let us wait for him here. If he needs our help, he will call for us."

So they waited, some sitting by the side, others standing on the path, but none would move beyond five yards of the group. Just before noon Nuing reappeared. He no longer had the jar with him. Everyone could tell that he had buried the jar because his hands and chest were covered in dirt.

"It is done," Nuing said to them, and they returned to the boats.

# 8

Libau came into the longhouse with two strangers following behind him. The sentry's face was solemn because the two visitors carried spears decorated with palm fronds and charms. It was a sign that their visit was an invitation to war. Libau had stood at the bathing platform to receive them from the moment they were heard while still a distance away. Every man had drawn a sharp intake of breath when they saw the standing spears and the fluttering fronds as the boat approached. The visitors had called out the customary greeting "Are you under taboo?" and Libau had responded with, "No, we are not. We have just buried a jar for the ghost of one man, but we are no longer under taboo."

When these two climbed out of the boat, Libau saw the rosette tattoos on their shoulders, signifying that they were ready to carry the weight of the world, and the tattooed ring on their thumbs to show that they were successful headhunters. The visitors were invited to come up to the house to officially declare the intention of their visit. Now Libau stood tall before the chief with these two men.

After introducing themselves as Jantan and Chad and that they were sent by Chief Biring, the older man Jantan said, "We would like to invite you and your men to join us for a war expedition."

"Who do you plan to attack?" Nuing asked.

Jantan said, "Three of my relatives were killed at the coast. We wish to go to the coast and wait for the killers."

"How can you be sure that they will be back? The winds might have brought them to the other side of the world by now," Nuing said.

Jantan nodded to show his respect, for this chief was experienced with the ways of the sea. "They will be back because witnesses of other attacks have seen the same men. They described seeing the same men."

Chad said, "They use invisible spears."

Nuing looked about him thoughtfully. He did not want to go to war. Even though the kingfisher Embuas had warned them, he could tell by the faces about him that some men would still want to go despite that. He had fought monsters and survived. There was no longer any need for him to prove himself. But these men were different. They wanted to be heroes. So they would go, under the leadership of another longhouse warrior if need be. Nuing saw that he could lose many good fighting men to Jantan. He took the next best course of action. He tried to disprove the visitors' information by showing his people that he was more knowledgeable.

"The weapons they used are not invisible spears. They are small hand canons."

Jantan and Chad shared a look. Nuing's resistance was unexpected. All the other longhouse chiefs had jumped at the opportunity of getting heads. Jantan said, "Your bravery is well known to us. There are many stories and songs about your fight with the demon huntsmen."

"Then you understand if I say that fighting demons is not a decision to make lightly."

Ratai was sitting among the women, among the silent crowd listening to the conversation between their chief and the visitors. Ratai could sense her father's reluctance. She wanted to speak her mind, to remind everyone present that Sagan was still unavenged, but she could not open her mouth to speak. The strangers made her shy and tongued-tied.

Even so, another part of her was angry that the others were silent, unwilling to speak up for Sagan. Had they forgotten him so quickly? She searched the silent faces about her, hoping that there was someone there who would speak out, someone who was older and more accomplished than her. Yet almost every face her gaze fell upon was silent and anxious. Only the young seemed excited by the prospect of a war expedition, yet they too were just as shy to speak out.

Ratai suddenly noticed a smell close to her. It was the stench of unwashed body besmeared with loamy clay and sour peat soil. She knew that it was Sagan's mother, and her body arched away from the older woman's presence. Then a hand blackened by dried mud grabbed her arm. Ratai was surprised by the quick pull. Just as she was about to jerk her arm away the hand let go. She turned in time to see Sagan's mother slip into a doorway. Sawai turned and gestured to indicate that she wanted Ratai to come into her room.

"Don't," Madu said. She had seen the gesture too. "She is mad. She might try to kill you."

Ratai shushed her sister then got up and kept her back bowed as she made her way towards Sawai's door. Through the corner of her eye, she could see Madu speaking to their mother and pointing her way. Maybe Sawai needed some comforting words, Ratai thought. She slipped in through the doorway but she only closed the door half of the way because her sister's warning was still fresh in her mind.

The room, Ratai saw, was in a terrible state. Baskets and cloth were strewn about, and the floor was powdery with dried mud tracks. Unspun cotton rolls were carelessly piled to the side, many frayed and grey with dust. There was no smoke in the hearth. This last situation troubled Ratai and it made her wonder if the lack of fire had brought in the madness. Beneath the smell of human sweat, she could smell rat urine. Immediately she went to the hearth, hoping there was a little burning ember left that she could blow back to life. The fire would keep the rodents out, she thought.

As Ratai blew gently onto the ashes to try and find a flame, Sawai paced the room. Suddenly she stopped pacing and turned Ratai to face her. She then dropped down to her knees, pulling Ratai down to the floor. With a feverish glee on her face, she said, "I found it." Quickly she covered her mouth and shushed herself.

"What have you found?" Ratai whispered back.

Sawai looked about her suspiciously, as though there were eavesdroppers in the room. "I found the jar," she said and giggled.

Ratai was seized by a sudden terror that made her head and nape swell. Almost breathlessly she said, "What did you do with it?"

"I broke the jar and scattered everything."

"You threw them about the cemetery?"

"No, I threw them into the river."

"Why would you do that? Sagan will return to haunt us."

"He should. He must," Sawai hissed fiercely.

Ratai wanted to say the right thing; she wanted to list out all the calamities that would befall the community because of what Sawai had done. But she could not. A part of her felt that what Sawai did was right. The people should be cursed; everyone should be cursed because they forgot Sagan.

The door creaked open wider. Ratai looked up and pressed her lips together on seeing her mother silhouetted against the doorway.

Nambi said, "*Indai* Sagan, I am glad to see you back. Have you eaten?" She stole a look at her daughter and was relieved to see that Ratai was unharmed.

Sawai clasped a hand over her mouth then she mumbled behind it. It was almost as though she was two persons at the same time: one longing to speak while the other wished to keep a secret.

Nambi touched Ratai's shoulder, indicating for her to get up and leave. Then she said to Sawai, "We are about to serve lunch outside. I will send in some food for you."

Sawai began to giggle behind her hand. Her mirth grew stronger and stronger until her face was red and tears flowed out of her eyes. Nambi pulled Ratai outside by the hand. Then she led her back to their family room. She said, "You must not be alone with *Indai* Sagan. Promise me, you will not speak with her alone again."

"But, Mother, she is grieving. She needs our kindness."

"We offered her love and comfort, but she rejected us. She would rather be alone. Now the *uging* demon has a hold on her."

Ratai wanted to protest. Yet another part of her shuddered. She too could have ended up like the older woman. She too could have isolated herself from everyone and been driven mad by the recluse demon. So she only bowed her head to show that she would obey even though she wanted to protest. Her tongue felt thick and heavy with fear.

Outside came the sound of people settling down for a community meal. Ratai followed her mother out. They went to the verandah to collect the pots of food that had been cooking on the hearth since that morning. Because Ratai was still single, she served food to the children and older women of the longhouse, making sure to stay far from the guests. Older men served the guests and the elders sitting about them. During the meal, the guests were invited to stay for a night before they continued their journey.

After lunch, Ratai sat among the young women as they listened to the guests speaking and sharing news about the other longhouses they had visited. After a while she began to notice a lot of whispering about the older man, Jantan. The girls had learned that he was still unmarried and that he did not have a sweetheart. Soon there was too much giggling and whispering for Ratai. She could not hear anything that the men were saying. So she moved away from the group of girls and edged closer to a group of older women. She sat behind *Inik* Jambi and turned her eyes away from the visitors, so that her interest would not be misunderstood.

"*Tuai*," Jantan said, "I have come for advice because you are like a tall tree growing on the summit of a hill, pointing towards the gods. You are the brave man who fought with demons and tricked the pig king. You are rumoured to be birthed by a curse, but you have wrestled a blessing out of the shaman snake. Our party would be blessed by victory if you agreed to lead us."

Nuing nodded thoughtfully throughout the speech. Then he countered, "I have planted roots in grounds writhing with worms. I have been inside the longhouse of demons. I do not feel like a tall tree, but more like Bejie's termite-infested stairway. My experience looks mighty like his stairway, but I fear that if you rely upon its magnificence too much, it will fail you just when you are about to achieve victory."

Jantan and Chad shared a look. It was unusual for a warrior chief to put himself down before his own people. Could this chief have received a warning from the spirits? Why would he not admit to it then? Usually if a man were to have been warned then there was no shame for him to admit it. It had nothing to do with his courage after all, but a warning from his guardian spirit.

Jantan then said, "If the omens do not assure you of victory then we understand your position. I, myself, and many of my friends have received good omens in our dreams and in our journeys in the jungle."

Nuing leaned forward and said, "Then you are free to go to war without me and my men."

Chad said, "We were about to do so, but both Jantan and I received a strange dream seven nights ago. That is the reason we are both here."

"What is this dream?"

Jantan said, "The Goddess Kumang told me to come here, because she said she has left a spear for me in this house."

Chad said, "I had the same dream, except that in my dream, I heard her tell him to come to your house to look for the spear."

A murmur rose among the crowd. Usually if a man or woman got a dream from a spirit, they would wait for signs that a spirit had actually appeared to them. But in Jantan's case, he did not have to wait for confirmation because Chad was his witness in that dream world.

Jantan continued, "That can only mean that you are the spear. The bards sing that you stole a spear from the pig king and that you are the only person who can use that spear."

Nuing shook his head. "The spear has been returned to the pig king. It is no longer with me. I am afraid, I cannot help you."

Ratai fisted her hand with frustration. She wished she had the courage to speak out, she wished she had the courage to rebuke her father in front of the people. How could he act so cowardly in front of these brave men? She was so frustrated and disappointed that she was close to tears. Surely there was a way that she could speak with Goddess Kumang, and ask her what Jantan's dream meant. Maybe if she got the answer, her father would finally agree to go to war. She was so angry she did not hear anything else for the rest of the afternoon. Then she returned to the verandah, to help the people there prepare the next meal. Usually the food for guests was prepared by only one household, but since these two men brought an invitation for war, many of the people in the longhouse were curious to know more, hence the festive atmosphere.

After chopping the bamboo shoot into thin shredded pieces, and while waiting for the natural toxin to boil away, Ratai noticed a group of young men, sitting around Bantak. They were talking quietly among themselves. She pretended to get something from the hearth closest to where they were sitting. They were so engrossed in their conversation that they did not notice Ratai was within earshot.

"We cannot disobey the chief," Bantak said.

One of the men said, "But father said the chief has no right to stop us if we wish to go."

"Who will lead us? Will another leader accept us?"

"We just need to learn where they will meet. Then we can ask to join them."

"Can we do that?" Ratai asked. The young men jumped to their feet.

"You should not be here," Bantak hissed and looked about anxiously.

Ratai leaned closer and said, "I want to go with you."

"I am not going anywhere," Bantak said and turned his face to the side. The other men walked away.

Ratai waited a moment longer, debating what to do. She was surprised at herself. She did not understand why she had asked to join them, but now that she had she felt a strong resolve to do exactly that. She returned to the other hearth and continued boiling the bamboo shoots. She was terrified of the growing longing in her heart, but it soon grew so strong that the fear was drowned by the longing itself.

For the rest of the day, Ratai went through the motions without thinking about her actions. She would sit with different groups of women and listen to the conversations among the men and boys nearby, but she remained tongued-tied. Many stayed up late to keep the visitors company or to listen to what they had to say, but Ratai felt more and more despondent as the evening progressed because she could not speak up. She felt as though all the energy had been sucked out of her body. So she went to bed right after supper was served, with the excuse that her back hurt.

When she lay down, she could feel something round and hard pressing against her back. She raised herself on her side and ran her hand over the kapok mattress. There was nothing there. She lay back down but felt the lump again. This time the lump moved and Ratai bolted upright. Was there a snake under her mattress? But it was not long. It must be a rat. She slapped down hard on the moving mass. And just missed it. She tried once more and missed. She tried a third time. Her fist hit the lump and the floor beneath her broke. She let out a scream as she tumbled face down.

"Oh, what a terrible mess!" a woman's voice said.

Ratai looked to the side and was surprised to see a rat.

"What are you doing in my house?" The rat said.

"This is my home," Ratai said and picked herself off the floor but when she was only halfway up, her head hit the ceiling.

"No, it is mine," the rat said. "Your home is above."

Ratai looked about her and realised that she was crouching inside a narrow space. Could she have fallen all the way through the lower floor? Then she realised that she was lying on top of a thin layer of unhusked rice grain. "Have you been stealing our rice?"

"I am no thief," the rat said. "I am *Bunsu* Tikus. All these rice grains came from me so I have every right to take as many as I wish."

Ratai took a deep breath. She had heard the story of Simpang Impang and about how he had received three rice seeds from the rat demon. She looked about her, "Where are your seven children?"

"They have grown up and started their own families. But they all still have the scorch marks that Simpang Impang gave them." The rat looked Ratai up and down. Then she said, "You should go back to your world. It will do you no good to stay here."

"Let me stay for a little while. I am very ashamed of my father. I do not wish to return now. I know I can be useful to you."

The rat sniffed. "Do not be too quick to judge. Even if your visitor looks brave, it does not mean that he was sent by the spirit."

"What do you mean?"

The rat shuffled about, moving the scattered rice grains to a corner where there was a pile of grain. Ratai picked up pieces of broken bamboo and put them to the side. Then she picked the rice grains stuck to her skin and reached forward to place them on the pile. The rat watched her for a moment then she said, "One man dreamed of the spear because he longed to be led by your father, the other lied about dreaming of it because he felt that his friend was right to dream of such a wonderful omen and he wanted to make sure that Jantan would succeed in persuading your father."

"Why would they not ask an augur or a shaman to confirm the dream?"

"Jantan received a charm, three petrified figs, from the Goddess Kumang. He has been adopted by her. So when he said that he dreamed of her, the elders in his longhouse believed him. They did not bother to confirm it with the goddess by watching out for omens." *Bunsu* Tikus added, "Your father's spirit sensed that something is not right, that is why he would not agree to join them."

"Father does not like Sagan. So he does not want to take revenge on his behalf."

"Sagan died because he and his friend would not listen to those who were wiser than them. Others already told them to be careful when they went to the coast, but they threw caution to the wind. They thought they were invincible, immortal."

"They were being brave."

"They were being foolish."

The rat returned to picking up the grains and putting them back into the pile. Ratai did not help her this time. Instead she sobbed quietly into her hands. Then she felt a soft touch on her knee. She wiped her eyes and looked down.

The rat was looking up at her then held up a grain of rice towards her. "Here. This is for you. You should go back upstairs now. Your family will start to wonder if you don't return. You may want to go to another longhouse though."

"Why?"

The rat let out a heavy sigh and looked about her home. "Because *Indai* Sagan released a curse into your community. This house will turn into a cemetery before the next generation is born."

Ratai gasped. "How can I stop this?"

"The only way would be to take revenge for Sagan and to bring back a head to appease him."

"I must tell my father," Ratai said.

The rat shook her head. "Your father must not go. He will die. Only you can go with the men and keep them safe. But you are a woman. No one will let you go." She pushed the grain into Ratai's palm. "Take this seed, Child. It is a charm to help you prosper in anything you choose to do."

Ratai received the *padi* seed and climbed out of the hole. She was surprised to find herself back in the loft, for she thought that she had fallen through the lower floor. When she looked down, the hole was gone. She wondered if she had been dreaming, so she looked down at her hand. There was a single grain in the middle of her palm. With her other hand, she reached up and took down a tiny pouch that was filled with magical cures and charms that she had collected over the years. To this she added the rice grain.

She could feel her sisters sleeping to either side of her. And the house was also quiet. She took a deep slow breath then lay back down on her mattress again. Her heart ached because she realised that the spirits did not want Sagan's death to be avenged. He had not sought their advice then he had ignored the wisdom of wiser and more experienced men. Ratai sobbed quietly into her hand.

\*\*\*

Jantan and Chad left early the next morning to deliver the news that Chief Nuing would only join their party if the omen was in his favour. Ratai did not go outside to see them off. She already knew what the spirits would tell her father. Instead she stayed inside the family quarter and began to put together a bowl of palm salt and a bowl of *kepayang* oil. She set these to the side and covered them with a patterned cloth as a sign that no one was to peek inside. Then she shouldered a burden basket and climbed down the trapdoor leading to the backyard.

Though the day had brightened, the garden was still covered in dew. She walked to the edge of the garden until she came upon thick layers of straight-standing thin stalks with spear-shaped leaves. One by one she pulled out the stem and the rhizomes of ginger snaking beneath the soil. She broke the stems off and shook off the dirt before tossing the rhizomes into the tall basket. Once the basket was full she squatted to shoulder the straps. Then, on looking up, she suddenly realised that the house was nowhere to be seen. She let go of the straps, stood up and looked about her, turning in circles. Panic and hysteria began to fill her chest. She forced herself to stand still and to stare down at the ginger. Then in a loud, strong voice she said, "Who are you?"

A man, his back bristling with porcupine quills, came out of the underbrush. He had tiny hands and tiny feet but a long stumpy body. He said, "I am Landak." Then he looked into the basket and asked curiously, "Is this all the ginger you have?"

Ratai blushed, a little embarrassed that she had been caught trying to do a project that she was not even sure would be successful. She squared her shoulders. "I am going to do a mordant bath."

Landak giggled. "You will fail."

"How dare you curse me?" Ratai retorted angrily. "I received the recipe from Goddess Meni herself."

"That may be so, but she did not give you a porcupine slave."

"Then I shall take one for myself," Ratai said, and she lunged at him, forcing him to fall on his back. His quills stung her, but she did not care. She kicked and punched his face, chest and stomach because his skin was exposed in these places. Then she grabbed the ginger stalks lying on the ground and began to whip him with it. The leaves were sharp and they cut into his tender skin.

He tried to turn right side up, but his legs and arms were up in the air and Ratai was sitting atop of him. He began to squeal and to cry.

Ratai leaned down and hissed into his face, "Give me a slave."

"Of course I will," Landak said. "Goddess Meni sent me to you, so you could have one of my quills. Why are you so rough?"

Ratai blushed. But she was not about to apologise. She stood up and said. "You did not say you were here to help me."

Landak rolled to his side, then got to his feet. His bruised face was glaring as he turned to look at her. Then he turned his back to her and said, "Well, choose one quill then. Quickly."

Ratai stared at the layers of flaring quills for a moment. One in particular caught her attention because the colours of ivory and black were brighter than the rest of the quills. She grasped it and pulled. Landak yelped then glared at her for a moment. Without a word he turned up his nose and marched away.

Ratai shouted a thank you. She turned back to her basket and once more saw her longhouse. She was back. She squatted down a second time to shoulder the basket. After sliding in the crown strap over her brow, she gritted her teeth and stood up. The dew was now gone from the ground but the day was dim because of the thick low clouds. The basket sagged with the weight of the ginger. Even though Ratai was used to carrying heavy loads, she had to bend forward a little so her back could bear some of the weight and the stretched strap would not cut into her shoulders.

When she climbed back into the house she found her mother stuffing palm cabbage into a bamboo tube. Nambi got up to help Ratai take the load off her shoulder. "Why do you need so much?" she asked her daughter on seeing that there were only ginger roots inside.

"I want to make a bath," Ratai said and looked pointedly to the freshly spun skeins of thread.

Nambi was about to protest because she was worried that her daughter was going to be punished by the spirits again for being insolent. Then she noticed the porcupine quill that Ratai grasped in one hand. It shone like metal but it had the texture of stone. She bit down on her tongue to stop herself from putting a curse on her daughter. Ratai's life had been strange of late. Nambi decided that maybe some spirit was now guiding her daughter and, as was the way with many spirits, they demanded secrecy. "Is there anything I can do to help?" Nambi asked.

"The salt and oil are ready. But I don't think there is enough. I need to clean and pound these roots too," Ratai said shyly, suddenly feeling overwhelmed by the importance of the activity she was about to undertake.

"Can your sisters help?"

Ratai was thoughtful for a moment. Was this going to be another failure? She would like her sisters' help because it would be less lonely. "Yes, I would like that."

Nambi went outside to call in the two older girls, Suma and Madu. Then she returned to the back to finish with their day meal preparations. The girls were busy brushing off as much dirt as they could from the roots with a coconut brush. But that was not enough, Nambi decided, so after she put their meal on the hearth, she took a basket filled with empty bamboo tubes and said, "I will bring some water for you to wash the roots with."

Suma said, "We can take these to the riverside."

Nambi shook her head. "No, people will ask too many questions."

Ratai said, "But I might have to boil the ginger outside because the hearth in here is too small. I need to boil them for half of the morning. People will still ask questions."

Nambi said, "Most people will be on their way out to the

fields before sunrise. I will make sure that the mothers send their children off to the fields so there will not be too much unnecessary chatter." Then she went out.

\*\*\*

Early the next morning, after the noise of neighbours on their way to the fields had subsided, Ratai brought out the basket of ginger with her sisters' help. There were other women there, sitting in front of the verandah hearth. They were all weavers. *Inik* Jambi, she saw, had prepared a boiled egg and a handful of popped rice in a small offering basket.

"We hear that you want to boil a bath," one woman said.

Ratai nodded shyly as she put down the basket. Then she said, "But I am not sure if this will work. I only know how to prepare the mordant bath."

Nambi turned to *Inik* Jambi. "You have been part of a *ngar* process before. Are we doing this right?"

"We need to wash our raw threads first; that is why I readied this offering. Then when we return we must cover the windows and doors to protect our work from prying eyes." She looked about her at the women. "There are so many of us. I think since Ratai looks like she has only enough materials for a single bath we should all agree to only soak enough thread for a single *pua* each."

The women assented with either a nod or a vocal *yes* then returned to their rooms to get their skeins of thread. They each came back out with a skein that was thick enough to fit into the grasp of two hands and looped to the length of a woman's height. *Inik* Jambi then showed them that they must place an empty trough below the long length of a ceiling beam. Then she showed them how to tie large wooden hooks along the beam and over the trough.

After this work was done, Ratai walked ahead of the group to the river, holding the offering in one hand and a skein of her mother's thread in the other. On reaching the bathing platform she made the offering by placing it to the side then she leaned forward and dipped the thread in the water. Each woman took her turn, making sure that each thread was wet through before they returned to the longhouse. On reaching the common gallery the women hung up the skeins on the wooden hooks over the trough. Then they returned to their rooms and brought out their ritual cloth to hang over the windows and door closest to the trough.

Some children turned up to watch the goings-on but the apparent seriousness of the affair hushed them into wide-eyed silence. Even Sawai was awed into silence. Then, with her head bowed, she returned to her room.

After the sacred space was built, a wooden mortar and a second trough were brought into it. One woman sat by the side and started to put in handfuls of peeled ginger. Two women took turns pounding them with pestles. There was not much talking, and if anyone noticed that something was not right she would either correct it herself or tell the closest person to do so. She would never point out the negative aspect of the problem because her words might curse the project into failure.

Some women went to the river to collect water. They poured these into the second trough. Others went into their rooms and brought out firewood. Every woman was busy going about doing whatever she felt was necessary. The first batch of pounded ginger and its juice was soon scooped up and added into the water-filled trough. The pounding continued with more ginger. After the last load of pounded ginger had been added, the women started squeezing the ginger fibres in the water. Their skin tingled with the heat and the refreshing scent of ginger filled the whole house. The water turned yellow then a milky gold.

While the last of the ginger was being squeezed dry and its spent fibre cast to the side, a large fire was started on the verandah hearth outside. Ratai scooped out the ginger water with a coconut bowl into three large clay pots. By this time, the sun was halfway to noon.

Two women had to lift each pot to place them over the fire. The pots were so big they barely fitted on the wide hearth. When they began to boil, Ratai used a stick to stir one pot. She felt that the sun was particularly bright that morning and the smell of ginger rising with the steam was overbearing. When she straightened her back to stir the next pot, she swooned. Nambi caught her and quickly brought her back into the shady common gallery.

Ratai accepted a sip of water from her neighbour *Inik* Jambi. Nambi said, "Maybe we should stop this?"

"No, Mother," Ratai said. "We are halfway done. I am all right now. I was just too excited last night and did not get a good night's sleep."

*Inik* Jambi said, "In my old longhouse the *Indu Ngar* covers her head with a cloth when she is outside during the ritual. She says it is to hide her from the eyes of wandering demons."

Ratai blushed when she realised that her neighbour was equating her with the high status of a Lady of the Mordant. Nambi, however, immediately got up and went into the family room. She soon came out with a piece of woven cloth about the size of a skirt. Ratai recognised it to be one of the special cloths that her mother often used to cover sacred works from prying eyes. Ratai allowed Nambi to put it over her head then went outside to continue boiling the ginger.

The day grew hotter but Ratai felt fresh and determined. She was not sure if what she was doing was right so having *Inik* Jambi close by talking about the mordant bath ritual that she had attended years before gave Ratai fresh assurances. She sensed rather than saw a change in the boiling water. The boiling bubbles appeared to be larger and the surface of the water seemed to have taken on a soft oily sheen, like the surface of a dewdrop. With the help of a few women, Ratai put out the fire and cleared the hearth of embers. The pots were left there to cool.

Then a few women, led by Nambi, began to serve lunch to those who remained in the longhouse. There was none of the usual noise and gaiety that accompanied such gatherings. For this meal it was quiet, as though there was a sleeping child in their midst. The women talked quietly among themselves about family and field matters. No one wanted to discuss the ritual or the design they planned to use on their cloth because they were all afraid that their words would jinx the process.

After the quick meal, Nambi went outside and touched the rim of the pots. "I think this is cool enough to carry in now." The water was still steaming hot but the pot was no longer so hot that it would burn through bark cloth.

They carried the pots, one after the other, into the common gallery and poured out the contents into the trough under the hanging skeins of thread. Then Ratai brought out the bowl of salt and kepayang oil from her family room. These were poured along the full length of the trough. Ratai straightened her back and stared at the water, unsure about what to do next.

*Inik* Jambi said, "Now we will all have to pound the bottom of the trough with a stick, so that the salt and oil will mix well."

Nambi asked, "What kind of stick, *Inik*?"

The old lady squinted and thought hard for a moment. Finally she said, "Any kind of stick. As long as you can grasp it in one hand." The weavers all dispersed and soon returned holding a stick each. Then they all took their places across from each other along the length of the trough. Ratai grasped the bottom of a stick and squatted at the head of the trough. She immersed her hand in the hot water and began to pound the bottom. The other women followed suit and soon there was a din of pounding reverberating through the full length of the house.

At this time, some men had started returning from their fishing or fieldwork. They looked curiously towards the noise and on seeing the hanging sacred cloths returned to their parts of the gallery without saying a word. The pounding continued until the water had cooled to skin temperature. When the women took their hands out of the trough, many of them commented that the water had given them a healthy glow. Some of the older women even claimed that the cramps from their fingers or wrist were gone.

"Yes," *Inik* Jambi said. "This water is very good. It can make us young again."

The women began to appreciatively wipe a handful over their face, neck, or shoulders, careful not to waste the precious water as they did so. After all, they wanted the perfect thread. Ratai then pulled out the porcupine quill stuck to her hair and dropped it onto the surface of the water. The quill barely made a splash on the water. It stayed afloat but the sharp end sunk below the surface.

Ratai frowned. "I think we need more oil." Nambi went back to the room and came out with a second bowl of kepayang oil. Ratai took out the quill and poured in about a fifth of the oil's contents. She started pounding the trough again. The other women helped her. A few minutes later, the oil emulsified into the mixture. Ratai again dropped the porcupine quill. This time it was level. Ratai let out a sigh of relief. "The bath water is ready," she said.

The women then reached up to release the skeins of thread from their hooks. After everyone was ready, they all let out a loud shrill shout and stretched out the skeins along the length of the trough. They pressed the thread down and rolled them on their side carefully, making sure not to tangle them against each other. They did this over and over until every single thread was soaked in the mordant bath. Once this was done to Ratai's satisfaction, the trough was covered with a rattan mat.

*Inik* Jambi open a cloth hanging over the gallery door and told Ratai to run to the river. All the other women rushed after her. They jumped into the river with loud happy shouts. It was an exhausting but satisfying day. Released from their hushed silence, the children too joined their mothers and sisters in the river, splashing and making merry.

By this time, more people were returning to the longhouse. Nuing looked about him with wonder. There were so many happy faces. He did not understand what was going on, but he accepted their happiness and he laughed with them to add to their blessing.

That night after dinner, *Inik* Jambi opened the mat and said to Ratai, "You must climb into the trough and tread on the threads."

Ratai stepped onto the thread. She walked atop it carefully, holding onto the hooks hanging down from the beam to keep her balance. Then two other women, at *Inik* Jambi's prompting, also climbed in. The three women walked in circles, squashing the thread and forcing the fibres to soak in more mordant. After a few minutes, they climbed out and covered the trough again.

For the next three days, the women continued this activity. Each morning, the ginger water was squeezed out of the thread and reboiled then added back into the trough with the thread. In the evenings three women would walk on them. When the rest of the longhouse occupants finally learned what the weavers were up to, nobody dared say anything bad about it. They sensed that it was a sacred ritual because a *puangar* would bring them closer to the gods. They had all heard stories about great warriors who owned cloth woven from the mordant thread. They told each other stories about cloths that were so red they glowed like fresh blood, and about the colour that was so fast they could be washed over and over without fading. To many who had never seen such a thing, it was an idea that filled them with wonder.

Early on the morning of the fourth day, the skeins of thread were taken out and squeezed dry for the final time. Then they were spread over two bamboo poles and left to dry outside on the verandah. When evening came, a simple offering was made at the drying area. For the next seven days and seven nights, the thread was left outside to sweat under the sun and to wash under the dew.

"What if it rains, *Inik* Jambi?" Ratai asked. "Will it not ruin the thread?"

"We will sleep outside here, in the common gallery," *Inik* Jambi explained. "This is our warpath, so there is no shame to sleep among the men." Then she turned to look sternly at the unmarried women. "Mind yourselves. When a man is about to go to war, he will not visit his sweetheart. You too must not receive suitors during this time, otherwise you will lose this war."

There were some giggles and glances exchanged among the younger women, but nobody revealed who their interests were. *Inik* Jambi, however, seemed to know which young women to throw warning glances to.

The week continued to stay hot throughout and Nambi interpreted this as a blessing from Goddess Meni. She was glad for it meant that Ratai's mordant would be successful. She felt that it was time for Ratai to be accepted as the perfect woman that she truly was. On the morning after the seven days and nights of drying and dewing, they again took the thread to the river for a wash. Again the threads were dried on the verandah, this time without pomp or superstition. Once the thread was dry, they rolled the skein into balls and stored them away to wait for the time for dyeing.

\*\*\*

While the women went about their work with the mordant bath, the men too were busy. They discussed quietly among themselves whether they would join Jantan or not. It was clear to them that Nuing was uninterested even though he promised to look out for omens. This did not sit well with the older men because good omens were known to be non-forthcoming when the intention to look out for them was not there.

A few days after the women had finished drying the thread, Nuing and three other elders returned from the jungle. They were solemn as they headed to the river to clean themselves. On their return to the longhouse, there was a large group of men and women waiting for them at the chief's common gallery.

Nuing sat on the raised platform and the other three men sat to either side of him. He nodded to *Tuai Burong* Nyaru to indicate that he should speak. The augur cleared his throat and said, "We heard Ketupong's voice on our third day in the jungle, but it sounded as though it was coming from everywhere. We could not agree if it was to the left or to the right of our hut."

Another man said, "One hawk came and flew in a circle overhead, but it was only one. There were no other hawks or hornbills that came to confirm its good omen."

Bantak said, "Is that not enough? Does it not mean that we can go to war?"

"We can go by our own will," Nuing said. "But the gods have not shown their blessing."

"Will they harm us if we go?" a young man asked.

Nyaru said, "The omens are not clear on that point. It does not say that the gods will curse us either with good or bad fortune."

Ratai listened with a sinking feeling in her chest. She could sense that the young men were disappointed. They all wanted to join Jantan, not because they wanted to take revenge for Sagan, but because they wanted an opportunity to prove their courage. She felt as disappointed as they were. She could not understand why the spirits would want to prevent them from going when war was such a glorious and courageous thing. Was not glory and courage good? Why would the spirits not want the people to prove themselves?

She did not speak up, however, because her disappointment was tempered by her fear of the unknown. Sagan had disobeyed and he had not listened to those with more wisdom. Because of that he was now dead and his mother had gone mad. Surely that was the sign of a curse. Then she remembered what the rat told her, that the house was under a curse because of what Sawai did with Sagan's funereal treasures. She felt confused and anxious because there did not seem to be a clear answer to their predicament.

The discussion among the elders continued until late into the night with people leaving and rejoining throughout. The young men's faces grew ever more forlorn as they too finally came to the conclusion that the expedition would not be a fruitful one. Ratai was starting to become less anxious as the night progressed. The tight knot in her belly relaxed and the repetitive discussion began to bore her.

A series of calls suddenly caught everyone's attention. They recognised this melancholic hoot, but it was always far away from the house. Yet this call now sounded like it was just above their heads. They all looked up to the ceiling and rafters. Each person tried to find the source of the ill-omen cry. The calls continued, now above them, moments later farther down the length of the house. It was a cry that even the little children recognised and it struck everyone with fear. The hawk-owl was a harbinger of death, for it sounded as though it was calling for their souls.

The augur's brow wrinkled into a deep frown when Nuing asked him, "What does this mean, *Tuai Burong*? There was no omen that tells us to go to war. What does this omen mean?"

Nyaru replied, "I must ask the spirits. I have never come across such conflicting messages before."

Though Nyaru kept his voice low as he made the reply, Ratai overheard. The fear and confusion returned with stronger fervour inside her. Could this be what the rat demon meant? That everyone in the longhouse was going to die unless they go to war. Yet if they go, there was no assurance of victory.

Ratai grabbed Nuing's arm and turned him to face her. "You must let us go to war. It is what the spirits want."

Nuing stared at her for a moment, surprised at the passion in her voice. "But there is no guarantee of success. Many of our warriors will die and fail."

"They will die a glorious death. They will be heroes and be assured of a good place in the afterlife."

By now there was a crowd around them listening in to their

conversation. Nuing said, "Are you deaf? Can you not hear the hawk-owl's call? It is telling each family that one among them is going to die before the next harvest."

Ratai hissed back, "We will all die if you don't send warriors to bring home fresh trophies to bless the house. *Bunsu* Tikus told me to leave this place because she said that everyone who remains will die."

Nuing frowned. There were gasps or cries of despair and fear from the listeners about them. "You cannot ask me to sacrifice our young men."

Ratai took a deep breath. It was now or never. "I am asking you to let me go with them."

"You are a woman," Nambi shouted, suddenly anxious and afraid for her daughter. "Your place is here in this house."

Ratai straightened her back and steeled herself before she turned to face her mother. Her gaze was proud and bold, like a seasoned warrior. "My place is where the spirits send me. I will go and be like one of the men."

Suma cried out to her sister, "But Sagan's spirit is appeased. You don't have to take revenge on his behalf anymore."

Ratai took a deep breath to give herself time to think. She did not want to expose Sawai's secret, but neither would her conscience allow her to remain silent. "*Indai* Sagan found the jar, and ..."

The shocked silence that greeted her pronouncement was so thick it made her ears smart a deep red. "What do you mean?" Nuing asked. "Did she ..." the action he was about to mention was so taboo that he could not bring himself to utter it.

Ratai nodded. She bowed her head in shame for not telling him earlier then just as quickly raised her gaze again to look into his face. "That is why I must go. Even if you will not let the other men go, you must let me go."

Unable to contain his incredulity, Bantak said, "You are a woman. You will only be in our way. We will have to take care of you and protect you."

Ratai turned to glare at him. "I do not need your protection."

Bantak said, "You will shame us. How are we to explain your presence in our group to the other men? What praise name should we give you? You have done nothing heroic. How are we to extort your qualities to them? You have never borne a child and your rice field does not prosper."

Ratai felt a pain so sharp in her belly that it felt as though Bantak had driven a knife into it. Yes, she was a failure. What right did she have to be a warrior? But her anger against his judgment rose so strong, it fuelled her pride. "You do not have to support me or to protect me. All you have to do is stay out of my way."

Bantak moved back an inch, startled and cowed by the fury in her face. He sensed that there was something else moving her. Something he could not understand but that which made the hair on his nape stand on end. But he was a man, he reminded himself. He was not going to recoil before her. So he stood his ground and glared back at her. He said accusingly, "You are the reason we are under a curse. Sagan went to the coast because he wanted to prove he was worthy to be your suitor. You turned up your nose at him and you would not even speak to him before he left."

Ratai felt sorrow welling up in her throat. She wanted to cry and thrash about like a child in a tantrum. But she could not allow herself that relief. Her pride held up her spine. Yet at the same time the same pride also cut into every muscle, making her appear stiff and trembling at the same time. Struggling to keep her voice even, she said, "He brought that curse upon himself. Now

I am going to fix it." She condemned the man she loved before everyone. Feeling the tears of regret about to burst through her being, she turned away and strode back to her family room.

\*\*\*

Dinner was quiet. But it was not the quiet of contentment or of satisfaction. Even the younger children could sense that something was different as they stole glances at their parents and Ratai. There was unease, a sense of waiting. Like when one waited for a thunderstorm on a hot sweltering afternoon. The day would be bright and hot, but the air humid and the white clouds thick.

After the meal and just as Ratai was about to get up to clear the mat, Nambi said to her, "Let your sisters clear the food away. Sit with me and your father for a little while."

The younger girls quickly cleared away the food. Then with a nod from Nambi, Mansau and Suma gathered the younger children and brought them outside to the common gallery. Even after they closed the door behind them, Ratai remained straight back and stony faced. She would not meet her parents' gaze.

Nambi said, "You ate so little, Child. That is not good for you."

"It is also not good to go to war," Nuing said. "War is nothing at all like the songs and stories you hear. Only the victors return to tell their tales. Those who die tell us nothing."

Ratai turned to face her parents. Seeing the worry on their faces, her stony expression softened and she said, "I know that your words are wise because you speak from experience. But I must go, and you must let me."

"Why?" Nambi pleaded.

Nuing studied the resolve on her face for a moment then said,

"Explain your decision to us. If we understand and are assured that you will return safe, we will let you go with our blessing."

Ratai fought the urge to break down and cry. She was afraid of the unknown and terrified of the fate that she could only imagine. But she must be strong and be self-assured, or else her father would insist on going, despite having been told by the spirits not to go. "*Bunsu* Tikus told me that the house is under a curse. That everyone is going to die. The only way to prevent this is by bringing home the head of one of the men who killed Sagan."

"Those men could be long gone by now," Nuing reasoned.

"*Bunsu* Tikus told me that they will return."

Nambi said hopefully, "She promised you victory?"

Ratai shook her head.

Nambi turned to her husband with horror. "You must stop her. You must go with the men in her place."

"Father must not go. The omens for him are bad."

"And what of you?" Nambi said passionately. "You are a woman. What do you know of fighting and killing other men?"

"You are right, Mother. I do not know. But *Bunsu* Tikus told me that all our men will die if I don't go with them."

Nuing looked from one woman to the other. Finally he said to Ratai, "Sempurai gave you to me as a blessing. I believe that he will protect you and bring you home."

"Thank you, Father," Ratai said and got up to leave the room. She ignored her mother's wail because she had no words or promises that could be used to comfort her. She knew that the only words her mother wanted to hear was her promise to stay.

# 9

Jantan could barely hide his surprise when he looked about him at the other men in Nuing's longhouse. He saw that many would not look him straight in the eye, and that others had turned their gaze down in shame. These men were clearly not happy to have a woman in their group. While Jantan was trying to think of a way to politely discourage the woman from joining them, his companion Chad said, "It is unheard of for a woman to go to war."

Nuing was about to explain when Ratai spoke up, "I was told by the rat demon that unless I join the expedition all the men from this longhouse will die."

Nuing nodded to show that he agreed with her. Then he indicated with his hand to encourage her to continue. She must stand up for herself now, he decided, while he was still here to act as her sponsor. Otherwise, she would not be allowed to speak at all during the expedition.

Ratai said, "My parents often tell me that I am a gift from Sempurai. Any man in this longhouse can be witness to my hunting skills."

"Yes," *Apai* Bantak said, though with a slight hesitation in his tone. "She hunted her first pig earlier than my son. If she goes into the jungle, she never returns home empty-handed."

Fighting down her shyness before the gaze of these two heroes, Ratai said, "I have been given the secrets of the mordant bath by the Goddess Meni and I was adopted by the Goddess

Kumang, who saved my life."

The women began to take turns recalling the story of how she came out of her fever and of how successful the mordant bath ceremony led by her was. Jantan and Chad shared a look between them a number of times. Nuing saw the reluctance on their face, so he said, "The omens for me were not good and I was reluctant to let my men go without me. But Ratai, my daughter, received different advice from the rat demon. She was told to go to save their lives."

Chad fiddled with his fingers for a moment. Then he leaned forward and said, "But *Tuai*. I have never heard of a woman who goes to war with other men. Women do not go to war for the same reason that men do not weave cloth. The work for either skill is equally dangerous and strenuous, but they are not the same."

The other men of their party nodded and mumbled among themselves. None had ever heard of a woman going to war. A woman may be exposed to war when her longhouse is under attack or when enemies come to her field, but her role had always been a defensive one. They conceded that the perfect woman was strong because she could carry heavy loads on her back and that she was brave because she could face demons and spirits that try to destroy her weaving. But war: war was the area of men.

Jantan turned to Ratai to try and reason with her. "Are you not afraid that you might never be able to wield the beater again? How will you capture the spirits you weave if your arm is injured? Enemies are not like wild pigs or deer. They attack you with swords and spears. They will not run from you."

Ratai hesitated for a moment. Then she said, "When Kumang adopted me, she told me that I will never weave a cloth."

Chad said, "How is that possible? She is the Goddess of the Weave."

"She is also the patroness of headhunters," Nuing said.

Chad was about to continue the argument but Jantan stopped him with a touch on the shoulder. Then Jantan turned to Nuing and said, "That is a good omen from the spirits. We will accept their blessings in whatever form it may come."

Nyaru the augur said, "The spirits can see more than we can. Maybe the omens are strange to us now because we can not yet see what is to transpire."

The men conceded to his wise words but they were still unhappy that Ratai was joining them. To put this problem out of their mind they began to discuss stories of past expeditions they had heard. They recalled stories of Lau Moa, the first leader to settle in the Skrang River. They talked about how his withered face had struck fear into the hearts of his enemies. And about how his courage had brought blessings from Sengalang Burong onto his sons. Again the story was retold about how his family received the proper incantations of the Gawai Burong, the feast of the Hornbill.

The discussion naturally moved to Lao Moa's daughter, Lantong, who begot Tindin, who went on to become a famed warrior. Bantak looked pointedly at Ratai, as though to remind her of another brave woman who had kept her place in the home and passed on the warrior spirit to her son. Ratai could feel her ears growing red as she listened, but she kept her head up and her expression proud.

Then they discussed the beautiful Remampak, whose father was killed by a Bukitan chief. She swore that she would marry any man who could avenge her father's death. The great Berauh Ngumbang came, killed Chief Ginyum and claimed his prize. This was what brave women do, they discussed loudly among themselves, a woman's role was to encourage brave men to go to war on their behalf.

Nuing felt that what the men were doing to his daughter was wrong, but he did nothing to stop them. He was half wishing that they could talk sense to her through their stories. It would not matter to him if the men died, at least his daughter would be unharmed. He felt that he could easily attract other men and other families to fill his longhouse, or that he could easily join another longhouse if necessary. Yet when he looked at his other young children, he realised that Ratai was their only saviour.

As the night wore on, another problem presented itself. If Ratai was to go to war, she had to sleep outside with the men. It was taboo for a man to be distracted by women before going to war, so they always slept outside, away from wife and family, before starting their journey. But Ratai was a single woman.

Nambi took her aside and said, "You must sleep inside with us tonight. You cannot sleep out here with the men."

Ratai was quiet for a moment. She understood her predicament well enough. Then she squared her shoulders. Her reputation as a woman was already ruined anyway. "I will sleep out here like the men," she said stubbornly.

Nambi next brought the matter to Nuing who took the time to ponder it for a moment. Then he said something to her. Ratai could see the surprised and shocked look on her mother's face. There was a slight argument between the couple. Ratai was relieved to see her mother relent.

Soon Nambi returned to Ratai's side and said, "Come with me inside. You must change into your father's clothes."

Ratai got up thankfully and followed her mother inside. She unwrapped her shin-length skirt and wound on her father's loincloth. She took off the string of beads around her neck and put on a large shell disk over her bare chest. She then slid off her dainty carved rattan bracelets and put on the thick arm and calf bracelets of shell. Instantly she felt strength growing inside her torso.

She loosened the bun behind her head then tied the long hair into a knot at her nape, letting the ends hang down loosely. Then she strapped on her father's *ilang*, the sword that he received from his father, Bujang Maias. Ratai had always wanted to wield it but now that it was hanging down at her side, she became wary of it. Finally her mother put a coat of wildcat skin over her shoulders. Instantly she felt protected by the stiff and tough pelt of the animal. She was proud and manly when she stepped out of the room to rejoin the men outside.

Ratai was surprised to hear the women ooh and aah their appreciation. She blushed when she heard some of them comment that she was the most handsome warrior they had ever seen. She returned to her place in the gallery and sat down cross-legged on the floor. Nuing nodded approvingly.

Jantan turned to Bantak and said to him, "Well, my friend. It seems that the chief's daughter can be a man after all."

Bantak nodded grudgingly. "Yes, you are right. She can fight and hunt better than some of us. That was why I was quite surprise when my best friend Sagan expressed his interest in her. No one else would."

Jantan asked, "So it was her sweetheart who died?"

"Yes, it was." Then with a hint of regret he said, "I might have been too harsh when I accused her of causing his death."

Jantan nodded knowingly. "Maybe you were harsh because you wanted to protect her. She may look like a man now, but she will soon learn that a woman has no place in war." Then he added, "Did the chief ask you to watch out for her?"

"No, he did not. In fact Ratai told me to make sure to stay

out of her way."

Jantan chuckled. "She is fierce and bold. Much like the Goddess Kumang."

"That may be so. But even the goddess asked for a champion when she found out that her parents were still alive and being kept prisoner by *Apai* Langit."

"Maybe Ratai's heart would not let her accept another?" Jantan said.

"You do not think ..." Bantak started to ask, yet stopped short because he would not allow himself to utter the word.

"I have heard stories of men who went to war or joined dangerous hunting expeditions because their sweetheart or young wife died. It was the only way they could think of to join her in the afterlife," Jantan said. Both men turned to look at her with pity then quickly turned their gaze away when Ratai looked in their direction.

Ratai could sense that she was the subject of private conversation among the small groups of people scattered about the common gallery. Try as she might to seem uncaring, when it was time for the men to bed for the night, she felt a slight panic creeping up to her chest. Who should she sleep next to?

Seeming to have wondered over the same predicament, her brother Mansau went to her side and said, "You should sleep on my bed. He pointed his chin to a narrow plank bed fixed to the wall. "I will sleep on the floor with the men." Then he slipped away.

Ratai did not argue or call him back. It was a solution for that night, and it made her think about future nights. She pushed the thought from her mind. She decided to solve the problem for each night as and when it came. She took off the coat and shell disk and unwound the sword from her waist. Then she lay on the bed and covered herself with her father's blanket. She hoped that she would dream of the black bear that had helped her father in the past. She slept, but dreamed of nothing.

\*\*\*

Ratai's arms ached from the fast-paced rowing. But she did not allow her discomfort to show. The more pain she felt, the more fierce she scowled, so that by the end of the day's journey she had begun to look as fierce as the men.

When they made camp that night, Bantak said, "I will go look for some meat, you should stay here and rest by the fire."

Ratai's back hurt and her arms were so sore it felt as though she could barely swing a stick. Her legs too were stiff from being cramped between two other rowers for hours. But she was not about to let the men think that she was any lesser than them. So she stood up, girthed on her sword and picked up her hunting spear. "I am restless. I am not tired," she said. This was what the heroes of epics would do, she reminded herself. This was what she would do too to earn the men's respect.

When she started going into the jungle, her hair and back were already drenched with sweat. She gritted her teeth in an effort to control the trembling of chill and exhaustion. No one offered to join her, so she walked into the jungle alone.

Even though she was used to walking in the jungle on her own, for the first time in her life she felt lonely. She walked without purpose; her only care was putting one foot ahead of the other. She did not listen for animals. She did not look out for peeping bamboo shoots or flexible palm trunks ripe with palm heart. She was not interested in food. She was a freak of nature, a tree that bore unnatural fruit. She was cursed because she stole a spearhead from Selampadai.

"It is a fate of your own choice," a tiny voice said from within a shrub of fern.

Ratai stopped walking then wondered if she had heard her own thoughts speaking to her. She looked about and saw a tiny nose sticking out of the shrub.

"Who are you?" she asked.

"I am your guide, Bulu Landak," it said. The small animal came out of the shrub and Ratai saw that it was a tiny porcupine.

"Are you my quill? But I left you at home."

"Your mother slipped me into your basket. She held me to her heart and she bathed me in her tears. Then she begged that I watch out for you."

Ratai was sad to hear of her mother's pain. The melancholia, however, soon turned to excitement. She had a spirit guide. She was going to be invincible, *mali lebu*. The men would have to respect her now. They must, once they knew that she had a strong protector. "What skill will you give me? How will you make me powerful?"

Bulu Landak looked down at her forepaws for a moment then she said, "Well, I can float straight if your mordant bath is good."

"I am going to war," Ratai said with a touch of impatience.

"I am good at hiding," Bulu Landak said. "I know how to hide you from bad spirits. That is how I protect weavers when they are weaving difficult work."

Ratai turned her back to the spirit and sat down on the ground with a heavy sigh. She felt defeated, useless. Her existence felt pointless. There was so much she wanted to do. She thought that the more she could do, the more she would be accepted and admired. Yet all her aspirations had fallen short of total success. She could do a mordant bath but she could not weave. She could clear a forest but she could not plant. No matter how hard she tried, she could never become a master at any skill.

Bulu Landak came to sit next to her and said, "I am useless. I can't do anything to help you at war."

Ratai's gentle heart instantly filled with pity. "You helped me with the mordant bath. You are not useless." Ratai's hope of becoming invincible went away, but she no longer felt lonely.

\* \* \*

It was already dark when Ratai finally returned to camp. She could smell fish cooking at some of the open campfires. She was tired but she had brought food. After a short rest with Bulu Landak she had continued hunting with renewed vigour. The adolescent sambar deer did not get a hint of her approach until it was too late.

She had slung the carcass over her shoulder. It was heavy but she did not mind the weight for the first mile. As the light began to dim she started to panic because she hated being alone in pitch dark. Bulu Landak, who had been by her side the whole time, started to glow, not brightly but with the soft glow of the moon. She led Ratai back to camp.

Assan, a young man from her longhouse, was the first to spot her approach. He got up and went to help her. The other men looked up then turned their attention back to the fire. Nothing was cooking there. They were all eating the ration they had brought from home.

With a wide smile, Assan said, "This is excellent. It has been a long time since I had deer meat."

Bantak said, "It is said that deer will make your spirit weak because it is a timid animal."

Ratai blushed and her heart skipped a beat. Had she brought bad luck to her company? Then she said defiantly, "My father brings home deer all the time. Nobody in my family is timid."

Jantan, who was listening from the next campfire, said, "It is the mousedeer that makes you weak, not the sambar deer." He got up and helped Assan carry the animal to the river.

Ratai sat down thankfully in front of her group's campfire. After a few moments of rest, she began to feel uncomfortable because though the men were talking to each other none of them asked her about the hunt. No one wanted to know if she had heard or seen an omen animal. No one was interested to learn if she had noticed anything unusual.

The rejection hit her hard. She was close to tears but was too proud and too stubborn to walk away. Then Uyut, the leader of their group approached the fire. He was dripping wet, clearly having just washed himself at the river. He sat next to her and said, "Ratai, you have brought back a feast."

"Thank you, *Ayak*," she said, calling him uncle not because he was related to her but out of respect for his friendship to her father.

"What did you do? Where did you go?" he asked.

Ratai was so surprised by the question she did not know how to answer it at first. Then Uyut said, "Don't be selfish. Share your story with us."

Ratai began her story from after meeting Bulu Landak. She did not mention her spirit guide because she felt that it was a secret. She talked about finding an animal trail and following it. "The trail led to a small cave and I saw some deer licking the stones."

Uyut nodded his head knowingly. "There must be bats living inside. Deer like going to these places because the rocks are salty from the droppings of the bats." The other men started listening with interest. Uyut raised his palm a little to indicate to Ratai that she should continue her story.

"None of the deer noticed me, even when I stood up to throw my spear."

Uyut asked, "Was the wind blowing towards your face or at the back of your head?"

"It was towards my face," Ratai said, after searching her memory for a moment. "I could smell the stink of guano coming out of the cave."

"What does that mean, *Ayak*?" Dujong, a young warrior asked.

Uyut started to explain, "You must always check the direction of the wind when you approach an animal. This is because *Bunsu* Ribut can be quite mischievous. The wind demon can carry your smell and sound to the animal if you don't watch out for him. That is why sometimes you can wait for a whole day at an animal trail, but if even the slightest wind blows your scent towards an animal, your hunt will not be successful.

Just then Assan returned from the river with the liver and heart of the deer. He lay them on a wide leaf on the ground in front of the fire. "There," he said. "You can start cooking that first. Ratai must be hungry. She did not take even a brief rest before going off to hunt for us."

Bantak would not meet Ratai's gaze as he took out a knife and began cutting the organs into chunks. Uyut started picking up the pieces and skewering them on thin sticks. Ratai leaned forward to help but Uyut said, "You should not be doing anything more. Go take your bath. By the time you return, the food will be ready."

Ratai hesitated for a moment. She was not used to not cooking or serving. But when she turned to Uyut to insist that she help, he gave her a stern nod, as though telling her that it was not a suggestion. She did not understand what he meant or why he would insist that she ignore dinner preparations. But she had promised her father that she would listen to Uyut about everything. So she got up and made her way to a secluded spot at the river.

She was self-conscious as she unwrapped her loincloth behind a bush. There were some men in the river but none of them was close to her. That morning, as they got into the boats, she had heard some lurid comments from a group of men led by Baling about her exposed thighs and buttocks. It was all that she could do to ignore them. She was glad when Jantan had reminded them to show her respect because she might save their lives in the battlefield.

After she had been in the river for a while she noticed two men from Jantan's group come close to her. The older man asked, "How many people from your longhouse have joined?"

"Twenty-three, including myself," Ratai said. Everyone already knew the number of participants from each longhouse. Ratai understood that the man only asked because he was being polite. She was young and inexperienced, so he asked her a simple question that she could easily answer. This way he would not embarrass or discourage her by her lack of knowledge.

The man said, "I am Oyong, and this here is my nephew, Nital."

Nital said, "We are Jantan's men."

"I am Ratai," she said, again stating the obvious. "I am with Uyut." It was comforting to her that she could have a decent conversation with him because her shyness would have made it impossible for her to say anything else.

"Jantan told us that you caught a sambar deer," Oyong said.

"It is only a small one," Ratai said shyly.

Oyong went through the same line of questioning that Uyut did, and this time when Ratai replied she remembered to tell them that she had found a salt lick in front of a bat cave and that the breeze was blowing at her face.

Both Oyong and Nital nodded to show that they agreed with her assessments then they shared their experiences of the day with her. By the time her bath was done, Ratai felt accepted and appreciated by both men. She returned to the camp with a light step.

More meat was cooking on the fire by the time she returned. Her empty stomach rumbled so loud she was worried that the others would hear. But no one teased her about her greediness as she took her place by the fire. It was a good meal. Even Bantak was in good humour. Each time Ratai looked up, she would catch Jantan's gaze. His boldness embarrassed her.

Uyut must have noticed it too because he said, "I've built a separate shelter for you, Ratai. You are one of us but you are still a woman. Your femininity might charm one of the men and weaken his resolve for war."

Ratai said nothing in reply but she threw him a thankful glance. Love and war were both strong emotions. They must never mix because the longing of love could distract a man during war, while the anger of war could lead to quarrels when there should be joy and tenderness.

By now the mosquitoes were buzzing about them more persistently so she too, like the men, began to start smoking. The smoke, however, made her feel sleepy. She decided to retire early for the night because she felt that she had proven herself enough for the day. She burned a roll of *selukai* bark and said goodnight.

When she reached the shelter at the edge of the camp, she saw that Bulu Landak had already curled herself up into a ball next to her blanket. Ratai waved the smoky bark about and then stuck the unburned end of the roll into a crevice at the base of the stick holding up the leaf roof.

As she lay down to sleep, the rumbling sound of a storm reached her ears. She saw the flash of lightning from behind her eyelids. She curled her legs up towards her belly and pulled the blanket over her face. She hated thunderstorms, especially storms with bright lightning. She felt the storm passing overhead and she heard the trees about her shelter creak loudly. She knew that she should get up and at least make sure that she was nowhere near an oversized tree. But she didn't want to get up because she was too afraid of the loud howling wind.

The leaf roof over her head shook and in the distance there was a loud crash. An emergent tree must have been uprooted, she told herself, growing more and more anxious by the minute. How she wished she were home now. At least if she was at the longhouse she knew that she would not be crushed by a tree because no large tree was ever grown close to the longhouse.

Another crash and another, Ratai pulled the blanket over her head tighter. The howling was distant, but it sounded horrible and frightening. The noise continued for a little more then it faded into the night like smoke. Ratai pushed the blanket away from her face. The night was bright and the air was dewy fresh after the stuffy heat of the thick blanket. Other than the sound of insects and one or two night birds, everything was quiet. Ratai soon fell into a deep, restful sleep.

\*\*\*

Ratai groggily sat up, wondering for a moment where she was.

She had been shaken out of her sleep. She turned her face to the east, downriver, and looked up to the sky. She was surprised that the Pleiades was still not out. That meant it was still late at night. Was it her turn to take the watch? She did not remember being asked to do so. She picked up the quill by her side and tucked it into the waist of her loincloth.

Uyut whispered, "Are you all right?"

"Yes, *Ayak*," Ratai replied sleepily. "Why would I not be?"

"Come away now," he said urgently. Then he added, "Bring your sword and shield. Leave everything else."

Ratai did as he instructed without question. It was cold and wet, yet it was Uyut's behaviour that chilled her. They crept quietly into the surrounding bushes. Ratai could smell sweat and fear all around her. Once her eyes got used to the darker shadows of the shrubs and foliage, she noticed dozens of men crouching behind the shadows. Uyut led her to their group. Ratai longed to ask if an enemy had found their camp, but she did not dare voice her question because the enemy could be close by and would hear her. There would be more than enough time to ask once the danger had passed. Now she must look and listen.

The warriors stayed crouched and hidden until the Pleiades came out in the east. But it was still too dark to tell friend from foe. They stayed silent for an hour longer, until the first fingers of dawn appeared on the horizon.

Then, slowly, the bravest and most experienced among them came out of their hiding places and begin to slowly search the area with their eyes. They moved with back bent, holding a spear or a sword in front of them.

Emboldened by the mens' confidence, the younger men and Ratai started to come out of hiding too. Carefully the group returned to camp. The light shone down clear where it was shady the day before. Slowly it dawned on Ratai; the trees were gone. There were no trunks, no branches, only a scattering of leaves. It seemed as though they had been plucked by the roots and thrown a great distance.

Ratai felt her chest tighten. She began to pant because it was hard to breathe. Then, when it dawned on her that what she had heard the night before was not a mere storm, fear took hold of her heart, squeezing it so tight that it began to pump faster and faster. Her hand sweated so much that the hilt of her sword felt slippery. Her legs and shoulders trembled so hard that her muscles started to cramp. It felt as though she was turning to stone. She wiped one hand on her loincloth then the other. The sword felt steadier now. She scowled and turned her face from side to side, ready to stare down any enemy, even a demon. Step by step her courage returned to her as she explored the empty camp. She was the first to discover a victim, or rather the pool of blood he left behind.

She called to Uyut, to show him the scene. After that seven other blood pools were found, all in the vicinity of that area. Jantan suddenly shouted for everyone to immediately break camp. No one questioned him. They rushed back to their shelters and campfires, staying only long enough to collect their belongings. The moment Uyut saw that all the warriors of his longhouse had filled the war boat he gave the order to start paddling downriver. They did not wait for the other boats.

He had heard the terror in Jantan's voice. Everyone had heard it. And he knew that everyone else was only willing to wait long enough for their own members and no one else.

# 10

Ratai watched the men, her eyes darting from face to face to try to read their minds. They were all standing in a circle around their leader, Jantan. He had asked Ratai and Baling to stand before him. Ratai looked about her and saw only frowning faces. Her breath became stuck in her throat because she could not tell if their frown was to her benefit or to her cost.

But Jantan was scowling at Baling, willing him with the might of his glare to accept responsibility for the calamity that had befallen them. He said, "Your men insulted a fellow warrior. The spirits have picked her as an important part of our success. Customs are important up to the point where it helps keep order and well-being, but when the spirit speaks and shows us a way out of the ordinary, it means that the enemy we will face is out of the ordinary."

Chad cleared his throat to break the silent tension. "We must part ways, but we must part with the bonds of friendship still with us. We already have too many enemies and too few friends."

Baling bowed his head with a mixture of shame and despair. If he persisted and stubbornly insisted that he and his men be allowed to fight, he knew that none of the other men would wish to fight by their side. So now he must decide. Should he swallow his pride and live or persist and die. Finally he said, "We will return to our home in the morning. For tonight, let us remain here with you in this camp."

Even as Jantan started to nod to show his approval, there

was a murmur of discontent from the other men. No, they did not want these taboo breakers to sleep among their midst. What if the demons return? This time the demons might think that they are all from the same longhouse because they share the same fire.

Jantan looked up and said, "They will remain with us tonight. All the men who insulted Ratai are now no longer with us. We will be safe."

The men were not convinced, but they dared not argue with their leader because they needed a show of strength now more than ever. Animals could be watching them; insects could be spying on them. They would tell the giants about how strong or weak they were. So there was no discussion among them about how unfair Jantan's decision was to their safety. They feared that if they were to break now because of this dispute more of them would die.

The men took the next course open to them, which was to show as much respect and deference as they could muster for Ratai. She was a woman, but she was a woman protected by the spirits. Maybe the same spirits would protect them too, they reasoned. Soto that end, Ratai was feted and entertained with many tales and praise. She was a little embarrassed by the attention but would not allow herself to shrink away with shy giggles like a young girl. She was a warrior after all, so she behaved like a warrior and accepted their words with bold humour.

Though sentries were set about the place, nobody slept that night. Even with their eyes closed, they listened to their surroundings carefully, sitting up and listening harder with every change in the symphony of insects. By the time morning light came, everyone was red-eyed from lack of sleep. Nothing had disturbed or startled them during the night and many took this as a sign of Ratai's protective scope.

*\*\**

Baling and his remaining men left at first light. They did not even wait to have breakfast first. Though it meant that the party was now sixteen men less, everyone let out a sigh of relief on seeing them leave. From that point on none dared say anything to put down another person, even as a joke. If an inexperienced warrior behaved inappropriately, he would be advised with minimal fuss. In addition to their fear of being punished by the guiding spirits, they were also now in a strange land. The spirits here did not know them and they were not sure if those spirits were friendly, so they did all they could not expose their fellow's weakness.

None of the larger trees were disturbed for either shelter or firewood because these would most probably be spirit dwellings. No one set a shelter or a blanket over an animal trail, because it was a hunting trail and no man wished to become prey to any demon that may be laying in wait there for a meal.

The next time Ratai went out hunting she was joined by Oyong and Assan. Not far from camp they came across wild pig tracks and followed them to a watering hole. The herd did not sense them coming, so they caught two pigs. It was still light when they returned to camp triumphantly. Both pigs were a good size, so everyone had enough to satiate his appetite for meat. Some men also caught a large catfish that was about the size of a six-year-old child. The leaders of each group took this to mean that the group was now no longer cursed, so the atmosphere was more relaxed that night.

They took to sharing stories and a few men began to sing. Even so, nobody talked about home or about the sweetheart they had left behind to go to war. The conversation was focused on great warring men and warrior gods. Some men even boasted about holding a great feast that would immortalise them in a story. Others were too shy to vocalise their aspirations, but they began to sit and walk like the heroes they fantasised themselves to be.

Ratai earned her warrior name early from the men because they believed that it was she who had protected them from the demon huntsmen. They called her the Maiden Who Blinds The Enemy "*Endu Engkerabun Munsuh*", and they feted her with stories of women from legend. Some men recalled stories they had heard of Sebai and Sinja who had joined men at war and broken through the fort of their enemy. They also spoke in awe of the mighty woman Dayang Ridu, who had led a dangerous migration to Padeh. Then they marvelled that they should see this happening now before their very eyes. They each made a note of how Ratai spoke, how she sat, how she ate, so that when they returned home, they would be able to compare her to a goddess of lore when they spoke of her to their children and grandchildren.

Uyut sat proudly next to a shy Ratai. If it was not for the older man, she would have got up from her seat and returned to her shelter. But he insisted that she stayed and that she sat with shoulders squared and chin held high because that was how great heroes carried themselves. The revelry continued until late into the night.

Oyong, however, had watched the goings-on with a frown of worry on his face. The moment he had a chance he said to Jantan, "Are you not going to remind them that we have not earned our victory yet?"

Jantan was thoughtful for a moment. He studied Ratai's flushed face for a moment then he said, "It is always good to praise the gods and the spirits who helped us with our joy. Let us allow them to celebrate tonight. Tomorrow we will be silent and stealthy once more."

Oyong nodded his head to show that he would follow Jantan's advice. The expedition had been unusual from the very beginning, so he should not expect everyone to behave in the usual manner. Even so, he listened carefully to everything that was being said, for he knew that the animals would be listening too. Nobody boasted about the heads they would get or about being part of a war expedition. Some boasted about their ability to hold great feasts but they did not specify what the feasts would be for. Most men only spoke about the past, about epic legends and heroic folklores. He was pleased to notice that even the youngest warrior was careful with his words.

One by one, the men began to separate themselves from the campfire and return to whatever rough shelter they had built for themselves. Ratai was feeling especially tired that night, so she too went to her shelter at the first opportunity. Yet once she was snuggled under her blanket, she could not sleep because she was too excited. She drifted fitfully in and out of sleep.

The next morning, Ratai felt ragged but she was glad to get up and go through the motions of getting breakfast ready. The mood was quiet when the group started to paddle downstream. They sensed that they would be entering enemy territory soon. They passed silent villages and, in the distance, oncoming boats would make for the banks ahead of them because no one wanted to pass a warring party. They did not slow until they neared the trading post.

In the river ahead was a single boat filled with ten warriors. One was standing on the bow, facing them. Jantan gave the signal for the other boats to stay where they were then he went ahead in his boat to meet the other.

Ratai watched the negotiation in front with as much interest as everyone else. She was too far to hear anything being said, but imagined the conversation by the way Jantan moved his body. For an anxious moment Ratai felt as though they had failed. That they would not be allowed to pass the sentries and go to the coast. That they would not be allowed to fight off the demons. She looked about her and noticed other frowning or scowling faces. She could sense the same anxiety in the other men. They had been through so much, surely the spirits were not going to let the men stop them from their expedition.

Jantan turned his body and waved his arm in a wide circle as though drawing them to him. It was a signal that they could pass the trading post. There was an audible sigh of relief as they set to their paddle once more. Even though it was towards the end of a long day, the boats travelled down at a good pace to show to anyone viewing from the banks that they were all strong warriors, like the great men of old who never tired or faltered no matter how long they had toiled or how hard they had fought.

As they passed the other boat, Ratai turned to look at the rowers. She was surprised to see that there were two women among them. Their gaze followed her with curiosity too. If it were not for their breasts, Ratai would not have recognized them as women because they were not only dressed like the men but also looked as fierce as their companions. One of them was covered in ringworm. It was all that Ratai could do to stop staring at her with awe. She used to hear stories from her father that warriors covered in ringworms were the most alert and the fiercest because they were always awake.

Suddenly, there was a cheer from the banks. It grew louder and within it was mixed the sound of deep trumpets and shrill war cries. Ratai set harder to her paddle. She was a warrior and a hero equal to the other men. The crowd was cheering her just as much as they were cheering the other men. She knew this because she had seen the other two women.

They paddled down the river for another four miles, far enough from the settlement to be left alone. They were now very close to enemy territory, so they do not want any distraction. Everyone said nothing but they all sensed it. The following day each of them would have to decide once and for all if they were to take part in the expedition proper. They each prayed to their totem spirit, begging it to give them an omen of victory. Camp was built hurriedly and quietly. There was little talking or discussion. Uyut, like other older and more experienced headhunters, collected his charges around their group fire and said, "You must refrain from useless thoughts and mindless conversations tonight. Make sure you keep your focus on getting a message from your *ngarong*. The guardian spirit that watches over you will see into your future and know if you will fail or be victorious. Listen to it. Be respectful when you ask for its advice. Maybe it will give you a charm that will protect you from harm."

Everyone, apart from the sentries, went to sleep early that night. Ratai slept but soon found herself waking in a strange place. She was standing on the river. It was hard like stone and it stretched to either side of her, disappearing into the distant horizon. There was no canopy above her head. She looked about her in wonder. Then she saw a group of people digging holes for a pillar to one side of the stone river. She walked towards them and asked the first person, a woman who was breastfeeding a newborn, "Where is this place?"

But the woman said nothing. She did not even look up but continued cooing to the suckling baby. Ratai went to the next person, a man with very dark skin. She asked him the same question, and, like the woman, he too did not look up. Then the man turned to the woman and said, "I have a good name for the baby. Let us call her Ratai, after my great-grandmother."

Ratai was so startled by what she heard, she suddenly found herself sitting up wide awake. It was not her turn yet for sentry duty, but she could not go back to sleep. So she got up and went to Assan's position at the edge of the camp. She coughed to let him know that she was coming to him.

When she reached his side, Assan asked, "Is there a problem?"

"I woke up early," she explained. "I couldn't sleep anymore, so I came to relieve you."

Assan gave her a quick smile. He was impatient to get to sleep and to get advice from his guardian spirit. Ratai stood at the position he vacated, making sure to stay well hidden. There she mulled over the dream wondering what it meant. Would she be victorious? All it showed was that she would have a descendant. But it did not tell her whether she should or should not go. She realised that there was no shame if she did not go, but there was no glory either. And she wanted the glory.

But she could die. A sudden cramp spread in her stomach. A chill started to fill her being, making her shiver to her core. She did not want to die, not now. She had not done anything significant in her life. Her hand instinctively went to her waist and she felt the porcupine quill tucked snugly in between the folds. Her spirit calmed. She was going to survive. She was still alive after all, and she realise that she would stay alive until she died. In her mind she was immortal because death was only a doorway to another life.

She could smell morning beginning to come into the world. And with that came the sense that men were waking and starting to move about. Soon the sound of wood being chopped reached her. Then there was a crash, quickly followed by another crash.

Ratai shivered with excitement; today the war leader was going to ask everyone if they would go or if they would stay behind. Bantak came to take over her spot.

Ratai returned to the campfire and began to feed it more wood. She could see some men erect two timber columns, which they then connected at the top with a beam. The doorway to glory, she told herself. Excitement filled her anew. She must enter it and fulfil her life's destiny.

Jantan started to call the warriors together. Oyong, Uyut and the other group leaders stood next to him as he addressed the group. "Friends, we all know why we have come this far. But last night I asked you to look deep into your spirit and to learn if you will be victorious in this war. If your spirit forbids you to go because you have committed a taboo then you must stay behind because your curse will bring a curse on the rest of us. If your spirit showed that you are fearful then you must remain because your fear will cost the life of one of us. If your spirit shows that you will fail in this quest, you may stay if you wish to save your own life. We all understand. But we will be honoured if you should join us, for your strength will bring us victory."

Ratai fisted and unfisted her right hand as though trying to decide if she wanted to grasp the ilang or not. She had felt brave and sure only moments before but now she was not so sure. She began to question her resolve and even the meaning of her dream. Did the dream mean to tell her that she must stay back or did it mean she should go? She could not decide and she doubted if anyone else could decide on her behalf. After all, it was her spirit and she was the only person who could interpret the language of her spirit.

The first warrior stepped forward with a great shout. He unsheathed his sword and made a mark on the surface of the crossbeam. Then he crossed the threshold and received a piece of fern from Oyong. A second warrior crossed, mimicking the first and making sure not to hit the same spot the previous man did. Ratai let out a curse under her breath; she would not be the last one to walk through that doorway. She let out a shout and followed the two men through, and received a piece of fern from her leader Uyut.

Then the crossing of warriors began in earnest. They went through in ones, in twos and each received a piece of fern. Finally, eighteen men were left on the outer side of the pledge doorway. To them Jantan said, "Thank you for being honest. Your spirit has warned you not to join us. So to you we entrust the duty of keeping our properties safe and to give news of the result of our expedition."

Jantan's words again reminded Ratai of her mortality. Who else but these men would tell her family that she had fallen if their expedition was to fail. The chill returned and her hands began to sweat. She tried her best not to shiver, not to show fear. She gripped the piece of fern in her hand harder, afraid that it would fall away and be lost to her forever. The feeling of tender leaves being crushed in her grip steadied her nerves. This was what she would do to the demons that murdered her beloved. This was how she was going to destroy them.

After a quick meal that night, the warriors who had decided to fight continued onwards, leaving behind those who had decided to stay. A group from the Julau River split into the other boats so they could leave their craft for the ones who stayed behind. If the group should return in the next few days then they would all return together. But if by some misfortune, nobody returned then these men would use the boat to bring news back to their families. Among the warriors were also those who had had bad omen dreams yet had decided to continue with the journey anyway for revenge. These left their war regalia with the remaining men, to be passed back to their sons or brothers.

Ratai watched the goings-on with bemusement. She had heard tales about them told in poetry and song in great metaphoric details. Now that she saw them with her own eyes, she struggled to understand them. Everything was so confusing. Her body felt conflicted too, one moment heroic and the next fearful. She felt like a hypocrite, a hero on the outside but a cowering coward on the inside. A new fear suddenly overwhelmed. What if the other men recognised her fears? Ratai frowned deeper to still the anxiety growing inside her belly. By the time they were ready to move on, a new sense of adventure had washed over her. Looking fierce did make her feel fierce. It did not take all the fear away but it took enough away to help her match the men's rowing fervour stroke by stroke.

After an hour of hard rowing, the pace slowed and they pulled up their paddles, letting the boats follow the flow of the ebbing tide. The river here was wider, and nipah palm grew thick to either side of the banks. The sharp staccato cries of Bejampong, the crested jay, were suddenly heard to their left. A cheer rose from some of the men. Despite her exhaustion, Ratai smiled and a new strength entered her muscles. The crested jay had blessed their expedition with its call. Surely his cries would weaken their enemies. The cheers, however, soon turned to cries of warning from the leading boat.

Ratai could see bubbles forming in patches between their boats. She did not understand what was going on, but she could sense the fear from the older men because of the scowling on their faces. She set again on her paddle. In front of her a pale long-bodied fish surfaced. The *labang* was half as long as their war boat. Terror washed over Ratai. She had heard stories of how a shark catfish could grow to be so large it would swallow a person in one gulp.

The pace did not slow until the sun lay halfway down the western horizon. Ratai's shoulders were stiff and her back ached but at least the blisters on her hands had hardened and no longer pained her. They found an opening in between the *nipah* palms and pulled their boats up into the foliage. They split into small groups to make camp, taking precautions to hide the light of the fire. This was enemy territory, so they must be invisible.

Unlike previous nights, no one went out hunting or fishing. They had all saved food from the day before and now ate this for dinner.

Even when the light went down, no one went to the river to wash. Those who had seen the *labang* surfaced had described it to the other men, so no one wanted to be in the water. Some men who had stood guard close to the banks said that they could see wide swirls and bubbles on the surface. "It is almost as though it is lying in wait for us," Oyong said.

Though she knew that the fish was in the water, Ratai still slept fitfully that night. Even Bulu Landak seemed to have abandoned her because the little porcupine did not appear. Ratai woke before dawn for guard duty. There was still some light from the moon, so she saw that the water surface no longer swirled or bubbled. For a moment she wondered if the fish had turned into a human and come on land. She had heard stories about the phenomenon before. Her eyes started to scan the men who were not sleeping and she was relieved to see that she knew all of them.

When first light broke out on the horizon, the warriors returned the war-boats to the river and resumed their journey.

By mid-morning Ratai noticed that the water was slowly

changing colour from the muddy ochre to a light grey. This strangeness worried her, but when she saw that the lead boat did not slow or falter, she was encouraged. She wanted so badly to ask Uyut but she was afraid that her question would jinx the expedition. Then recalling that the Goddess Meni lived in a black lake, she decided that maybe a different god lived in this place.

At noon, when the sun warmed the crown of her head, Ratai heard the sobbing cries of a kingfisher that chilled her. It came from the left bank. Again the more experienced warriors cheered.

Uyut, who was sitting at the stern, said, "Embuas has put a curse on our enemies. They will weep over their dead."

After a few more miles, Jantan signalled that they should make camp. Here the nipah palm had given way to a mangrove jungle. Except for the smallest craft, all the other boats were shouldered and carried into the forest. Three men, Chad, Nital and Assan, then went ahead to scout the coast.

All activities were done quietly. Everyone moved as little as possible and there was barely any talking between the men. They studied the sky, the water and the movement of the branches above their heads. When a snake or a lizard moved close to any one of them, instead of killing it for his meal, the warrior would use a stick or the back of his knife to move it away. For one, the smell of cooking would be carried in the wind. Killing the animal without purpose might also invite the demon of waste into his life. After all, he had joined the war to prosper, not to have all his material wealth wasted by the demon.

Towards sunset, the sentry by the river waved his hand to signal that the scouts had returned. A few men came out of hiding to help them shoulder the boat and moved it out of sight.

The warriors who were not on guard duty gathered about Jantan and the group leaders, to listen to the scouts' report.

"What did you see?" Jantan asked.

"We saw two large ships. Each one had two sails," Chad said. "They were partly lying on the sand and I could see some men scrubbing the bottom."

"I counted about forty men on shore," Assan said.

"Before we reached the coast, we saw some men at the river," Nital said. "They were making so much noise, we heard them before we saw them. I thought they were having a festival."

Chad nodded. "Yes, they were laughing and joking. I think they were feeding the *labang* we saw yesterday."

"Feeding it?" Jantan asked.

Assan shuddered. "They threw a body from their boat and I saw the fish swallow it."

Chad said, "I think there is more than one shark catfish. I could see the water boiling about them and their boat was rocking from side to side."

Ratai felt the blood drain out of her. She could feel herself being swallowed by the fish, being eaten alive. Then she remembered her dream and felt comforted. She did not have any children now, but the dream promised her that she would have a descendant.

"Tell us about the men," Uyut said, breaking the enchanted horror that seemed to have taken hold of the group.

"They dressed like Melanau traders," Nital said. "They had cloth tied around their head and they wore calf-length trousers."

"Some of them were so black they looked like they wash in indigo dye, and others were deep brown like belian wood," Assan said.

"Yes," Nital said, "but a few men were very pale, with long hair that looked like rope."

A murmur rose from the group. Those were clearly not normal men. "One man was strange," Nital said. "His hair was thick and yellow and it circled his face."

"What do you mean?" Jantan asked.

Nital twisted his face side to side, in an effort to find the right words. Finally Assan said, "He looks like a fowl with feathers all flared and ruffled. Like a rooster about to fight." Was this the demon that Bantak saw, a voice asked from among the throng.

"Maybe he has not shaved because he is in mourning," Uyut suggested.

"No, this is different," Chad said. "His whole behaviour was different, like an animal. At times he would jump about like a monkey then curl by the fire like a dog. One point he sniffed the air and looked towards us."

Assan shuddered. "I thought we were going to die."

Ratai could feel a tight squeeze in her heart but she could not tell if it was excitement or terror. This was her suitor's murderer. There was no doubt about it. She wanted so badly to go to the coast now and get his head, but her feet would not move. It was as though they had grown roots and fixed her to the ground. The struggle within her was so strong she started to tremble.

"I think we must wait another day," Uyut said. "At least until we hear from Kelabu Papau."

"I only saw them building rough shelters against the wind," Nital said. "I think they only plan to stay a few days."

"If the diard's trogon does not hide our approach, that demon will sense us," Oyong said.

"Even if he were a demon with the powers of a god, it does not matter," Jantan said. "Bejampong, the crested jay, has already promised to weaken them, and Embuas, the banded kingfisher, has divined that they will be mourned. Victory belongs to us."

There was a murmur of approval among the men. Ratai could sense the air changing as the mood of the group lifted.

There was no fire that night and, though the mosquitoes and sandflies tormented them, there was also no smoking. Chad's description of the animal-like enemy was still fresh in their mind. They each imagined him patrolling the river on a boat, scampering from bow to stern and sniffing the air like a hungry hunting dog.

No words of doubt were allowed to fester among them. Each time a young warrior wondered about the enemy feeding the *labang*, an older man would remind him of Sengalang Burong's omen of success. They encouraged the youths to accept the warpath god's pronouncement, lest the offended spirit would curse them with death. Though the night was silent for the most part, the atmosphere was tense with anticipation.

At the darkest point of night when thick cloud covered the waning moon, Ratai heard a rustle then she felt a touch on her shoulder. It was time to move. Now dressed fully in warrior raiment, she followed the form she sensed ahead of her. She lined up with her companions and lifted the war boat. Silently they walked to the edge of the riverbank. The craft was slid in, making barely a ripple. After every person had climbed in, they began to paddle. Not with the usual gusto, but with great care, making sure not to splash the water.

Ratai wondered if the catfish would tell the animal-man that they were coming. She quickly pushed the thought away from her mind, lest it created doubt and jinxed her. Instead she returned to the vision of her dream, focusing on the face of the suckling babe who was about to be named after her. The promise of the spirit comforted her.

Each boat followed the one in front of it by sound and feel. They were totally enveloped in darkness and it was so thick Ratai felt as though she could taste it. In the pitch dark, her other senses began to sharpen. She could just make out forms and movement in front of her, but the vision was only good for two feet or so. The air started to taste a little different and the breeze grew stronger. The boughs and leaves on land swished and whipped about, giving her a sense of the direction of the bank. Then the boat suddenly swayed to one side and a man at the bow slid into the water silently. He led the boat to land.

When Ratai climbed out and stepped into knee-deep water and alluvial mud, her toes curled with fear. She could not see enough to know what to expect. All she had was her imagination and it was filled with vicious demons and hungry monsters. She let out a loud sigh of relief when she finally climbed onto dry ground. Soon they started moving again, trusting only the person in front of them. Ratai could feel the fear creeping back into her skin. She forced herself to keep moving ahead as noiselessly as possible. Her fear did not matter now because she would soon be in the thick of it.

After about a mile or so of creeping in the dark, the sound of sleeping men reached her ears. The group stopped and crouched down. Ratai was surprised then almost instantly became wary. She willed all five of her senses to search her surroundings. Men only slept like that when they felt safe, and they were only safe if they had good sentries in place. Some moments of tenseness later, she felt the group moving forward again.

The breeze was moving downwind, so Ratai stayed low to the ground. She hoped that her scent would mingle with the smell of rotting vegetation.

A sudden shout erupted from the beach. Ratai froze. In the breaks between the tree trunks and the men in front of her, she could see a thick mane of yellow hair bobbing up and down around the campfire. "Wake up! Wake up! Wake up!" he screamed. Then there was another shout as a man swung a whip against this mad dancer.

"Curse you," the man shouted. "Curse you to die. It is still night, you fool!"

The whipped creature whimpered and crawled on all fours to a group of men who had sat up when the commotion started. They were in a row and Ratai could see that their feet were tied together. The creature went to the first man and this fellow kicked sand into his face. One after another the next five men shooed him off in similar fashion until he reached the last person.

This man patted the sand then lay back down. The creature lay next to him. Ratai shuddered because even though she was a distance away from it, she could see that the creature was looking into the foliage, looking straight at them. She sensed that he knew they were there.

The group moved closer. This time the slave man stirred because the creature lying next to him had started growling. He sat up and squinted into the dark. Jantan let out a sudden war cry that made Ratai jump up to her feet. Every warrior stood up with sword brandished and shield held forward. They charged, each striving to outrun their compatriot. The race for trophy heads was on. The pirates were not ready to meet them. A few rushed to one of the ships and tried to pull it back into the sea. But the tide was low and their number was too few. These men were cut down without a fight.

Ratai could hear shout after shout coming from various directions, as one warrior after another announced his kill, his ownership over a new trophy head. Ratai chased after a small thin man. Then when he turned to beg for mercy, she realised that he was a boy. She cut him down anyway and let out a shout.

There was chaos, as warrior after warrior scrambled for his prize. Ratai looked about. She saw pirates running and warriors chasing after them. Then she noticed a group of men standing about the spot where the demon-man had been. She squeezed her sword-hilt and marched towards them. Then she stopped and stared.

The demon man was growling like a dog and snarling at them. She saw that he was bleeding from gashes and cuts that had been inflicted upon him. But he still fought, yet not for his life it seemed because he could have easily run into the open jungle behind him. He acted as though he was guarding a most precious treasure.

Then Ratai looked at the man cowering behind this creature. He was dark-skinned and bearded like a man in mourning. She realised that this was the man who had shown some kindness to the creature. The other slaves had already been killed, their heads claimed. This man was still chained to the dead man next to him. He could not run, but he gibbered, "Mali! Mali! My name is Mali!"

Jantan came forward, grabbed the demon-man by the throat, lifted him up to expose his chest and then stabbed his heart with the sword. The demon-man let out a final snarl before rolling back his head and slumping forward. Jantan pulled out the sword, swung it and severed his victim's head. He let out a victory shout. Then he turned his gaze to the slave Mali, and he lifted his arm to strike. But Uyut held him back with a touch to the shoulder. "Wait. Let me buy this man from you."

"Have you not got a head?" Jantan asked, surprised at the request.

"Yes, I have killed one man. But I would still want to buy this one from you," Uyut said. Then he added, "I will give you the other head, if you give me this man alive."

"He is nothing, a slave," Jantan said.

"The other man I killed was a pirate. Maybe even his owner," Uyut said.

Jantan lowered his arm, and stepped aside to let Uyut take the man. Uyut tested the iron chain and realised that he could not break it. So he cut off the feet of the dead man. Once the ankle was separated, the chain slid out. He dragged the still cowering slave to his feet.

Ratai watched with wonder as Uyut walked past her. Why would he exchange a trophy head for a live man? She thought that only the people of the interior took live prisoners because they needed slaves to work in their fields.

The men started to disperse and returned to the bodies they had cut down. Ratai too returned to the boy's body. She cut off his head. A few members of the expedition were wounded, and their companions tended to them. Five men of their party were also killed. Their companions pulled their bodies into the brushes. Then they came out with heads and walked some distance off.

By now Ratai had returned to Uyut's side. "What are they doing, *Ayak*?"

"The return travel will take too many days, so they cannot bring the bodies back. They are burying the heads away from the bodies. This way if an enemy should find these dead men, they cannot take the heads as trophies." Then he said, "It is taboo to hang the head of your kindred at your longhouse column. Your home will be cursed, and you will never prosper."

Ratai looked down to the slave who was cowering at Uyut's feet. "Why do you let him live?"

"The creature protected him. There must be a reason."

"Maybe there is no reason. Maybe the creature only cared for him because he is kind."

Uyut shrugged. "I do not know why I saved his life. Maybe

because his name is Mali. It means taboo. What manner of taboo he is, I do not know. Anyway, I have no sons to help me with manly work. My daughters are too young to be married, so they have no husband who can help me. This one here can."

Uyut then looked down at Ratai's hand that was awkwardly grasping a freshly cut head by the hair. "You cannot carry it like that. After those men return from burying their kin, we will have to move away from here. You must find a wide leaf to wrap the head in, so the blood will not soil our boat too much."

Ratai walked up to the bushes to find a wide leaf as advised. There were four other men from her longhouse who were also looking for leaves for their trophies. She felt proud to be among those who would be returning with a prize. Even if everyone fought as bravely as her, not everyone got a trophy head to bring home. This was proof again that the spirits had blessed her.

"You did well," Jantan said from behind her as she was wrapping the head.

"It is only a young one," she said, trying to hide her shyness. Daylight was starting to fill the sky. Inwardly Ratai cursed the sun for not giving her a few more moments of darkness to hide her flushing face.

"It does not matter. A life is still a life. He would have grown into a man, and it would still be one life." He then took a deep breath, ignoring the awkward silence between them. Then he said, "The Goddess Kumang brought you back to life, I am told."

"Yes, she adopted me."

"Then we are spiritual siblings. I too have been adopted by the goddess."

Ratai felt a lump of disappointment in her throat, though she could not understand why. Yet it was not the disappointment of disdain. She swallowed the feeling down. "Were you ill too?"

"No, I was meditating at the foot of a hill. She came to me in the form of a hill mynah, and she called me her son."

Ratai chided herself for thinking that Jantan was a handsome man. Had she forgotten her beloved Sagan so quickly? He was the reason she was here, the reason she risked life and limb for revenge. Yet this conversation with Jantan made her feel protected. She had been feeling more and more isolated lately because she felt different and out of place. Talking with Jantan made her feel that she was not that much different anymore. His pride and confidence became her pride and confidence.

They returned to the group together. Ratai was no longer awkward as she strode with the trophy in her hand. She was relaxed and her back was straight and proud. Some men had gone to the ships and collected everything they thought to have value: jars, cloths, knives, plates and strange items that they had never seen. These were split among them after a tenth was set aside.

As soon as they could, they returned to their boats and paddled upriver, away from the beach. They all knew that it was unwise to linger because they could not know if these pirates had allies in the area. Before they were even halfway to previous night's camp, they landed and built a fresh fire. The treasure-filled boats were moored fast and extra sentries were assigned to keep them safe. Uyut set Mali to work building and tending the fire.

Oyong found a small stream farther in, not far from the bank. In this running water they cleaned the heads of brain matter. Uyut taught Ratai how to pry out the vertebrate bone under the nape. Then through this hole she cleaned out the brain with a piece of rattan that had been shredded at one end. He also taught her to scrap off the fleshy parts from the face. "Try to clean off as much as you can. A little bit of flesh is not a problem because the smoke will dry it. You don't want too much flesh though because you will get maggots."

After Uyut was satisfied with Ratai's work, he cleaned a thick stem of vine and coiled it into itself like overlapping loops to form a kind of loose basket. He passed this to Ratai and said, "Use this skull holder to hold the trophy over the fire. Make sure it is not directly above the flames, because you want to smoke the head, not cook it."

Ratai received the *ringka pala* gratefully. When they reached the fire, she could see that a few heads were already being smoked. Some, like hers, were in skull baskets, others were tied to the cross stick by their hair. There was even one that was still wrapped in its palm leaf. She said nothing. She made no comment. Everyone had a right to treat their trophy as they saw fit. It was not her place to advise them. Uyut, she saw, only offered his advice to those who asked, and only those of their longhouse asked for his opinion.

Assan, however, was curious about the differences. At one point he asked Uyut which technique was best.

Uyut replied, "The *adat* does not specify. The spirits, however, insist that we welcome them with a festival and that we take care of them after we hang them up at our columns. How the head is prepared is more a matter of longhouse custom. If you criticise the customs of another house, you will create more trouble than good." He looked pointedly at Assan, as though to warn him about his chatty tongue. "So if you see anyone who does anything differently, do not criticise him. Watch what he does, learn from him if you can, but do not judge it. His life is different, so it is only natural that he would do things differently in his land."

Then he turned to Ratai and said, "That is why a wise man is a widely travelled man. He searches everywhere for better ways of doing old things, and for better things to take the place of old things. We call him Orang Kaya if he is prosperous, and we call him Raja if he has power over his domain. A man who never learns new things will never be rich or powerful. Even if his father was rich and powerful, he will lose everything if he is not wise."

Ratai said, "What about a woman? What will you call a woman who is wise, rich and powerful?"

Uyut twisted his head about for a moment, as though trying to squeeze out a memory from some far flung past. Finally he said, "A few years ago, when I visited the trading post, I heard of this new word Rani. It is the name for the wife of the Raja."

"But what is she called, if she is not his wife?" Ratai asked.

Uyut scratched his head. "Why do you ask such difficult questions? It is not natural for a woman to be rich and powerful without a rich and powerful husband."

Ratai's excitement faded. She noticed Mali watching them and she felt that he was judging her. She was too proud to walk away so she turned her gaze to the fire. She could see the skull holder between billows of smoke. It made her trophy look larger than anyone else's. Then she realised that she was like that head. Covered in trappings to make her look grand, for both her father and grandfather were known as *mali lebu*, or invincible. But she herself was small, much like her trophy, which was the smallest one at the fire. Her courage and achievement, she realised, would always be inferior because she was a woman. She wanted to cry, to wail aloud because she had strived so hard, and suffered so much to get that trophy. She knew that she had toiled as hard as the other men, even more than some of them, but she would never be as good as the least of them because she was a woman.

After the thought occurred to her, she lost all interest in the goings-on. She began to shrink back from the group and kept to herself. Nobody noticed and nobody bothered because everyone was excited about going home and telling their sweethearts about their adventure. Then some young men from Song and Mambong began to brag to each other about the beauty of their beloved, about how skilful or green-thumbed she was. An experienced warrior reminded them not to speak carelessly but one of them said, "The expedition is over. There is no more taboo to observe. Mind your own, old man." Then they went a short distance away to continue their conversation.

Jantan looked up to the darkening sky then to the drying heads. "I think we will make camp here tonight. It is too late to return to the others."

Ratai and Uyut got up to help collect firewood. After going into the jungle a few yards, they saw a fire. They could hear loud voices boasting to each other.

Uyut sniffed. "It must be those fellows again. How can they be so careless? Their leader should advise them not to make so much noise or they will attract trouble."

Nital, who had followed them, said, "Well, let us remind them then." As they neared the campfire, they saw that there was meat cooking on the open flame. The five men were eating with gusto. Then one man spotted them and called out, "Come join us. There is plenty of meat."

"When did you have time to hunt?" Uyut asked curiously.

"We found this campfire," another man said. "The one who made it must have heard us and runoff."

One man pulled a piece from the fire and passed it to Ratai. She took it reluctantly. She had no appetite for the food for she felt fatigued with grief. There was no more desire, no more will to do anything. She wished she could lie down now but did not want to bring attention to herself by not joining in their merriment. So Ratai steeled herself and forced herself to eat. The moment her teeth touched the food, she gagged. The meat smelled rank. She could not understand how the other men could have eaten this stuff.

Uyut, who had taken a seat next to her, asked, "What is wrong, Ratai? Is the food not good?"

She grimaced. Then she whispered to him, "This meat smells rotten."

"Maybe you got a bad piece. You can have mine," Uyut offered.

Ratai shook her head with a scowl. "No, it smells bad too."

Uyut smelled the meat in his hand. Then he looked at Ratai, then at the other men who were eating voraciously. He threw down the piece in his hand and stood up. He shouted to the jungle in front of him. "Hoi! Show yourself. Who are you?"

Nital, who had just pulled a piece for himself and was about to eat, also stood up with surprise. The five men who had found the campfire did not even look up from their meal. It was almost as though they were blind and deaf to everything that was going on about them. All their attention was on the food.

"It is only us," a woman's voice answered timidly from among the trees. "Please don't hurt us. We have only come to make sure that our darlings are well."

Suddenly one of the men from Song lifted up his head and said, "I know that voice. Is that you, my love? Is it you, Embun?"

A young woman came out from behind a tree. Then there was more giggling as she pulled out another woman from behind a shrub. Then three other women came out. They clung to each other like shy girls as they walked towards the fire.

Uyut pulled Ratai to her feet and he dragged her back. She looked to him questioningly. She was horrified to see the open fear on his face. He was beyond hiding his terror behind a scowl. Nital too had put the meat back on the fire and edged back, not daring to turn his back to the women.

All five of the women were beautiful and perfect in every way. Ratai could not understand why Uyut and Nital were moving away from them like they were enemies. Yet Uyut's grip on her arm was so hard that soon she too felt afraid. Once they were a few yards away, they turned and ran back to camp. Along the way, the two men hissed at the other men who were out collecting firewood and, without question, these too quickly returned to camp.

Jantan was surprised when he saw everyone return empty-handed. "We must leave now," Uyut said.

Jantan reached for his sword. Nital grabbed his arm and said, "This is not something we can fight."

"Women," Uyut started to say. "Those men from Song and Mambong have conjured up their sweethearts."

Suddenly there was a flurry of activity as every man began to pack his things. The inexperienced warriors were confused, but they were too afraid to ask what was wrong. They sensed the fear in their elders and they knew that the worst place to discuss a terror was in its presence. So they followed their elders' lead.

The heads that were still smoking over the fire were quickly wrapped in leaves and stuffed into baskets. Though there was a lot of activity, nobody made a sound. Then from the jungle came the sound of men screaming in pain and terror.

Everyone froze. Suddenly there was a rush for the boats. Mali did not need any prompting to run after his new master. They paddled upstream as fast as they could. Then they heard a cackle, like the laugh of a mad animal. This was soon followed by others. The branches of mangrove trees began to snap by turn in their direction. The front boat moved to the centre of the river, leading everyone to the swirling water. There they waited and listened as the boats swayed and turned with the flotsam and jetsam of the jungle.

The scream of the animals called to them from the banks. Though the watery distance from shore kept their hunters away, nobody felt safe at that place. They knew that there were more monsters in the deep.

No man travelled by night, unless he was hunting. Only hunters travelled at night. Even among the demons, this was so. They knew that they were now at the mercy of the river, for they were like a herd of pigs out in the open and visible to any spiritual hunter. Ratai could feel something large rub against the bottom of the boat. Her companions tensed, for they sensed it too. But nobody dared to make a comment, or to speak about it to the fellow next to him.

Ratai pulled out the porcupine quill from her loincloth and squeezed it tight against her chest. It let out a dim glow, and Ratai calmed down. Then there was more light for a breeze blew towards them, bringing fireflies that landed on the twigs and branches swirling in the water.

To the fireflies Jantan said, "Thank you *Akik* Sengalang Burong for the courage you have sent us. Thank you for your protection."

Ratai stared at these insects with wonder. Surely they must have come from the longhouse of the warpath god because it was said that his back wall was covered with fireflies. Could they be here because of the heads in their boats? If she returned home safe, she must make sure to give a grand feast for the trophy head.

There was little sleep that night as they kept watch on the sky, the water and the jungle. Even though they felt assured by Sengalang Burong's sign of protection, none wanted to curse his blessing by being careless. The gods were fickle. They might promise you success but if you did not do your part they would reverse the promise.

When dawn broke, the noise of the night changed to the songs of the gibbon. They were all glad to hear it. Jantan went from boat to boat asking for an elder man to join him. When he passed by their boat, Uyut exchanged places with Nital. The boat barely rocked as they stepped from one craft to the other.

Ratai watched anxiously as the ten men paddled back to shore and crept back into the jungle. The sun warmed her back and dried off the dew of the night. Her eyes searched for them between breaks in the trees and her ears strained to listen to the sounds in the air. She let out an audible sigh of relief when she saw them come out of the jungle and back into the boat.

Jantan signalled for the boats to follow him, so they returned to be the side of the bank and continued their journey upriver. By noon, they reached the camp where they had left the men who had not joined them.

They were exhausted but still wary. That night the victorious war party was silent, and far more sombre than before their battle.

# 11

Nothing came to them during the night, so everyone was calmer in the morning. While breakfast was being prepared over the fire, Uyut and Mali went out on a boat and returned some hours later with a large pile of isang palm leaves. Uyut then taught Ratai how to weave the strands into a headband and armbands. "You must put this on to show that you are a successful headhunter."

Ratai smiled wide. She felt grand in her costume of leaves. She felt like a hero of epic stories: brave, strong and potent. She saw other warriors piling on the leaves. Only those who did not go to war did not wear leaves. Those who got trophy heads, like herself, wore a band of standing palm leaves over their brow as well as bracelet bands of the same material around their upper arms and calves. Those who went to war with them but did not get trophy heads wore leaves on their arms and calves.

Uyut also made Mali shave his beard and eyebrows because having facial hair was a sign of being in mourning. This was a victorious expedition, so all signs of bad omen must be cast off. They would be passing villages and the trading place on their way home. Everyone must learn about the success of their expedition. Everyone must see how grand and brave they were.

Each time they neared a village, the lead boatmen called out loudly and the villagers came out of their homes to look at them. Then those who had trophies would stand up and shout victoriously. There would be a cheer in return from the sentries on the banks. From these men, word would spread into the interior of Jantan and his warriors' success. This story would be passed down from generation to generation, and with each retelling, the warriors would grow stronger and larger until they would become like gods. Many myths would spring from their story, of how their guardian spirits called on gods to help them and of demons who gave them charms to protect them.

Ratai felt wave after wave of pride each time she stood up to show that she was heroic. When they reached the trading place, the other boats gave way to them. Their lead boat slowed in front of a boat filled with sentries. They were invited to come ashore where a feast had been prepared for them.

Once on land, Jantan offered a tenth of the loot they got from the pirates to the chief of the trading place. The foreign traders of Sina, Indoo and Java stood back at a safe distance but their curiosity kept many of them close enough to hear the goings-on. The traders who had come out of the interior milled about the warriors asking for stories that they could retell back home in their villages.

The two warrior women that Ratai had seen days before now came to sit with her. They introduced themselves as Subang and Bliong. Their father was the leader who guarded the trading place. After their brother was murdered while he was drunk, they had joined their father to find his murderer.

"Have you found him then?" Ratai asked.

"No," Subang said. "The Javanese sailors said he had run away back to his country beyond the great lake."

"One day," Bliong said, "we will build a large ship and travel to his land and kill his family."

Ratai felt that this was a difficult feat to carry out to fruition, but she kept her thoughts to herself. It was not her place to say what was possible or impossible. Only the gods could do that.

"What of you?" Subang asked, looking up at her crown of palm leaves with envy. "How did you get your trophy?"

Ratai shrunk inside. She forced herself to square her shoulder. "He was a very fast runner. So am I. That was how I managed to kill him."

"You must be faster than everyone else," Subang said.

"Yes, I was," Ratai said, and felt convinced of it. Suddenly, the size of the head no longer mattered. Jantan was right, it was one life and it was a good one to hang at her column.

The rest of the night was passed with great festivity. Many of the men were eager to return home, so they continued their journey early the following day. The festivities, however, were repeated in village after village over the following days because some men at the trading post had rushed back to their longhouses to tell their people about the brave heroes who had vanquished demons. After a week, when they were about a mile from Ratai's home, they made camp in the jungle.

Early the next morning, the sound of drums and brass gongs reached them. The heroes donned fresh palm leaves so that they would smell fresh and virile when they did a mock attack at the house. Nuing had been watching out for them and had seen them make camp. So that morning, they were ready for the heroes.

The heroes let out a loud war cry when they came within sight of the longhouse. Ratai could see her father standing tall on the bathing platform in full war regalia. She stood up, proud to show him, to show her people, that she was one of the heroes. Everyone on the banks cheered. The people stomped their feet and shouted. Their daughter and sons were bringing home blessings, no curse, no bad omen had a place in their home that day. They stomped and shouted to chase away any remaining ache or sickness in their body. There was nothing to sorrow for, nothing to be anxious about because their daughter and sons had returned with blessings.

At the foot of the house, a pig was already tied down and ready, waiting to ritually wash their feet which might have been soiled with a bad omen. Jantan speared it then climbed into the longhouse. Then the others followed, each touching the sole of a foot to the head of the sacrificed pig. When they reached the top, they were offered rice wine to drink. This too was meant to ritually clean them before they entered the sanctuary.

When Ratai entered the house, her mother was waiting with a winnowing tray that had been covered with a sacred cloth. After drinking some wine, Ratai put her trophy upon the tray, and her mother led a procession of women up and down the longhouse. They showed the prize that had been brought back home by their warriors. There was singing, dancing and drinking. Rambunctious children ran about but were careful to stay out of the way of the strangers. Soon the smell of smoke brought the scent of food into the house, whetting everyone's appetite.

Mali was looked upon with suspicion when he first came into the house, but once Uyut had sent him to his wife, Mali immediately set to work stoking the large fire on the ground in front of the longhouse and carrying water for his new mistress. He worked hard and without complaint. Uyut was pleased with his new slave and was impressed at how much initiative he had. He seemed to know exactly what needed to be done and did not wait about to be told what to do. Uyut returned to the festivities with a light heart. He congratulated himself for having gained a hard worker. Maybe Mali would not bring spiritual blessings but at least he could help lessen some of Uyut's burden.

The music and feasting continued ceaselessly, as though to overwhelm the fear and the strife that the warriors had experienced during the expedition. It was done with such noise and fanfare that it made the older boys dream of joining an expedition and it made the men who had stayed behind wish that they had gone with them. The women, who were generally shy and modest in front of male visitors, were suddenly bold before these men. Every woman wished that they were married to a hero or at least to one who strived to be a hero. They dressed in their best and poured their heady charms on the men.

The older folk did not reprimand their daughters and granddaughters. Some even encouraged them. The feast was a good time to make alliances between families, between longhouses. Every woman, however, made sure to decline politely if a man they did not like should indicate interest, for an insulted warrior could do great harm, not just to her but also to the community.

During the feast, the *tuai burong* put some meat into the mouth of the trophy heads on display. He also fed the existing heads on the columns. The women sang a lullaby to the heads on their tray or in their arms. They sang their best verses to persuade the spirits of these heads to serve them and to bless their fields.

\*\*\*

Early the next morning, Ratai climbed into a small boat with her sisters Suma and Madu. Placed in front of each of them was a medium-sized basket filled with upright empty bamboo tubes. It seemed foolish to go upriver just to bathe but there were so many people coming and going from the bathing platform that it would be impossible to wash properly.

Ratai did not mind the bother, however, because she missed

the company of the two girls. They chatted about things that happened while she was away. "Mother was so worried," Madu said. "She wiped the floors clean everyday and she swept at least twice a day."

"That is why I came back safe," Ratai said. "Nothing in our *bilek* had caused me to slip or to trip during the expedition. You must remember that for yourselves next time when you marry a warrior or a traveller."

"What of you, Ratai?" Suma asked. "Which will you marry?"

Ratai blushed but she kept her head high while her two sisters giggled. They finally reached a quiet spot where they often fished. The tide was low that morning, lowering the tideline to expose part of a rock bottom mixed with mud. Ratai steered the boat towards the river cliff and they all climbed out onto the exposed bottom.

When Suma repeated her question, Ratai replied, "I don't know. Maybe I will marry a woman."

There were gasps of surprise. Then Suma said thoughtfully, "It does make sense. You are a successful warrior and you are a good hunter."

"And don't forget, Sister," Ratai said, "I am a terrible farmer." They all burst into laughter.

"If only I can marry you," Madu said. "I would like that very much."

"There is no pig big enough that we can sacrifice to neutralise that taboo," Ratai said. And they all laughed.

There was a cough behind them. Madu let out a squeal of surprise and they all turned to see Jantan smiling down at them.

"I apologise," Jantan said. "I heard chattering and I thought you were monkeys."

Suma and Madu blushed a deep red then Madu scoffed. "We

are not monkeys and we do not sound like them."

Jantan smiled teasingly. "Yes, they sound nicer."

Madu stomped her feet and was about to make a reply when Ratai said, "These are my sisters Suma and Madu. *Endu*, this is Jantan. He is the warrior who killed the demon."

Suma turned her face away shyly. Madu was remorseful but then her face brightened and she said, "Are you going to marry Ratai? She is a headhunter too."

Jantan chuckled. "If she will have me, why not?"

Ratai's face turned a bright red. She could not understand Madu's preoccupation with marriage. Maybe it was because of the mass number of warriors who were visiting them now or because of the incessant talk among the unmarried women about finding a sweetheart. She stammered, "That is not possible, I think."

"Why?" both sisters asked at the same time. Jantan too was surprised with the open rejection.

Ratai scrambled about in her head for a good reason not to be interested in Jantan. He was a visiting warrior after all and the last thing she wanted was to cut down his pride in this manner. Then an idea occurred to her. She said, "Because he is also adopted by the Goddess Kumang. She came to him during his meditation and she called him *anak*. We are spiritual siblings, so it is impossible for us to marry."

Jantan's face was still red but he smiled and nodded as though to agree with everything Ratai had just said.

Then Madu said to him, "I have another sister."

Suma pulled a sharp breath then she pinched Madu's arm. Her victim yowled and slapped her hand away.

Jantan let out a loud laugh, louder than was necessary, and he said, "I am going to continue my hunt. I will leave you to your bath." Then he walked away, back into the jungle.

Once he was out of sight, Suma turned to Madu and said, "How could you have said that?"

"Why not?" Madu said as she stepped into the river. "You are beautiful and skilful. Everything you plant grows abundantly. You will make a perfect wife for a hero."

"Madu is right," Ratai said. "He will never be put to shame by you. There will always be food in his home to serve visitors, so he will be known as a great and prosperous leader.

Suma was quiet and thoughtful while they bathed. Ratai and Madu splashed water at each other then at Suma. But Suma only turned her face away from them. After they had washed they began collecting water in the empty bamboo tubes. They then lined the tubes upright into their baskets before making their way home.

When they reached the house, they were surprised that it was so quiet. Once inside they found the reason. The men were drunk senseless. Despite herself, Ratai had to smile. This was a good omen. It meant that they had satisfied the needs of their visitors beyond their ability to receive them. Madu giggled when she saw her father and brothers lying on their backs and snoring loudly. There were still some men who were up but their speech slurred and their movements were unsteady.

When the young women went into their *bilek*, they found that their mother too was drunk. Though she was still awake, she covered her eyes with one arm to keep the light out.

"It is a good feast, Mother," Ratai said.

Nambi waved the other hand weakly, to acknowledged that she heard but did not have the energy to respond. Tambong was curled up next to her, for it was her usual naptime.

The baskets of water were placed in the back room then Suma went outside to check the wine placed around the gallery column.

There was only a half of a bamboo tube of wine left. She collected the empty tubes and returned to the back room.

"Aren't you glad that Father got those new jars?" Suma said to Madu as she lifted a mat covering the wide mouth of a large jar.

"I still wished that he had got the silver pins for my high comb instead," Madu said wistfully. "You and Ratai have nine each. I only have five pins."

"You can have mine," Ratai said. "I don't use them anyway." She picked up an extra bamboo ladle by the side and began to fill one of the empty tubes with rice wine.

Suma frowned. "How are you going to welcome the gods if you don't have pins for your comb?"

"I am not graceful and I don't dance," Ratai said. "Madu makes a prettier welcome maiden than I ever will."

"You should not talk about yourself like that," Suma said.

"This wine is still cloudy," Ratai said to change the subject.

"Mother made them right after you left," Madu explained. "They are still quite new. Do you like it?"

"Yes, it is sweet," Ratai said.

Suma smiled. "We found some ripe wild pineapples."

"And sugarcane," Madu added. "That is why we have the only female *tuak* in the house."

Ratai smiled good-naturedly. She was proud of her sisters because they were very good foragers. Even if she and her father were never to catch another fish or animal, she knew that the family would never go hungry with these two about.

"We must remind father to get some more yeast from the trader," Madu said coyly.

"Why? Is there another feast soon?" Ratai asked.

"Mother might have to make more wine soon," Madu said. "After all, you are both of marriageable age."

Ratai rolled her eyes back and shook her head. Suma turned her blushing face away. Neither of them made a reply.

\*\*\*

After three days of continuous eating and drinking, the visiting warriors finally got into their boats and began their trip to the next longhouse.

Ratai was exhausted, yet she still had too much nervous energy to rest. So she started cleaning the gallery in front of their room, scrubbing off the spilt food and drink as well as vomit with a rough coconut brush. She collected all the split bamboo tubes that had been used for cooking and carried them down to the back of the longhouse. There was already a large pile of splintered and burned bamboos there. It was a very satisfying sight for it meant that the feast had gone well. Any spirit who saw it would realise that the longhouse had gone through a successful *enchaboh arong* ceremony. There were now fresh trophy heads in the house and they would do well to keep away from this place.

People returned to their farms in the days after. Work was still hard but their hands felt light because of the blessing of the new heads. Every home that had a warrior testified to the others about the extra acreage they had cleared or the extra jungle produce they had collected. Some claimed that fish swam willingly into their nets because of the charm of the new trophies, others claimed that they could feel new strength course through their bodies throughout the day.

Ratai likewise felt invigorated. The experience of having gone through the expedition and of having returned with a trophy had made her more confident. She was surer of her place in the longhouse, in the farm and in her home. She spoke with more forcefulness. She no longer felt herself inferior to the women for being unskilled in feminine pursuits, nor did she feel inferior to the men for not being a physical man. She was Ratai: the female who had the gall to steal a spearhead from Selampadai. Even her younger brothers were asking for her advice for fishing and hunting now. They were no longer embarrassed to be seen with her in the jungle. When she returned from her work in the farm or from hunting and fishing, she would weave baskets and mats. Soon there was talk again of doing another mordant bath ceremony because some of the young girls who had caught the interest of a warrior wanted to weave a *ngar* cloth to impress him.

One day, while Ratai was resting at home to honour the second new moon since her return, a boat arrived at their landing place. In it were six people, four of them being older men and women. The sentry recognised Oyong and allowed him and the group to come up to the house. A few young men from the house helped them carry the basket loads of food and wine that they had brought.

Instantly, like a bolt of lightning, the news spread through the longhouse. The women recognised the sign. This was an enquiry party. They all wondered whose hand was about to be asked.

Oyong made his way straight to Nuing's gallery. The baskets of food and wine were carried into the chief's room and placed behind the door, unopened. Nambi came out to invite the women into the privacy of their *bilek*, while Nuing stayed outside with the men. Soon his sons, Mansau and Betia, came out to serve wine to the visitors.

One of the old men said, "Your family is blessed with many children, Tuai. You are very prosperous."

Nuing replied proudly, "I have seven children. Two sons and five daughters. They are all healthy and strong."

"A sacred number," the old man said, "like the sisters of Pleiades and the daughters of Grandfather Sengalang Burong."

Oyong began to introduce the man, "This is Karong, *Tuai*. He is our friend Jantan's uncle. Our old chief died four years ago because of an illness, so his uncle has taken over fatherly duties."

Though Nuing knew exactly what those duties were, he asked the question, so that they know they could make the request known to him without repercussion.

Karong began, "Well, my nephew Jantan is very interested in forming an alliance with you through one of your daughters."

"Does he know my daughter's name?" Nuing asked.

"He says they are all beautiful. He will love the eldest who accepts him."

Nuing nodded. Jantan had not visited his loft at night, so it was his way of saying that he did not wish to force himself on the woman of his interest. He was unsure of her feelings towards him, but he was sure enough of his own feelings that he was willing to risk a rejection.

Nuing got up and went to the door. He whispered the request to Nambi. She collected her three elder daughters, sat them down in front of the female visitors and said, "The brave warrior Jantan would like to marry one of you. He said that he would take for his wife the eldest to accept him."

"It is impossible for me to accept him." Ratai said. "Even though Jantan is a brave and handsome man, like the God Keling himself, I cannot accept. He is also adopted by Kumang, so we are spiritual siblings."

Nambi nodded then turned to her second daughter. Suma, however, said nothing. She tried her best to hide her blushing face, but her red ears betrayed her. Madu shook her shoulders. "Say something. Say yes. You are meant to marry him."

Jantan's aunt, Pandak, said, "Well, even if the durian cannot speak, we can tell that it is ripe from its smell."

Suma was so embarrassed, she could feel tears forming in her eyes. She got up and hurried into the back room. Madu followed her, urging her to give a positive reply quickly otherwise the entourage would return without her answer. Nambi went to the door and told her husband that Suma was willing.

The conversation after that was far more relaxed. More people from the longhouse joined them. The gift baskets were opened and the food and wine from the visiting party was served to everyone who was there. There was sweet glutinous rice, yellow with turmeric or sticky with honey. There were small packets of roasted fish coated in herbs and wrapped with ginger leaves. Boiled eggs, dried jackfruit and banana. There were also gourds filled with honey and basket loads of smoked fish and meat. Everyone in Nuing's longhouse marvelled at the richness of Jantan's land. Many among the crowd commented that Suma was going to have a happy life in her new home.

However, Nuing was unwilling to let his daughter follow her husband. "Our land is closer to the coast," he said. "My daughter is used to the easy life. Whatever she lacks, I can get for her from the Malay traders. Seashells, beads, silver pins and belts. She lacks nothing in this place."

Oyong whispered something to Karong, and the other man nodded. Then he said, "Jantan lost his mother when he was very young, before he even owned a loincloth. He has also lost his father. He says that if you are unwilling to let your daughter go to him, then he will come here to you."

All those who had held their breath now released them with a sigh of relief and a laugh of joy. Yes, it was a good match. Suma was beautiful and skilled, and they were going to gain a brave warrior. Their longhouse was going to be famous.

Karong took out a piece of cloth from his basket and said, "It is only a simple thing. A skirt that was woven by my wife. We hope that your daughter will find it pleasing." The cloth was finely woven and patterned with rain-filled clouds.

Nuing received it with both hands. A woman in the crowd came forward, took it from him and went into Nuing's apartment to show it to the women in there. It was now official. Jantan was engaged to Suma. The guests stayed for the night. They left the next morning with a promise to return with the groom in twenty days time. Nuing took out strings of raffia rope and tied twenty knots into each of them. Then he sent out men to invite relatives and allies from the other longhouses to the wedding. Some went by land, others towards the coast and two groups crossed the wide main river to go to the tributaries on the other side.

Nuing kept one string for himself, hanging it against the wall facing the gallery, where everyone could see. That same afternoon the whole longhouse gathered in his gallery to find out which visitor they were going to host.

The next day, the first thing Nuing did before he began preparations was to undo one of the knots from the raffia rope. Nineteen more days to the wedding. There was a lot that needed to be done. His daughters were pounding the husk off the rice to prepare them for wine brewing. There was still plenty of yeast because his wife Nambi had been diligently growing the culture with rice powder that she had rolled into balls then sun-dried for many days. She had also sun-dried plenty of sweet jackfruit and rambutan flesh that she could add to the brew to sweeten it.

"Oooh *Tuai*," *Inik* Jambi called out to him. "I wish you would let me adopt one of your daughters. I only have sons and grandsons to help me prepare for the feast."

"Your daughter-in-law can help," Nuing said with a smile, clearly knowing in advance what the answer would be.

"She is heavy with child. All she wants to do is sleep. Her back aches, her head is heavy, but she eats more than me. I think I will have another grandson. I wish she would give me a granddaughter now."

"Are your sons and grandson not helping?"

"Of course they are, but they only do what is necessary. I am ashamed to show my guests how hard my life is because there is so little feminine beauty and comfort in our home. Our *tuak* will be bitter and male. Our rice is barely ever pounded properly now. Many of the grains I cook are still covered in husk."

"I will help you, *Inik*," little Tambong said. She had been listening to their conversation the whole time.

"You are such a little blessing," *Inik* Jambi said and reached out her hand. "Come help me crush some mustard greens. We are going to pickle them with salt and rice."

"I like pickled mustard," Tambong said as she walked away hand in hand with the old lady.

Nuing smiled. *Inik* Jambi was exaggerating her problems. He knew that there wereplenty of other women who helped her because they were her kin. But she always came to him with the same excuse, so that she could ask for Tambong's help. She was very close to the young girl.

Over the following weeks people travelled for miles, spending two or three nights away from the longhouse to collect as much food as they could. Logs of palm hearts were carried home on bent backs. Any meat or fish caught were either smoked or fermented in brine water. The farms were scored for maize, tapioca roots, beans and young gourds. Vegetables or fruits found in the first ten days were either pickled or dried. Those that were collected later were kept in cool places so they would stay fresh.

Boat after boat went up and down the river searching for firewood and fresh bamboo tubes. Their chief's daughter was about to be married to the brave warrior of another longhouse. No matter how tired they became during the search, their pride of entertaining their guests until they vomited due to the great volume of food and wine was what kept them focused.

Nuing also readied the groom's gift. His daughter was marrying a man from Kapit, who came from many rivers and hills away. He went to a dusty corner under the ladder going up to the loft and unwrapped a brass cannon that he had bought from a Malay at the mouth of the river. It was the length and thickness of his leg. The cannon was still as magnificent as he remembered it. The pivot handle was carved into a fin and the body etched with scales. The gaping mouth of the catfish was the mouth of the cannon. Then he set a blowpipe next to it. It was not carved, but polished black and its wooden handle was as hard as iron. The cannon would act as a bridge to let Jantan's spirit cross to their land, and the blowpipe would act as a rail to prevent his spirit from falling off the bridge.

Nuing could not help but be a little sad as he handled the two items for he had always imagined that Ratai would be the one who would marry a brave warrior from a distant land. He bought the cannon and blowpipe specifically because of this expectation. He did not want to be separated from her, so he meant to use these items to persuade the groom to stay at his longhouse.

Still, it was one of his daughters who was getting married. His smile returned as he remembered this. Then he promised himself that he would return to the coast soon, to buy another cannon. There was still one more thing he needed for the dowry: the dainty white blooms of the areca flower. This would be collected a day before the wedding itself, so that the blooms would still be pretty for the ceremony.

The days passed quickly and by the eighteenth day people had already started arriving at their bank. These were those from the farthest houses. Some had been in their boats for five days. Before going up to the house, they bathed in the river to clean off the sweat and dirt. Visitors who travelled by land also bathed first before they went into the house. Then they changed into their clean good clothes. They put on ornaments of shell, rattan and bone. The women who had adventurous men in their family also wore beads and silver.

Uyut went out to meet them at the landing with a small basket of food offering and a live fowl. He conducted a quick *miring* ceremony, a short prayer and a wave of the fowl, to welcome them. Then he hung the small basket on a pole that had been stuck into the water by the side of the landing place.

There was a great noise of music and drumming to scare away any bad omen. When the visitors reached the longhouse, another fowl was waved over their head to bless their entry. They were offered wine to drink. The welcome was friendly but informal because they were not the wedding party and they were there by the bride's invitation. A member of the family hosting them led the party to his gallery. The male guests sat at the gallery and the women went into the room. After spending a little time there, to show respect to their host some of the guests then spread out to the rest of the longhouse, to meet their kin and to renew old friendships.

Everyone asked for news from each other, and the latest news from Nuing's people was the expedition that some of them had joined. By this time, Mali had become so familiar with the way things worked that he needed no instruction from Uyut. He was so industrious, the visitors watched him with wonder as he stacked firewood next to one outdoor hearth after another. He worked so quickly, he appeared to be caring for the embers and the rows and rows of smoking food all by himself. They had never met a man with such dark skin before, so he stood out even among the body of sun-browned men.

One man asked Uyut, "Do you know what land he is from?"

"He said his fishing village was at a place called Silanka. Some men took him when he was little and sold him as a slave."

"He never tries to escape from you?"

"No. He says his home is so far away they crossed the salty water for five moons before he saw land."

"He must be from the land of Ribai."

"You are very lucky. My slave kept trying to escape," the first man said.

"What did you do to him?" Uyut asked with curiosity.

"When my father died, I took his head and used it to unseal the spiritual box."

Everyone there nodded. It was a wise course of action and it saved the visitor the trouble of looking for a victim outside his longhouse and risking a blood feud with another community.

"Will you sacrifice your slave too one day?"

"No," Uyut said. "I do not think so. Mali is so hardworking and attentive, he is now like a son to me."

"Are you thinking of adopting him? I have heard stories of a man who had adopted his slave because he had no children."

Uyut chuckled. He would neither say yes nor no to the question. And the questioner did not press for an answer. He was pleased with himself for having asked a question that Uyut obviously had never considered. Uyut excused himself from the guests and made sure that they had enough food and drink to keep themselves entertained while he saw to the preparations. Throughout the day, and the next few days, he watched Mali, to study his attitude and his demeanour. He mulled over his guest's question. It was a tempting proposal.

\*\*\*

On the morning of the twentieth day, there was a commotion of drums and gongs coming towards the longhouse from downriver. A fort built from sacred cloth had been set up at the door from the end where the visitors would enter. After it were two more forts, one in the middle of the longhouse and the third at the other end. A spear had been laid across the open door to ritually block the entrance.

The moment the groom's party was heard, Suma was sent to hide in *Inik* Jambi's room. For the past few days, the older woman had insisted that Suma show as little of herself as possible to the visitors and she absolutely forbade Suma to go outside now. "Nobody must see you now, until you are presented as the bride. If you show yourself to them before the rite, your face will be less radiant because they have become familiar with your beauty."

Uyut again went out to meet the visitors after they had washed and dressed. He brought with him offerings to the spirits. This time, a group of young men followed him. On reaching the landing place, he greeted them, asking, "How was your journey? Were the omens good or ill?"

"We encountered no bad omen. We saw no signs that prevented us from coming here. And we heard nothing that would put a stop to our ceremony today," Oyong replied.

Again, a *miring* ceremony was conducted, and the offering was added to the dozen other offering baskets hanging on the pole. This was a rich longhouse, overflowing with rice and eggs. So they were not stringent on the number of times they conducted the *miring* ceremony with each new arrival. After the offering was made, the young men came forward and helped their guests carry in the food and wine that they had brought with them. This was their wedding too, so they were expected to feed their guests.

The visitors marvelled at the lush fruit trees and rows of *lemba* leaves and *taya* cotton plants. They looked up in awe at the cotton tree. They congratulated Jantan for having chosen a bride from this prosperous place. To be so blessed, the people here clearly lived by the ritual customs that pleased the gods. The groom's entourage was all dressed in their best; the men with feathers bristling from their caps, and the women with silver pins sprouting out of their hair. The shells and bells lining the hem of their woven skirts made a great noise as they rattled. They made sure to walk slowly and to sway from side to side so that everyone who watched their approach would note how magnificent they looked.

At the bottom of the steps was a live pig strapped down to a piece of thick bamboo. Uyut passed a spear to Karong who was leading the entourage. The pig, as though sensing its end was near, began to struggle and squeal. Karong touched the spear to a spot behind its foreleg then pressed his body weight down onto it. The blade cut easily into its thick flesh. The pig gave one last involuntary kick then lay slack against the rope. Karong was then offered a cup of wine. He drank it down in one gulp then touched his foot to the head of the pig before climbing up the ladder. The groom followed next. He too drank wine and touched the pig with his foot before going up. Both wine and blood washed his spirit clean.

On reaching the floor above, the spear was taken away and the fort opened to them. A rooster was waved over their heads to welcome them and to bless them. After the *biau* was a long line of people waiting for the groom and his entourage with cups of wine. They walked and drank their way down the length of the house to the middle fort then, after they persuaded the people there to let them through, they walked and drank their way to the third fort. Only after that did they turn back and walk to the bride's gallery. During that time, a few men took turns walking in front of Jantan as they walked along the length of the house so they could get to the cups before it was his turn to drink. In this manner, Jantan was able to reach his future father-in-law's gallery still relatively sober.

The walls to either side of the gallery were lined with sacred cloth and every column was circled with gourds or tubes filled with rice wine. In the centre of the longhouse, to one side of Nuing's gallery where the wedding couple would sit, was a jar so large two men could fit into it. It was filled to overflowing with tuak. The challenge was set. The visiting party must finish every drop in that jar before they return to their land. The visiting women then made their way into Nuing's *bilek*, for it was not yet time to celebrate with the men.

When everyone was seated, Nuing welcomed them with food and wine. No one talked about the wedding. This was a subject that they all viewed with great shyness, so nobody wanted to be the first to broach it. Just the thought of having to ask Jantan boldly about his intentions made Nuing blush.

So, instead of asking, he offered them a copious amount of wine. Though the walls of the gallery were covered in sacred cloth, the groom challenged at each one of the forts and wine served for the ceremony, neither one of the party wanted to speak about the wedding. They all pretended that they were just entertaining normal guests who happened upon their house. They played music, they danced, they challenged one another with ludicrous poetry, and aggressive teasing.

When evening came, the drinking cup was put away. Roasted, smoked, fermented and brined meat and fish were brought out. Pickled palm hearts, bamboo shoots and mustard greens were placed side by side with fresh fern and mushrooms. Though the women moved in and out of the rooms, none of them served the male guests outside. This was not a feast to welcome warriors, so the single women were expected to keep their distance. Any man who wished to get to know one of the ladies must first enquire from someone who lived in that house. This way he would be sure that his interest was available and not held back by taboo.

The drinking continued after dinner. The night grew deeper and despite the raucous noise, the children fell to sleep on their father or mother's lap with exhaustion. Hours after the last child had fallen into a deep sleep, the noise suddenly quietened and a cup was filled for Nuing.

He was quite intoxicated, but not enough to quell all of his shyness. He held the cup in front of him, towards Karong and asked, "Who are all these brave birds you brought with you? Who are these hornbills? Their courage stands high and flutters in the wind like feathers. Why have you brought them here?"

Karong accepted the cup from him, drank it in one gulp then replied, "I am embarrassed by my business. My shame is beyond description. I have tried to find words to describe why we are here, but the words would not come. I am almost ashamed to say it because Sempurai is your protector, and your father is as strong as Keling and is as rich as a Malay trader. I cannot tell you why we are here yet."

The cup was filled and returned to Nuing. He took a drink from it then refilled the cup. He looked to Oyong and asked,

"Our friend Karong will not tell me his business here. Do you know why you are here?"

Oyong received the drink, then he said, "I only know my business. Karong has asked us to come, to help his nephew Jantan to open the gates, to split the clouds so the sun may shine down. I thought it strange that he would need my help, because he is as strong as Laja, whose column is covered with smoked trophy heads. When he faces an enemy he is as fierce and as potent as *Bunsu* Remaung, the demon tiger who has sharp teeth and long claws. I cannot understand why he is so afraid to open the sky himself. So that is my business here, to help my friend enter your home." He drank, refilled the cup and passed it back to Nuing.

The questions continued to and fro and during that time the names of the gods were invoked and their pursuits compared to either the groom's or the bride's skill and ability. In this way all who attended the wedding learned the history and pedigree of both bride and groom.

When the cup was passed back to Nuing after all were satisfied that the bride and groom were equal in skill and blessings, Nuing said, "I can see the brave bird now with open eyes. The hornbill is brilliant in his warrior colours. He is dressed in the horns of rhinos, the claws of wildcats and feathers so magnificent I almost mistook him for Keling, the warrior guardian. I almost mistook him for brave Laja, Keling's cousin."

Karong said, "Our hornbill thought he spotted a porcupine with pretty spines, hiding behind the columns of your house. It looked rare for it was covered in flowers of happiness. He is here to ask that you show him where this porcupine is."

A shout pierced the night and it was followed immediately by other shouts. The groom's party had finally admitted that they were there for the bride. For after all, a porcupine is like love.

Even if you tried to hide it under a basket, its quill would still show. Nuing smiled brightly. His face was red from both wine and happiness.

Nyaru shared a look with Nuing then he turned back to Karong and said, "We know the porcupine that you seek. You came days ago, to tell us of your intent. We have waited many days for you to come. But you have not come. So we locked the porcupine away. Because we promised her to you, so we have hidden her from curious eyes. But we have hidden her so well that now we cannot find her."

Karong said, "We are prepared to look for her." He turned to Oyong, who had set out the bride gift: a hand axe, a spear and a knife. "See, we have the axe that we can use as a ladder to reach her and a spear to pry open her door. And this is the knife that will be used to open her mosquito net. But our hornbill falters, he is unsure. He is afraid that he will fail."

Nuing said, "Maybe this will help his spirit to cross." Assan picked up the canon and placed it in the middle of the group. Dujong placed the spear next to this. Then Nyaru placed long bunches of areca blooms on top of the two items. "See the canon is strong and sturdy. He can use it as a bridge to cross to my land. The blowpipe can be the rail that keeps him safe on the bridge. And our areca palm welcomes him with its fragrant blooms."

Karong touched the canon appreciatively. Then he said, "This is exactly the gift that Belang Pinggang requested for when he married Gupi, the daughter of Bada." He turned to Jantan and said, "If these items had helped a demon cross from his land into this world then it will help your spirit travel here safely." Then he turned back to Nuing and said, "The areca tree in your land has flowered profusely. It is a sign of good things to come. Their union will be successful."

A man let out another victory shout and there were smiles all about. The betrothal ceremony was a success. Both parties were happy, the land was happy. There was nothing to stand in the way of the bride and groom. Nyaru, the chief augur, stood up and began to recite the laws that governed festivals. There must be no fights between them because they were now kin. There must be no curses because the wedding had been blessed. Any man or woman who broke the rule of conduct would be fined.

The door to *Inik* Jampi's room opened and everyone turned their attention there. A woman came out with a tray of areca nuts, and behind her was the bashful bride with two other women leading her. Suma was dressed with so much colour and silver that she looked like a bird of paradise. The tattle of shells and bells sewn to the hem of her skirt was music to all the single men. Jantan was so startled by her resplendence that he pulled in a sharp breath and stared with dumb awe. Everyone laughed with joy because this was exactly the reaction that they had hoped from him.

Jantan tried his best not to stare at Suma, as she took her seat on the brass gong beside his. She looked at everyone but him. She could not stop smiling and she was trying her best not to giggle with joy. *Inik* Jambi, considered a skilled and prosperous woman, picked an areca nut from the basket placed before them. The other elderly folk nodded with approval at her choice. Then she cut it in half. Even though the nut was not perfectly halved, everyone said that the two halves were equally perfect. It was their way of telling the couple that they were equally matched.

Then the betel nut halves were put in a small fine basket and the basket was wrapped in cloth. This was passed to the augur, Nyaru, who began to sing a lullaby to it. The baby is beautiful and perfect in every way, he sang. She will have bountiful harvests and she will be protected by the spirits. Her hearth fire will never go out.

Ratai watched Suma and Jantan turning their gaze and smile to everyone but each other. She watched the proceedings with a smile frozen on her face. She should have married first because she had a suitor. But he was dead. In an effort to push the thought away, Ratai turned her gaze to the panels of hanging sacred cloth. But there was no comfort there too because she remembered how her mother used to tease her about having to hang up these same cloths for her wedding. How did it all go so wrong, she wondered as she watched the crowd blessed the couple with their loud enjoyment of the wedding ceremony. Why was fate so cruel to her? Maybe she was really cursed from the day of her birth. Was that not why her birth parents had abandoned her in the forest of bamboo?

Ratai crinkled her eyes and arched her lips into a deeper smile. It helped hide the stinging hot tears pooling behind the lids. She could not understand why she was feeling so much pain. She should be happy for them: her foster sister in the flesh and her foster brother in the spirit. Yet the pain in her chest and the sudden rush of heat and dizziness in her was undeniable. She missed Sagan. This happiness she saw happening should be hers. She knew without being told that other women watched her with pity. She was the elder sister, she should be married first.

Her being alone, being unloved, was a sign of unhappiness. It was a sign that she had grown far too familiar with. At that moment, when surrounded by joy, Ratai's only recourse to her disappointment was her sense of duty. She noticed that many of the bamboo tubes near her were empty, so she collected them and refilled them with wine from the large jar in the middle of the house. She served wine to the women who had come to congratulate the bride to be, and drank with them. She sent her brothers to serve the men outside in the common gallery. She helped her mother get the fire ready, and to wash and clean the raw foodstuff. She decided that they were running low on food, so she climbed down the trapdoor and went to the back garden. She got down on her knees and stuck a sharp stick into the soil at the base of a tapioca tree. There, in that moment of solitude, Ratai started to cry. She missed Sagan. She missed the feeling of longing to see him, and then the sense of shyness when he was finally near her.

Ratai could not tell how long she was outside. She only came to her senses because of the relentless mosquitoes biting her. She grabbed some soil and rubbed it all over her exposed skin and over her face. Then she continued digging for the roots. She grabbed armloads of tapioca roots and carried them to the bottom of the trapdoor. Then she returned to the garden to bring some more. This time when she returned her father was waiting for her.

"We have more than enough, I think," Nuing said.

"There are many hungry guests. The celebration must not stop until the day Suma leaves to visit her in-laws," Ratai said.

Nuing nodded. "Yes, you are right." Then he looked at her face. "Why are you so dirty?"

"There are a lot of mosquitoes. Maybe I am not ugly enough for them to shun, so I have made myself uglier."

"You have never been ugly, Child," Nuing said tenderly.

Ratai turned her face away and again returned to the garden. This time she busied herself among the herbs, cucumber and maize. She tried so hard to keep her grief inside that her back and neck felt stiff from the effort.

Nuing did not go back up to the house because he had a sudden urge to comfort her. It felt like the most natural thing to do even though he felt that it might embarrass her. Acknowledging her pain was akin to admitting that he could see her unhappiness. And if he admitted to seeing her unhappiness, it meant that she had failed. Despite that, he decided that his place was by her side and that it was his duty to assure her that the unhappiness she felt was only temporary.

So he went to her side and his voice shook when he said, "You are as brilliant as the morning star. I know you are because there was once a time in my life when I had wanted nothing but the morning star. I have stopped longing for the morning star since you came into my life. So you must be that star. You are a gift from the gods."

Ratai's busy arms suddenly slowed and they fell by her side. She went down on her knees and covered her face with her hands. Nuing stood next to her as she wept. He looked to the house, he watched the sky. The stars were starting to come out. He could not see either the belt of Orion or the cluster of Pleiades. Yet he imagined seeing a serpent pointing towards it, a hunter's bow. His first child was magnificent, like the stars in the sky. Her joy was his, her pain was his. She was not of his flesh, yet he felt as though only they understood each other.

"Maybe you try too hard," Nuing said. He realised now that he had acknowledged her failure, he must do everything he could to help her. She was his child after all. "You are never meant to be mediocre. Sagan was not a man of adventure. He was not your equal."

Ratai began to cry harder. Between sobs she cried, "Then the gods should have made me hate him. Not take his life."

The cicadas' symphony grew louder and mingled with the noise of laughter and music from the longhouse. But Nuing only heard his daughter's weeping.

# 12

It had only been one day since Suma left to visit her new husband's land. Already the people in the longhouse were returning to their work in the field. The sacred cloth had been folded away and the gongs returned to their spots along the walls in the room.

Ratai was glad for the return to normalcy. She had spent the whole of the previous day cleaning the floor and she had gone to the farm in the morning to clear the weeds that had been neglected for the past two weeks. She was now going through her normal evening chores cheerfully and even took time to answer Tambong's endless questions.

"Will Suma ever come home?" Tambong asked for the tenth time.

"Of course she will. She will come back in a few weeks."

"Why must she go?"

"Because she must meet her in-laws. She must show them that she is a skilful wife. "

"What will she do there?"

"She will collect food, clean and cook. Just like what she does here," Ratai answered. Then she frowned and studied Tambong's face seriously. "Do you know how to clean and cook?"

Tambong shook her head.

"Well," Ratai continued, "then you must learn. Or nobody will marry you."

"I want to be a warrior. Just like you."

Ratai laughed. "You still need to clean and cook. Everyone must learn that. It does not matter if you are a headhunter or farmer. "Betia, the younger brother, walked in with fresh bamboo tubes. She turned to him and asked, "Do you know how to cook, Betia?"

"Of course," he replied. "I will go hungry in the jungle if I can't cook. I am not an animal. I don't eat raw meat and leaves."

Tambong squeezed her brows together for a moment then she turned to Ratai and said, "All right then. You must teach me how to cook."

Ratai showed her how to clean a catfish, then how to stuff the cut pieces into a bamboo tube. She taught her how to crush wild herbs and ginger to be stuffed into the same tube with the fish. After water and nipah palm salt were added, and its opening stuffed shut with a roll of ginger leaves, the tube was placed on the fire next to a tube of boiling rice. Ratai took Tambong's hand in hers and taught her how to turn the tube every now and then so the tongues of fire would not burn a hole in the bamboo. Tambong was so engrossed in what she was doing that she did not say a word throughout the lesson.

When the family came together for dinner that night, Ratai told everyone that Tambong had cooked the fish. The young girl sat up straight and proud while everyone praised her for the wonderful meal.

"*Indai*," Tambong said as she looked up at Nambi, "you must teach me how to plant rice too."

"You should learn how to pull weeds properly first before you plant rice," Madu said.

Tambong's shoulders fell, causing everyone to laugh at her despair. She did not like pulling weeds because it was backbreaking work. It seemed so menial and unimportant. She could not understand why the weeds could not be left alone. Worst of all, she could not understand why the weeds looked like rice sprouts but did not grow into rice stalks.

Nambi said, "Well, Child. You must learn everything in stages. Nothing you do will be successful if you don't learn to do the simple things properly first."

Ratai smiled wryly. There was nothing she could say on the subject because she herself was such a failure at planting rice. After dinner was cleared away, Ratai went outside to the verandah to enjoy the cool breeze. It was dusk so she was surprised to see Mali still working outside. She stared curiously at the mound of wet clay that he had build just yards away from the banks.

Her gaze followed his steps as he trudged back from the river with a large clump of clay on one shoulder. A few people next to her made a snide remark about what a dirty fellow he was. He liked to dig in the dirt, they said.

An old woman said, "My son tells me that he goes to the oiliest and dirtiest part of the river upstream and digs the soil there." As proof of her tale, she pointed to two mud-encased baskets leaning heavily against a fruit tree not far from the mound of clay. "*Indai* Tupang was furious. She cannot understand why her husband lets their slave become so dirty."

As though sensing that he was being criticised, Mali returned to the river to wash. Uyut had just finished his bath but he stayed for a few minutes to talk with Mali.

Then *Inik* Jambi said, "He also collected the ashes from our kitchen hearth. Did he also ask for yours?"

"Yes, he did," the other woman replied. "You should see the pile of charred wood and ashes he collected from our feast. He keeps them under the house."

"Poor *Indai* Tupang. Did she say why her husband is allowing

Mali to do this?"

The other woman shrugged. "She said, he said that Mali promised to cook him some iron."

Ratai was just about to walk back to the room because the mosquitoes were starting to bite. But the moment she heard the word iron, she asked, "Is that true, *Indai* Aso?"

"I doubt it very much," the other woman, *Indai* Aso said. "I think he is just trying to find a way to escape. Or trying to find a way to hurt us."

"But he seems to get along well with *Apai* Tupang," Ratai said. "Even my brothers like following him about because they say he has many new ways of doing things."

Despite trying her best to ignore Mali and his activities, Ratai lingered outside because of her curiosity. There were many people who lingered outside too, particularly about Uyut's common gallery. The young men pestered Mali, demanding to know what he was building. He explained, "I am building a kiln. A special kind of hearth to cook iron."

The moment he said that, he was suddenly surrounded by people. Everyone wanted to learn how to cook iron. The children asked where iron grew. Adults asked if they could cook iron into knives and machetes. Some complained that his kiln was too small. They should have made a bigger one so they could make large iron pots, like the ones the Malays used to cook their food.

The people knew about iron, but they had never given any thought as to where it could have come from. They got their knives and spearheads from the Malays or the Penans. And all that they needed to know was that as long as they were good hunters and farmers, they would be able to trade their produce with these people for iron. Mali knew how to cook iron and how to forge knives. These young men passionately called out their requests above each other's voices.

"Be quiet!" Nuing suddenly shouted above the riot of voices. "You should all listen when you are learning. Not make impossible suggestions."

Mali was taken aback. He was not used to his words being listened to.

"Do you know how to make clay pots and bowls, like the ones the Malay sells?" *Inik* Jambi asked.

"Yes, we can use the kiln to make those things," Mali said. "It is useful for other things made of clay."

"Can you build a forge too? Will it take long?" Uyut asked. He was so excited by the prospect that his face was turning red. Only blacksmiths had forges and kilns. Again he silently congratulated himself for taking Mali alive.

"It depends on the weather. If it is hot and dry, it will take only a few days. But if it rains, the water will wash the clay structures away."

The questions resumed again, this time more restrained and focused. Mali explained what he planned to do and how he would go about it. Many of the men offered to help, because they wanted to learn.

Come first light the next day, there was a group of men outside with Mali. The slave picked an open spot and went down on his knees to dig a shallow hole with a deer horn. Then he dug a channel coming out of it. He broke off a piece of clay about the size of his fist and began to knead it until it was smooth. The other men began to imitate his actions. He placed this along the edge of the hole. The other men did so too. Mali squished the lumps together and smoothed them into one piece. Then he moulded more lumps and repeated the process of smoothing the base until he reached the shallow outlet. He placed a stone into this opening, then lay a clump of clay atop it. By now the other men had caught on to what he was doing so they too smoothed and blended their clay lumps with the one next to it.

"What is he making?" Mansau asked when Uyut approached the group.

"He is building a small kiln," he replied.

"What is that?"

"A type of hearth to cook iron," Uyut said, a little unsure about his own answer. He had seen a kiln at the trading place he visited when he had collected enough pelt or jungle produce to make the long trip worthwhile. But he recalled that it was as big as a hut. This kiln was tiny in comparison. He wondered if it could be of any use. Yet he was also terribly curious about the building process, so he said nothing.

When Nuing came out to join them there were five men, including his son Mansau, working on the kiln. Mali would either smoothen the edges or add tiny bits of clay to form a smooth wall. They stopped at noon when Mali declared that the structure was high enough. The chimney shaped kiln was waist high and as wide as the embrace of a man.

Then Mali dropped some twigs and dry leaves into the chimney. He lit a small fire in a coconut shell. When the flames started to dance without coercion, he dropped the contents into the chimney.

"We can bring more wood so you can make a bigger fire," Mansau suggested.

Mali shook his head. "No," he said, "the fire must be small or this will ..." He touched the rim of the chimney and made a show of a piece breaking off. Then he looked up to the sky. It was clear but they could all see that he was worried about rain.

Uyut said, "Help him build a shed over the chimney. Otherwise the clay will melt away when it rains."

This the young men understood. They all knew that if you submerged a sun-baked clay pot in water, it would melt back into clay. So without further explaining, they all got up and went to the jungle. Mali stayed behind to keep an eye on the fire. By evening, there was a simple thatch roof over the chimney.

For the next few days, the longhouse was abuzz with wonder. Some claimed that Mali was making a fool of Uyut, because no one had ever seen a kiln like the one that Mali had made. Others said that they should wait it out, maybe the people from his land did things differently. *Indai* Tupang's attitude towards Mali changed on the third day and she became less harsh with him after he made her a gift. While waiting for the chimney to dry, he had carved an intricate hairpin for her out of bone. Now she was the envy of every woman in the longhouse.

Every few hours, Mali would tap lightly on the chimney, to check for its doneness. When it started to give out a hollow ring, he put out the fire and explained to the men that it would be ready for use in three days. Then the next morning, Mali went into the jungle. His self-appointed apprentices had been watching out for him and they followed without being asked. When they noticed him breaking off thick branches, they started to chop a tree but he stopped them by shaking his head. So they began to chop off the thicker branches instead. Then they used vine to tie the branches into heavy bundles, which they carried back to the longhouse. When they noticed Mali breaking the wood down to three-foot lengths they did likewise. Soon there was a good pile placed next to the kiln.

Early the following morning, Mali again went to the river to get more clay. This time he had company, so he got a good amount in about an hour's time. He started standing the branches up, and leaned the outer layers into the inner one so that they formed a dome shape. Over this he lay a thick layer of dry leaves and grass, then slapped on an equally thick layer of clay. There was a good bit of jostling and joking as the men put on the clay because it was messy work.

After the stack was covered, except for a small hole on top, Mali used a stick to poke seven holes into the bottom of the dome. He said that seven was a good number and the others agreed with his wisdom. Then he blew another fire to life in the coconut shell. He dropped the flames down the top of the dome. When red and orange flames began to show through the bottom holes, Mali resealed them, leaving only the top open. This, he explained would reduce the size of the fire. If the fire was big, it would make ashes, if it was small, it would make coal.

The next day, the people all milled about when Mali cracked open the dome. The inside was all black, and the wood had shrunk into a third of their original size and turned into coals.

"Why don't you just get the burned wood from the hearth?" Mansau asked.

Mali broke one of the coals in half to show that it was dry and black to the core. "Because this will make hotter fires. You need a very hot fire to get good iron."

Then from a basket he took out some of the oily scab-like crusts that they had collected upriver. He poured the crusts into an old wooden mortar. They were rather dry because they had been left outside for days. He began to pound them to dust. He placed handfuls of these onto wide leaves. Then, next to the chimney, he placed an upright log with the help of two men. The round surface was wide and flat. Mansau and Assan helped him carry a heavy cone-shaped rock with an equally smooth and flat-bottomed surface. They placed it on top of the log.

"What are you going to do with this?" Assan asked.

"I am going to make a hammer," Mali replied, moving his arm in a hammering action.

Mansau asked, "But this is heavy, you need at least two strong men to swing it."

Mali smiled and winked. They had come to recognise this to be a sign that he was going to do something exciting. He crossed three sturdy branches in front of the log and tied them together where they crossed, forming a rough three-legged stand. Then he strapped the stone to another sturdy stick and lay this stick atop the crossed branches. The contraption looked like a bird with its head down and its tail up in the air. Mali went to the tail end and pushed the handle down. Almost effortlessly, it seemed, he lifted the stone. He released it and the stone fell down with a thud. The young men let out a cheer.

Uyut flushed with pride. He would not have been prouder if Mali was his own son. The men ate together that night, with great noise and excitement. Everyone could sense that something special and important was going to happen the following day.

The next morning, Mali fired up the chimney with coal. Then he blew air into a hole at the bottom of the chimney with a thin bamboo pole. Two other men joined him and soon the flame was roaring. No one there had ever seen or heard anything like it before. The roaring fire coming out the top was red, but if they looked inside, it was so white it was like the sun. They let out a cheer with every roar. Mali told his apprentices to keep blowing as he poured in the red dust from the day before. He added more coal, then more dust, and a final layer of coal onto this. The men took turns in twos or threes blowing into the hole. Mali continually added coal to the flames. Even when lunch was brought out to them, the blowing continued.

Ratai had gone to work in the field that morning. When she returned late that afternoon, her curiosity got the better of her so she approached them. As she got closer and the searing heat from the chimney reached her, Ratai began to shudder. She suddenly remembered meeting Selampadai, the creator god. She remembered how he had poured out liquid iron, which was red and hot like fire but moved like water, into the clay people.

Mali said, "Do not stand too close, Princess. The fire will burn you."

"Why do you call me that?" Ratai said sharply. "My name is Ratai. Call me by my name."

Mali fell to his knees and bowed his head. Ratai was instantly enraged. She could not understand why this man was so weak. He was teaching them new and amazing things, yet he cowered before them. She wanted to beat him but he was Uyut's slave. She felt all eyes watching her, so she walked away keeping her head high.

When the sun went past the halfway point of the western sky, Mali stopped the blowing. He folded a long piece of bamboo strip in half and used this impromptu thong to reach into the chimney. Everyone let out a cry of awe when he pulled out a bright red molten blob.

He dropped it onto the upright log and told Assan to lift the stone. When the stone was up, he rolled the soft blob to a spot under the stone then he told Assan to drop the stone gently. Sparks flew as the stone hit the bloom. Those standing nearby jumped a step back and drew a laugh from the others. Mali nodded and Assan lifted the stone again. Mali turned the bloom then the rock fell back on it, crushing and cracking off more sparks and crust.

"What are those?" Uyut asked.

"It is bits of dirt and ash," Mali said. "It is of no use to us."

Uyut stared at the pieces of slag suspiciously. They did not look like dirt and ash to him. Then his gaze again turned to the red-hot ball under the hammering stone. Soon the black layer of skin stopped forming over the surface of the hot mass. He could now see that is was hot and clean and was of the consistency of thick honey.

Mali continued to turn the mass, which was starting to look squarish, and Assan kept pounding on it. Soon the red began to turn darker and the mass seemed to become harder though still malleable. Then the mass started to ring each time it was hammered. The people let out a cry of awe. Both Mali and Assan were drenched in sweat but it was clear to everyone that they relished the attention. So the crowd cheered them on, as though they were in competition against someone else. Finally, Mali indicated to Assan that he could stop.

The red-hot ball was now a thick sheet of shiny iron.

"But it is not a knife," Betia said.

Uyut let out a laugh. He did not wait for Mali to explain because this part was familiar to him. He said, "We can use fire to melt it again, then beat it into any form we wish."

Mali looked up and smiled. Yet unlike a proud and skilled man, his shoulders remained bowed. Ratai watched him and she stared at the kiln he had built. A plan started to form in her mind.

# 13

Suma stared outside the window with a slight frown on her brow. Almost half of the front garden was covered in a layer of dust and ash. In the middle of the disorder was a simple thatch roof over the kiln. She could hear a ringing yet she still could not believe that Mali was actually beating iron that her brothers said he had cooked out of red mud.

"It is amazing, don't you think?" Ratai asked from her side.

Suma shrugged. A little annoyed that so much attention was being given to a slave. She felt that her brave husband Jantan deserved more attention than Mali. After all, Jantan was the hero and Mali was a mere slave.

Suma said, "I do not understand the fuss. Everything is dirty and dusty because of that slave." Then she added, "Jantan thought it was funny that our brothers are running about to do his bidding."

Ratai was taken aback. She had never heard any manner of bitter comment from her sister before so the statement came as a surprise. But then Suma had been saying many surprising things since her return. Trying to distract her, Ratai said, "Did you enjoy visiting Jantan's home?"

"Yes, his family was very kind. His grandmother was very pleased that I come from a line of famous warriors. She was also surprised that my sister is a headhunter." She then went on to tell Ratai about the attention she got from the other women. Many of them did not know how to starch the thread properly, she said, so she had shown them. She had also taught them how to weave a mat in the ginger design that Ratai had made. "It was all very pleasant." Then she added, "I wish the people here would show Jantan as much respect."

Ratai said, "But we are showing him respect. He is a hero and the men listen to everything he says with great attention."

"Look at our brothers and their friends. All they want to do is spend time with Mali. Since I returned last week, Mansau has not been to the farm or to the jungle with father." Then she turned to Ratai accusingly. "You have been watching this slave non-stop too."

Ratai blushed, understanding her sister's unmentioned accusation. "I am only curious. Don't you find any of those things he is showing exciting?"

Suma turned up her nose. "He is dirty and noisy. I don't see what is exciting about any of that."

Ratai walked away. It felt pointless to argue with her sister. Suma had been testy lately. Maybe she was just disappointed that their brothers were not helping with the building of her new room, Ratai thought. The people had helped them put up the pillars, lay the cross beams and even line the thatch roof. Now that the heavy part of the building had been completed, everyone had returned to their own activities; the family was expected to get bamboos for the floor and bark or planks for the walls themselves. It did not help that Mansau would rather work at the forge with Mali than collect the building materials with their father and Jantan.

Ratai was feeling more and more frustrated by the day. There was so much work for Mali and there were so many men always about him that she had not had an opportunity to speak with him privately. Maybe she should ask Mansau for help, after all he was very close to him.

The more Ratai thought about her plan, the more excited she became. But she tried to keep her expectations in check because she had not even asked Mali the question yet. She had seen large ships at the trading place. She wanted to learn how to make one because then she could cross large rivers and lakes with it. Maybe even the sea. Her mind was full of ideas and it latched onto every little bit of memory she had. But after some time of daydreaming about her perfect life, she could no longer tell if her vision of how a ship looked was real or just a figment of her imagination. But she did not care. She was going on an adventure and nobody was going to stop her.

"Why are you smiling on your own?" Jantan said. "Are you in love?"

Ratai blushed, first with embarrassment then with resentment. "Why do people assume that I am in love when I am happy? There are many other things to be happy about." She walked away in a huff.

Jantan's gaze followed her then he turned away when his wife called him.

That evening, after dinner, Ratai pulled Mansau aside and said, "I need to talk to Mali. Could you ask him to speak with me a moment?"

"Why don't you go ask yourself?" Mansau asked.

Ratai blushed for a moment. The idea had never occurred to her. Then to hide her embarrassment she said, "Because I am a woman and he is not a relative." She squeezed his arm. "Just ask. I will meet him outside when he is ready."

Mansau shrugged and went outside. A while later, he poked his head back into the room. "Sister," he called and waited for Ratai to look up, "Mali is outside now."

Ratai got up and went outside. The people who were lingering in the gallery looked up from their work or conversation. Ratai could feel their gaze. She tried to look cold and harsh so no one would ever mistake the intentions of her conversation for something it was not.

Mali kept his head bowed but his ear inclined to her. She asked, "Do you know how to build a big boat, like the ones at the trading place?"

Mali looked up with surprise. "I cannot make a ship because you need special tools and skills for that." When he saw the disappointed look on her face, he said, "I do know how to build a boat that is big enough for a home."

"A home?" Ratai's look of incredulity suddenly turned to excitement. "A home on the water?" It had never occurred to her that she could live in a boat. She had always assumed that boatmen travelled along a river during the day and made camp on land.

"Yes," Mali said. "I come from a fishing family. We lived in boats. My father used to trade with people along the coast. That is, until we were attacked by pirates."

"Is that why you are a slave?" Mansau asked, his eyes wide.

Mali nodded and he wiped his eyes. Mansau was about to ask more but Ratai stopped him with a touch on the shoulder. She had seen death and it had haunted her since her return. She did not want to imagine her family being snatched away from her one by one either – by the sword or by the chain –so she understood that Mali might not want to be reminded of his family.

She said, "I would like you to teach me how to build such a boat."

"But you live in a good and safe home," he said. "Why would you want to live in a boat?"

Ratai could sense that others were listening to their

conversation. A sudden idea occurred to her, maybe she could get others to help her build it too. "Well, if you are going to keep making iron and clay pots then you must find a way to trade them or they would just lie about uselessly. A big boat will be a good way to carry them to the trading post."

Mali nodded. "Yes, you are right. I have taught your brother here everything I know about making iron. I think I can help you build a boat for a while."

Nuing said with a worried frown on his face, "But we do not have a tree big enough to make a boat that my daughter can live comfortably in."

Mali turned his body sideways to include Nuing in the conversation. "We can make planks for the boat."

"But the boat will leak," Nuing said with a raised eyebrow.

"We can use wood resin and rope to seal the boat," Mali explained.

Nuing thought for a moment then he said, "I understand what you mean. I use the smashed core of rattan to seal my bark boats. They work well."

By now there was a group of men standing about and openly listening to their conversation. An animated discussion soon followed and before long there were volunteers offering to get the planks.

Ratai was pleased with the response. All the men were excited about this new activity. For the rest of that night, the house was abuzz with discussion about the boat. How big was it going to be, how wide? What type of wood should they use and many more questions came up.

The next morning, Ratai and a group of men went into the jungle and a few men returned with rolls of rattan. Later in the day, there was a loud commotion coming from the river. Soon

Ratai could be seen walking along the bank ahead of a group of men. They were pulling on a rattan vine that had been tied around a large log. Behind them was another group of men dragging a second log.

After they had dragged the logs onto the bank, Mali fixed stakes to either side of one log so it would not roll. Then he built a narrow platform to either side of it. He also took pieces of wood and began to cut them into plugs shaped like axe-heads. Mansau and Ratai stayed behind to help him while the other men returned to the house.

The next morning, Nuing got onto the platforms with one foot on either side. He leaned down and began to cut into the log with a machete. Mansau drove the plugs into the cut Nuing had made and drove them into the log with a stone hammer. Bit by bit the log began to split open. This process was repeated over and over across the full length of the remaining timber until it split in half. Then they took the half and repeated the process. They did this until they got multiple wedges from one log. Then the sections of wood were carved and smoothened until they form even flat planks.

In the meantime, Mali made a few clay bowls and put some bog iron dust and hearth ash into them. Then he covered the bowls with more clay and dropped them into the kiln. Assan and Ratai offered to blow air into the kiln. While the crucibles burned, Mali began work on a pair of bellows for the forge. He cut two wide bamboos to length and then he split one in half. He cut out all the stem walls inside the bamboo except for the last one at the bottom. He then cut open a hole near the bottom on one side. Into this hole he inserted a small bamboo tube that had been hollowed out. He put sap around the hole to fix the smaller bamboo in place as well as to seal it. Then he resealed the sides of the bamboo halves with resin before putting the halves back together. He wrapped a raffia rope tightly around the tube.

He explained, "I do this so that the tube will be airtight."

Then he took a piece of stick and some stiff chicken feathers. He showed Mansau that the feathers must be tied in such a way that it stiffens when waved down but becomes slack when waved up. After tying the feathers around the stick, he stuffed the newly made piston into the tube then he pulled. The feathers bent inwards. He pushed. The feathers stiffened. From the small bamboo tube, Mansau could felt a strong flow of air blowing into the palm of his hand. He asked to be allowed to make the second bellows, carefully re-enacting every step that Mali had taken. When Mansau had put together the second tube to Mali's satisfaction, Mali placed the two bellows side by side with the air holes pointing into the forge. They no longer needed two men to blow into the fire with bamboo tubes. Now only one man was needed to push the piston up and down.

By now the iron ore had been burning for at least half a day in the crucibles. Using the bamboo thongs, Mali pulled out the crucibles and left them on the ground to cool. They all went to the river to wash and returned to the longhouse for dinner and to rest.

Early the next morning, Mali started a fire in the simple forge and tested the bellows by blowing the embers back to life with it. Once he was satisfied that the fire was burning hot enough, he broke the crucibles open. The men jostled among themselves to get a first-hand view of what might come out of the clay balls. There was shiny iron mixed with grey slag.

Mali collected the shiny bits on a piece of flat stone then he placed the stone on the fire. Assan was working on the blowers, moving the piston up and down by turn. The bits of iron began to melt into each other. Mali pulled out the stone and began to gently tap the soft metal with a stone mallet. Pieces of remaining grey and black slag began to peel off its red-hot surface. He beat it over and over and when it began to cool he returned it to the fire. He explained to everyone that he had to keep doing this until all the black and grey bits were gone. "This way the iron will be hard and strong."

They all watched in awe as he stretched and pulled on the metal with the stone mallet until one end was pointed and sharp while the other was roundish and blunt. Every now and then he would plunge the item into a trough of water then return it once more to the fire.

"Are you making a spear?" Uyut asked.

"I am making a needle that can pierce holes in wood. We have to sew the pieces of wood together to make a boat for Ratai."

At this announcement there was a burst of wonder and questions. Uyut recalled the time when he had seen boats in the trading harbour that had seams. He had told the people that some merchants sewed their boats like women sewed blankets and everyone had laughed at him. Today he felt vindicated.

Once the large needle was cool, Mali wrapped a raffia rope once around the shaft. He positioned a stick across it forming a cross. However, instead of tying the stick down in the middle, he tied one end of the rope to one end of the stick and the other end of the rope to the other end of the stick. The contraption looked like a bow with the arrow tied in the middle of it. He placed a piece of bark on the top and pressed the whole contraption down on a piece of wood. He pulled the stick towards him. The needle turned one way. Then he pushed the stick away, and the needle turned the other way. They could all see that the needle was boring into the wood.

There was a loud cheer, and suddenly everyone wanted an iron needle that could bore into wood. In the next few days, while Mali worked on making more needles, the men collected wood and began to carve frames for the inside of the boat. In the evenings, after dinner, they would wind raffia or coconut fibre into twine as thick as a little finger. They also pulped the core of rattan vines into a rough rope.

Suma watched the activities with growing bemusement. She was clearly unhappy because nobody was offering to help her husband. Even her father sometimes would rather join the boat building then help Jantan.

That night during dinner, unable to contain her discontent, she said, "How much longer is your boat going to take, Ratai? My home needs building too."

Ratai turned inquiringly and was surprised to see Suma's livid face. "I am not sure. We have just finished putting up the frame. Mali said that we will begin to bore the planks tomorrow."

"Well, I hope that we will not starve this year because barely anyone is going to the farm now to tend to their fields."

"That is not true," Nambi said. "I go to the field every day and none of the fields I pass are ever empty of people."

"But you go alone," Suma insisted.

"Your father sometimes comes with me. Other times there is Madu and you."

"Yes, and it is hard work without everyone else," Suma said. She did not look at anyone as she spoke. Instead she kept her angry eyes looking down at her food.

Jantan said, "I will be putting up the last of the walls tomorrow. We can start living there soon."

"But your loft is not up yet and not all of your floors have been set down," Nambi said.

Jantan smiled. "After I put up the wall and the door, I will gather more bamboo for the back room. It will not take long to finish. The hearth is ready so we can start cooking there anytime."

Ratai could sense the resentment coming from Suma and she felt guilty for it. She chided herself for being selfish, for not noticing that Suma needed help too. But everyone was so excited to learn all those new ideas from Mali. Some of the things he taught were things that they had always wanted but were all beyond their means. Now he was showing how those things could be made.

Nuing was surprised by the resentment he sensed. Then guilt hit him. He should have done more to help, but he was so engrossed with Mali and his new ideas. Even in the evenings they could talk about nothing but the boat or the forge.

"I will help you put up the rafters," Nuing said. "Suma is right. We should have asked if you needed help."

Jantan's face turned red. "I do not need help. I can finish the room on my own. It is only a matter of doing it fast or slow."

Ratai shrugged. She would not offer her help. After all it would seem strange if she helped Jantan while others were helping her finish her boat. The rest of the evening was quiet. Both sisters were resentful of each other since they each felt that the other was being unreasonable and unfair.

The next day, Mali showed Ratai how to bore holes into a plank and then to cut tiny grooves from the hole to the edge. He said, "You must make sure the holes on the other plank face this one in a straight line. The groove will make the twine lie flush to the planks so it will not slow down the boat or collect rubbish when it is riding on the water."

Ratai nodded to show that she understood what he was trying to tell her. If the twine sewing the pieces of planks together stuck out, it would cause drag in the water and make it harder to move the boat. She had scraped enough dugout boats to a smooth finish to understand the concept.

Mali had made three other boring pins so Ratai did not work alone. Assan and Dujong were also working hard. They each had a piece of bamboo that were all of the same thickness. This was what they now used as a measure for the distance of one hole to the other. After a few hours of hard work, they had enough planks to put together in the bottom of the boat.

Mali placed a piece of waxy rope between two planks then lined them together, making sure to put the grooved holes outside the boat. He also lined the holes so they were just across from each other. Then he folded a coconut leaf spine over a piece of raffia twine and threaded it through the first hole. Ratai pulled the rope from the other side. Then she threaded the rope into the hole below the first one. Mali received it from his side. He placed the waterproof rattan rope in between the two planks and threaded the raffia rope over this rattan one, holding it in place. They repeated this over and over until they reached the end of the plank. Each time before he overlapped the raffia over the rattan rope, Mali would wrap the thread over a piece of hard wood and pull hard on it. This tightened the thread and forced it into the groove, so it would lie flush to the plank.

More and more people started to collect about the boat-building site as the day progressed. All other activity was forgotten as they made comments about the work that was being carried out. Mali and Ratai's actions were committed to memory for future reference or to verse for stories. Even Mansau and Betia could not keep away even though they were supposed to be helping Jantan lash down the last bits of his floor that day.

By the end of the day, the first parts of the bottom of the boat were done. Ratai flushed with pleasure. She had not dared hope because she was afraid that Mali had over promised, but when she saw how watertight the planks were, she was encouraged to dream again. She now stood in the middle of the frame. The depth of the boat was about half her height and the length was easily twenty feet. It was so wide she could stretch out across its width comfortably. It was a good size and she could imagine travelling and living in it. Ratai was already imagining where her hearth would go and where her bed would be. It was wonderful, beyond her dreams.

"Will I have a roof and walls?" she asked excitedly.

Despite himself, Mali smiled. "Of course you will. I will make it like a house with windows that you can open and close. I will also build shelves so you can store your jars of food and wine."

She turned and smiled her perfect black smile at him. Mali blushed and looked down. Then she walked away. His gaze followed her. He shook his head, as though to strip a vision off his mind, and turned back to carving the plank that he had pick for the gunwale.

\*\*\*

Ratai lay back on her pillow and looked up dreamily at the darkness above her. She could not see her charm pouch, but she knew it was there. The rat demon's promise was true. Everything she touched would prosper. She was feeling happy and was too excited to sleep. She turned to smile at Madu who was snoring softly next to her. Her fingers played with a bit of tacky resin as she imagined which stitching hole she would stuff it into tomorrow. Her back still felt stiff from stuffing the holes with coconut fibre and resin. There was only a little more left now. Her father had already started rubbing the wood with oil, both inside and outside, to make it waterproof. This afternoon, Madu was folding and threading together leaves to make the thatch roof. Mali had also started carving something that he called a rudder. He explained that it is difficult to control the direction of a large boat with just a small paddle. So he made a very large paddle with a handle that was as tall as a man. This would be placed at the back of the boat to steer it.

Ratai searched her childhood memory to try to remember if she had ever seen such a thing in the larger boats. She recalled seeing protrusions at the stern of boats that looked like fish tails when they were lifted. It made her wonder if the rudder for her boat would look like the arrow-tail shape of a carp or the fantail shape of a snakehead.

The rafter creaked. Ratai tensed up. She waited for the suitor to move on, but he remained. Then she felt her toe being shaken. Ratai sat up and wondered who it was. No man had given her any indication that he was interested in her. Was this man someone from another longhouse? They were hosting some visitors who were curious about the things that Mali was doing. Maybe this man was one of them.

"Who are you, Stranger?" she asked in a low voice. Her first instinct was to shake her sister, but then she thought better of it. She had suffered enough embarrassment, she did not want to go through it again.

"I am a hunter on his way home, but I was struck by your charm and chose to stay," he replied in a nasally voice.

"What is your name?" she asked the next customary question half-heartedly. She was in no mood to toy with love, especially now when her boat was so close to being ready for the river. Yet if this man was a visitor then she must treat him with respect because he might become angry and start a quarrel with the longhouse.

"I am a man with no name. I am happy to receive any name that you might give me."

Ratai began to feel a little annoyed. She wanted to stop this game now. Maybe she should pretend that she was tired. "You are very kind, Stranger, but I am too tired to think of a fine name for you now. I am trying to finish a boat and it is very hard work."

"You are cruel. You are chasing me out even before the floor under my buttock has had time to warm."

Ratai stifled a giggle. But she must not encourage him to stay. She tried another tactic. "Why don't you return after I finish the boat? Maybe then I will be less tired."

"But I love you. I love you enough to risk my life," he replied earnestly.

Ratai was surprised. His voice had trembled with passion and emotion. He seemed so sincere.

Then he continued, "I will give up anything for you, even my life."

His earnestness made the hair on her nape stand on end. She replied, "Then let this time be a test of your love. If you truly love me, you will wait and you will return. If your love is only a passing passion, then you will find another sweetheart to love."

"Very well," he said. "I will return after the boat is finished."

He turned on his heels while still in a squatting position. Ratai could just make out his silhouette. Instinctively she leaned forward and pressed the blob of resin between her fingers onto the back of his loincloth.

She waited for him to leave the loft before she lay back down on her mattress again. Her heart pounded. She must find out who he was so that she could decide whether she should encourage him or not. She tossed and turned for most of the night, trying to think of what to say to him if she did not like him.

The next morning, the whole family sat down together for breakfast. Even though Suma and Jantan now had their own room, Nambi still insisted that they ate together. Ratai was happy to see that Suma was more content. She was glowing and dreamy at the same time. Then at the end of breakfast Suma announced that she was with child.

Nambi let out a shout of joy and Nuing smiled so wide his eyes teared. The younger children started talking all at the same time. Ratai and Madu clapped and laughed. Then Nambi started giving instructions to her daughter about what she could and could not do. "You must make sure to follow them," Nambi said, "so that your child will be born healthy and strong."

"But I feel so tired and lazy all the time now, Mother," Suma said.

"It will be like that for the first few months," Nambi replied. "You should go back and rest."

Suma got up and her husband followed her out. Ratai looked up and her eyes fell on the blob of resin on the back flap of Jantan's loincloth. Instinctively she clasped her hands over her mouth to stop a scream and she looked down so no one would see the shock on her face. But her father saw. After the door was shut behind them, Ratai got up and started clearing the room. She went about her chore automatically. Then she took a machete and a smaller carving knife and went out.

Ratai made directly for the boat. She felt dirty and wrong. She was glad no one was there yet. Mali must have gone to the fields with Uyut and his wife. That was what he usually did in the morning.

Ratai started filling the stitching holes with fibre and resin. She used her porcupine quill to stuff the spaces between the wood and the raffia rope. She felt the structure move a little but she did not turn to see who had got into the boat with her.

"Child," Nuing said, "what bad omen did you see this morning?"

Ratai stopped her work and turned slowly. "It was not a bad omen, Father. Only a taboo."

Nuing sat back, and was silent for a long moment. "Last night," he began, "the rafter creaked."

Ratai was relieved that her father had guessed the right reason, yet she was also anxious about what he would do now that he knew the truth. She did not want him to fight with her brother-in-law. Not now, especially when Suma was so happy.

"Father, it is all right. I will keep rejecting him. We are spiritual siblings anyway. We can never be together."

Her father looked at her. "But Suma will find out. She already blamed you when your brothers did not help Jantan build their room. She will blame you for this."

Ratai's face turned red and her eyes started to brim over with tears. "I will leave the moment the boat is ready for the river. She will not find out because I made him promise not to come back to my loft until I have finished the boat."

Her father watched her face for a moment. Then he said, "Let me talk to your mother."

Instantly she reached out and grabbed his wrist. "No, Father. This is my shame. This is my fault. Please don't let anyone else learn about it."

He patted her hand and said, "You have done nothing wrong, Child. It is not your fault." Then he climbed out of the boat.

Ratai remained on her knees, sobbing. Then she squared her shoulders and turned back to work. By the time Mali joined her, he found that she had finished waterproofing all of the stitch holes that they had sewn the day before.

\*\*\*

With his head bowed in shame, Nuing sat across from his friend Uyut. The other man too, would not look at Nuing because he could not believe that such a terrible taboo was happening in their house.

Finally Uyut asked, "What will you do?"

"I tried talking to my wife. But she was so shocked by what I told her, she did not wish to discuss it." After a minute of silence, Nuing said, "My child wants to leave for good because of this man."

Uyut said, "You must chase this other man away. Jantan is a mere headhunter. Ratai is a gift from Sempurai to bless you, to bless us."

"Ratai will not hear of it. She loves her sister. She is happy that her sister is happy." Nuing let out a loud sigh, "If only there is a man she will marry."

Uyut said, "All the bachelors say they are afraid of her. She is fierce, they said. She is too knowledgeable. Nobody feels like her equal."

Nuing chuckled bitterly. "Sempurai has played one of his tricks again. He has made her unnatural, like him. He is half-god, half-demon. She is a woman who is manlier than most men."

Uyut smiled then his face became serious. "She works well with Mali."

Nuing stared at his friend for a moment. "He is a slave. You cannot make her marry a slave."

"She can buy his freedom from me. I will only ask for a coconut bowl of uncooked rice."

"No," Nuing said. "People will think that my daughter has done the unthinkable or that she has something shameful to hide. I will pay you three *guchi* jars."

"Are you sure?" Uyut asked with disbelief. A *guchi* jar was considered to be of great value because it is was round and was the size of a human head.

"He is a man with many skills, so it is only right that I should pay you that much," Nuing said. Having agreed on the price of Mali's freedom, both men returned home.

\* \* \*

That night, after dinner, Nuing invited both Nambi and Ratai to go out frog hunting with him. They lit two resin torches and Nambi slung a medium-sized basket on her shoulder. The pond was about a mile from the longhouse. It had been raining during the day so the area was quite wet. They shone the light in front of the frogs, and when the creatures were mesmerised by the flame either Ratai or Nuing would catch them by hand. Each catch was dropped into the basket under a layer of wide yam leaf. Once they had a good-size catch, Nuing invited both women to sit for a while because he had something to say to them.

"I have struck a deal with Uyut to buy his slave's freedom," Nuing said.

"Why would you do such a thing?" Nambi asked perplexed.

Nuing had expected this question and had thought long and hard for a good answer. "He is not a man of this community. And he has many skills. I thought he would make a good husband for Ratai."

Ratai protested. "But I do not want to marry him. I do not want to marry anybody."

Nuing let out a sigh. "If you marry him then no one will visit your loft at night."

"Why can you not find a man from among our own people?" Nambi asked.

Ratai kept her eyes down. She knew what her father had to say but could not, so she answered her mother. "Because no man will have me. No man wants to starve or be naked."

"They are fools," Nuing said angrily. "They are fools to think that you cannot provide for them."

"It is true, Father. I cannot plant and weave."

"There are many women who cannot plant rice or weave," Nuing said. "Their families are not hungry or naked."

"I can teach you and help you," Nambi said. "You only need more time."

Ratai looked up and gazed into her mother's face. Then she said, "I am sorry, Mother. I can never be the perfect woman. I have tried for many years and I have failed."

"Then what do you want to be?" Nambi said, her face frowning deep with grief. "What do you want to be, Child, if not a woman?"

"I have a boat now. I want to be a trader. I will sell the iron we make and buy jars or ornaments."

Nambi was about to protest but Nuing held her back. Then he turned to Ratai and said, "Think about my suggestion. If you are agreeable to it, I will make an announcement."

"What if Mali does not agree?" Nambi asked.

"He gets along with Ratai," Nuing said. "He will not reject an opportunity to be free."

"What if he mistreats her?" Nambi asked

Ratai let out a frustrated sigh. "Mother, I am strong enough to take care of myself."

Nuing chuckled. "You forgot our daughter is a headhunter. He would not dare hurt her."

Ratai got up and shouldered the heavy basket. Without turning she said, "You can tell *Apai* Tupang that I wish to buy Mali's freedom so he can be my husband." Then she walked homeward. Nuing and Nambi followed her from behind.

\*\*\*

Ratai would not meet Jantan's eyes when Nuing made the public announcement that Ratai wished to buy Mali's freedom. Mali had been warned the day before by Uyut that he would be set free and married on the same night.

Everyone gasped when Nuing brought out the three *guchi* jars and placed them before Uyut. They were each about the size of a human head, either green or brown and shiny with glaze.

"It is not easy for me to give up Mali," Uyut said. "He has brought much new knowledge with him and he will make me prosperous if I keep him as my slave."

Nuing replied, "I understand. That is why I offer you two jars to buy his freedom and one jar to show that we are now family. My daughter Ratai wishes to live in the boat he built her, so it is only right that he should marry her so he can travel with her as her husband and keep her character safe."

Ratai raised her proud head and looked boldly to Mali. The other man caught her gaze and bowed his head deferentially. She could not tell if he was agreeable to the wedding or not, but she did not care. She needed him to protect her character from Jantan's lust. She had felt this need strongly when Mansau complained to her that whenever men from Jantan's longhouse had asked him about her, he had always discouraged them. It was only natural that they would ask him because he was a member of her family. Yet his misrepresentation of her character would eventually start a rumour.

Mali was the perfect choice, Ratai admitted, because the men did not discuss private matters with him. And they could not ask him about her either because there was nothing Mali could say on the matter. They would all have to accept Nuing's reasoning as a matter of fact. Jantan could say nothing either, without exposing his own debasement.

So Ratai felt safe. The awful secret would stay hidden. Then her attention turned to the many adventures she would have travelling down the river. She wondered if the boat could also sail up and down the coast. Mali would know what to do, she thought to herself. By the time she turned to look at him again, she was flushed and excited. Mali smiled in return, appearing glad that she looked happy. Everyone who saw the exchange felt glad for both of them. Maybe they had fallen in love during the long days of working on the boat, they whispered. Remember how proud Ratai had behaved around Mali, they reminded each other. Then they recalled how she would spend all the daylight hours by his side, hewing planks and carving them. Many had thought then that she was strange, but when considered in light of her interest in Mali, her behaviour now appeared natural. Everyone was happy for Ratai, because it seemed as though she had found happiness once more.

Jantan said, "I don't understand how you can allow this, Father. This is a family of great reputation. How can you allow a slave to be one of us?"

Nuing let out a shout. It was loud and furious and it cowed everyone into silence. He went into his room and came out with a spear. He shook it in front of him and declared, "Tonight Mali will be my son-in-law. I have bought his freedom. If any man or woman dares to call him a slave from this day forth, I will strike them down with this spear. He is a free man! He is my son-in-law!"

Then he stomped to one end of the house and made the same declaration. He turned back and stomped to the other end of the house and repeated the declaration. Each time he spoke and shook his spear, he would be answered with a loud shout from the people, to show that they too stood by his declaration.

The couple was married that very night. There was no lavish ceremony like the one that Suma had because Mali did not have a family that they needed to impress. Even though married, Mali continued to sleep in the common gallery with the bachelors for the next week, until the boat was ready to go onto the river. From that day forward, Mali became known as Mali Guchi to show that his freedom had been bought with the small but valuable jars.

\*\*\*

Ratai ran her hand appreciatively over the carved gunwale on the side of the bow. The wind had picked up and she marvelled at the raised mat sail that had puffed up and become filled with wind. Her father had helped Mali tie bamboo poles together and her brothers had helped him raise the mast and set it in the boat. The cover of thatch next to her rustled and reminded her of the many clay pots and knives that it was sheltering from the elements. Among them were also two large baskets of unhusked rice.

This was a good boat and Ratai was amazed at how well it floated. There were no leaks at all, so they only needed to bale out water when it rained. Her husband now stood at the stern, having rested up the long oars that he had been steadily pulling on since that morning. He was now holding the handle of the rudder, keeping their course steady.

Ratai walked along the middle of the boat towards him. She took a step up onto a bamboo floor and ducked her head under the roof. Then she passed jars of uncooked rice, smoked meat and pickled vegetables that her mother had insisted she bring with her. Truly this was a floating home, she thought to herself again, feeling a bubble of excitement growing inside her belly.

Mali Guchi stepped back when she reached him. And he bowed his head respectfully. She stood next to the rudder, on the other side, and put her hand over his. His head snapped up with surprise. Ratai turned her face away from him and looked towards the horizon ahead. Her hand, she kept upon his. He did not move his hand away and he could feel that she was navigating the boat together with him. He took a step forward and stood next to her.

"I am a free man," he said with awe, as though realising it for the first time.

"Of course," Ratai said, annoyed that he still brought this matter up. "I will never marry a man who is not my equal." Then, as though for the first time, she noticed the features of his face. It was the same face as the father of the newborn child in her dream. She looked away, feeling suddenly shy. Her gaze was transfixed on the horizon ahead of them.

Mali Guchi looked at her, admiring her proud and beautiful profile. To him she was like a princess, like a rani. He marvelled that he was her husband. Then, like her, his gaze turned towards the horizon and he dreamed of their future together. For the first time in many long years his dream was full of hope and happiness. It was an exciting dream, filled with travels and adventures that were only matched by hers.

# Acknowledgements

My heartfelt thanks to Philip Tatham of Monsoon Books for being so supportive of the Iban Dream series. Three books, spanning more than six years, and for each he had put together a strong team of editors and cover designers. I appreciate that you never tried to change any part of the stories and accepted them exactly as they are. For this reason, the manuscripts have stayed as close to the Iban storytelling style as I can possibly make them.

My appreciation also goes to my mother Jimah Agah and my siblings, Shanton, Dorita and Kelvin, who have provided me with everything I need during the most difficult times while I was working on the manuscripts. To my extended family members Phyllis, Patricia, David and Patrick Mowe: thank you for your encouragement and advice. I am also indebted to my cousin Rebecca Rabbu and friends Betty Yong and Lucy Tang, who persistently checked up on me every month or so, to provide me with social nourishment.

My life is blessed. There are no words to express my gratitude and my love to all of you

# Iban Dream series

### IBAN DREAM (VOLUME 1)

Orphaned as a young boy in the rainforests of Borneo, Bujang is brought up by a family of orangutans, but his adult future has already been decided for him by Sengalang Burong, the Iban warpath god. On reaching adulthood, Bujang must leave his ape family and serve the warpath god as a warrior and a headhunter. Having survived his first assignment — to kill an ill-tempered demon in the form of a ferocious wild boar — subsequent adventures see Bujang converse with gods, shamans, animal spirits and with the nomadic people of Borneo as he battles evil spirits and demons to preserve the safety of those he holds dear to him. But Bujang's greatest test is still to come and he must rally a large headhunting expedition to free his captured wife and those of his fellow villagers.

### IBAN JOURNEY (VOLUME 2)

A curse hangs over Nuing's life. He may be the youngest son of the great headhunter Bujang Maias, but he is rejected by his longhouse community. When the people's fear of him becomes unbearable, Nuing leaves them together with his best friend Gunggu. Nuing and Gunggu wander the land until they eventually meet and are accepted by a group of travellers made up of cursed individuals. Soon after, however, the worst possible scourge befalls Nuing when he kills a demon huntsman. Follow this Iban traveller as he experiences the hidden world of Iban spirits and gods in his quest to find a way to defeat an army of Antu Gerasi hell-bent on revenge.

# Iban People
# and Traditions

The following photographs of Iban life in Sarawak date from the 1950s to the present day. For more images, please follow the author on Facebook at *www.facebook.com/IbanDreamByGoldaMowe*.

ABOVE On the exterior verandah of an Iban longhouse in Sarawak, the liver of a pig is being inspected to see if the omens are favourable. [Photo©Peter Mooney]

ABOVE AND BELOW An Iban warrior dance in a longhouse depicts the terrifying of the enemy before an attack. The *parang* (machete) at the dancer's waist is unsheathed as the dance develops.
[Photos©Peter Mooney]

ABOVE The author photographed with Iban heirloom lanji and sintong baskets. Short sintongs are used by women to collect ripening rice clusters. Once these baskets are full, the rice is poured into the tall lanjis, which are carried by men. The bigger the lanji basket, the stronger the man. [Photo©Rebecca anak Rabbu]

BELOW The back of a longhouse in Sarawak. The lack of an open verandah at the back prevents enemies from sneaking in, and there is a loft to store rice. [Photo©iStockphoto]

RIGHT An Iban headman.
Each longhouse has an
elected headman.
[Photo©Peter Mooney]

BELOW A Kelabit
longhouse feast.
[Photo©Peter Mooney]

ABOVE Throwing the large and heavy net weighted all round the edges while poised on a narrow plank on an unsteady Iban longboat requires perfect balance. [Photo©Peter Mooney]

BELOW Ibans hauling a longboat upriver through rapids. [Photo©Peter Mooney]